Whe

The .... Trilogy

Book 2

By

Joshua Griffith

ISBN: 9781723918445

Contact Joshua Griffith on Facebook
Follow him on Twitter

Cover art by BooksGoSocial.com

To Stacie: You're my greatest inspiration in every aspect of my life!

Table of Contents:

Chapter One

Chapter Two

Chapter Three

Chapter Four

Chapter Five

Chapter Six

Chapter Seven

Chapter Eight

Chapter Nine

Chapter Ten

Chapter Eleven

Chapter Twelve

Chapter Thirteen

Chapter Fourteen

Chapter Fifteen

Chapter Sixteen

Chapter Seventeen

Chapter Eighteen

Chapter Nineteen

Chapter Twenty

Chapter One

The screams grew louder as another small section of skin was magically peeled off the man's body. Zordic methodically walked around the cold, steel table with malice in his black eyes. His fists were clenched so hard, his black claws dug into his palms. It had been nearly a month since he had sent Derek and his crew to eliminate those who had escaped from his jail. Their orders were to bring back the shape-shifter, whose blood he craved more and more with each passing day. But his men hadn't returned, and Zordic could only assume that the escapees had banded together and killed all of his men. They could very well be gunning for his head next.

Zordic looked around the dimly lit room, double checking that all the blood sigils were in place and that nothing was out of place. With the rituals, of late, Zordic had decided to add black candles in every room to help protect him from the witch who had escaped jail. She had the knowledge of how to call him to her, so Zordic wasn't taking any chances. In magic, names mean power, especially over demons. When a witch or whoever has the true name of a demon, like Zordic, that demon can be summoned easily and even forced to do the witch's bidding.

Zordic knew if the witch tried to summon him, it wouldn't be for social chats or making deals. No, she would be out for his head and that wouldn't do. He had bartered for several charms that would help cloak him from magical detection or magical conjuring, hoping to block her spells.

The demon looked down at the man on the steel table. The man was a shape-shifter, and Zordic ran a finger over the gaping hole in his flesh. The man grimaced in pain and struggled, but he couldn't escape his restraints. Zordic licked the man's blood from his finger and felt...

Nothing!

Not even a buzz, he thought disgustedly. Certainly not the euphoria he was seeking.

"You don't have what I'm looking for," Zordic said in a monotone voice as he flicked his wrist over the man which made another chunk of skin peel off.

The man screamed and arched his back, hoping he could shift but to no avail. "Release me, dammit!" the man howled his rage at Zordic. "If I don't have what you seek, then why keep me here, you sadistic fuck?!"

"My reasons are my own, and you're correct. I am a sadistic fuck. I enjoy my work, but you don't understand. You do have something I want."

"And...what might...that be?" the man asked as sweat covered his whole body. Shock was setting in from the pain, and he began to pant hard.

Zordic leaned down. "I'm going to take your life essence and add it to my ever growing collection," he said coldly as he stared mere inches from the man's face.

The shape-shifter did the only thing he could. He spat in Zordic's face.

The demon pulled back and let an evil, toothy grin spread across his visage as he snaked his tongue out to lick the spit off his face. "You're a feisty one; I do admire that about you, my friend, but the fun must go on. Don't you agree?" Zordic flicked his wrist three consecutive times and made more flesh magically peel away on different parts of the shape-shifter's body.

The shape-shifter screamed loudly and thrashed his body, letting blood fly from his new wounds. He had chunks of flesh peeled off both thighs, and most of his chest was gone, along with his abdomen. Now Zordic started on the man's arms.

"Just...kill me. Kill me...NOW!"

"No, this is too much fun; plus, I need to vent my frustrations out on someone, so it might as well be you, my friend," Zordic said with a malevolent smile as he flicked his wrist again. Tears streamed down the shape-shifter's face as he howled in pain once more and felt the world going black. Zordic sneered as he jammed his claws into the shape-shifter's open wounds, forcing him to wake up.

"I will *not* have you sleeping and missing all this wonderful fun we're sharing together, my friend. It's quite rude to do that, you know?"

"I'm not...your fucking...friend!" the shape-shifter growled through gritted teeth.

"Why sure you are. I don't let just anyone on my table of fun. Now, shall we get started or not? You're beginning to bore me. Where did that feistiness go?"

Zordic bent down and used his clawed index finger to slowly cut into the exposed muscles of the shape-shifter's chest, running it from nipple to nipple. The shape-shifter started to squirm, but Zordic held him and said, "Now, now, I haven't finished your new tattoo—stop squirming. I want to make it look perfect for you, my friend." He ran his clawed finger all the way down to where the shape-shifter's navel should have been and then back up to his chest, carving an inverted triangle into his flesh.

"FUCKING DEMON," the man screamed angrily. "RELEASE ME, SO WE CAN HAVE SOME REAL FUN!"

"Ah, there's my feisty, little friend — back from the dead," Zordic smiled and clapped. "All you shape-shifters are so much fun to play with." His smile faded. "Unfortunately, though, you're not the one I'm looking for, so it's high time you shed all that skin of yours. You should be used to it, being a shifter and all." The man yanked hard at his restraints, but they didn't give even an inch.

Zordic took a couple of steps back and extended both his muscular arms, quickly rotating both his wrists. His eyes went completely black, and they glowed as he concentrated. The shape-shifter had a look of horror on his face as he felt every inch of his skin ripping from his body, bits of it sliding off his carcass onto the table and floor. He screamed as he watched his own face peel off and slide up past his eyes.

The demon swept his hands apart, and all the shape-shifter's skin was flung in every direction, putting him in full shock.

Zordic held a clawed hand over the center of the inverted triangle he had carved in the man's chest and chanted. Slowly, the demon had the man's life essence pooled into the palm of his hand. The shape-shifter gasped in shorter, rapid breaths, and his head lolled back and forth. As the man's mouth gaped open in mute protest, he released his last breath and died.

Zordic stepped away. He held out his hand and an ethereal globe materialized. Placing his other hand over the top of the ethereal globe, he let the life essence drift slowly inside. The globe sparkled and shimmered. It thrummed with the life essence as it filled up. Once he was done, Zordic had the ethereal globe dissipate, and it went back to his personal storage.

He looked down at his handy work. He had enjoyed all the torture and extraction of the life essence, but none of it compared to the thrill and euphoria of that special blood — that *special blood* which had gotten away from him. Just the mere reminder of it sent the demon into a frenzied rage. And with each passing day without that special blood more rages burst violently out of him, and he found he had less control over them.

He bellowed out in anger and frustration that his men hadn't recaptured that elusive prize by now. He sighed heavily. Just after one taste of that escapee's special blood, Zordic had become hopelessly addicted to it. No heroin or meth had ever addicted anyone so quickly or so completely. He had to have more of that special blood. He craved it — even in his sleep, he craved it! He had to have it, and he vowed to do anything to get it.

He stared at what was left of the man's carcass on the table. The torture and murder of this shape-shifter had been a waste of his time, he knew that. But he did see the silver lining in the fact that he had rid the world of another supernatural being.

All supernatural creatures could easily pose a threat to his plans to rule over all of humanity like a god. He had all his P.A.N.E.L. squads in the Portland area and surrounding towns searching for shape-shifters, in particular, so he could test their blood.

He had no idea who the shape-shifter with the special blood was. Zordic had never seen him. While inspecting the cells from which the prisoners had escaped, he had made the mistake of tasting the blood left on the walls and floor. He had tasted it so he could identify the escapees.

A witch had been in one cell and a necromancer in another. According to his taste buds, neither of them had left the blood behind. But two others had also escaped with them — a gremlin and a shape-shifter. It was this shape-shifter who carried within his body the powerfully addicting blood, and Zordic was determined to recapture him and feed on him.

"Gordon! Come here, my child!" Zordic bellowed out.

A young blond man who was in his mid-twenties entered the room. He was dressed in the crimson red P.A.N.E.L. squad's uniform. He wore black combat boots and had an inverted triangle badge with his name carved on it. Gordon did his best to walk towards Zordic without slipping and falling in the blood and skin that pooled all over the floor. He made it to Zordic without incident. "Yes, my master?" he asked and took another step forward. "What is it you — OOOF!" Gordon went face first on the floor, his head missing the steel table by mere centimeters.

Zordic put clawed hands on his face and slowly shook his head in disbelief. "Good help is so hard to find after an apocalypse," he groaned in a defeated voice.

Gordon grabbed hold of the steel table and pulled himself up, coming face to face with the flayed shape-shifter and nearly fell again. He struggled to stand without slipping. Suddenly, Zordic's evil figure loomed over him, frightening him. Would his master flay him for his clumsiness? With his heart thudding violently in his chest, and terror finding a home on his face, Gordon asked, "Yes, my master, what…is it you require?"

"I require competent individuals who can catch the right shape-shifter for me," he growled.

"I take it he wasn't the right one?"

Zordic's anger and rage got the best of him, and he slammed his fist into the flayed shape-shifter's chest. He ripped out his heart and screamed, "DOES IT LOOK LIKE HE'S THE ONE I WANTED?"

Gordon cowered as Zordic flung the heart at him, hitting him square in his chest.

"If he was the one I wanted," he growled through gritted teeth. "He wouldn't be in this condition, now would he? I want him alive. I sure wouldn't kill him. Do you not have a brain in that little skull of yours, Gordon?"

The young man stood shaking so hard, he thought he would faint.

The demon glared at him as he said coldly, "You better mind your tongue, or it will be you on my table next."

Gordon gulped hard as a tsunami of fear sent terror in wave after wave washing throughout his whole body. Gordon finally regained what little composure he had left and said, "Forgive me, my ever generous and gracious master. I didn't mean to offend you in any way." He dropped to his knees and grimaced when his pants made a sick, squishing sound as they soaked up the carnage of blood and skin. "You may take me next then, my master, to make up for my ignorance."

Zordic scowled at Gordon. As he weighed the benefits of a sacrificial offer against the loss of a trained soldier, he remained silent for a full minute, his black eyes glowing with rage as they bored holes into Gordon's soul. Finally Zordic's eyes started showing his irises, which were inverted red triangles, and he let out a heavy breath. "Arise, my child. Your offer will be rejected for now…as long as you don't patronize me again. This will be your one and only warning, for a fate worse than his awaits you if you cross me again."

"You are too generous, my master," Gordon said as he slowly rose up.

"I need you to get this place cleaned up for me. Gather several more of my children to help with this." He stopped for a moment as he considered something. "Is there any more shape-shifters waiting for me?" the demon asked with a malevolent smile.

"We'll get it cleaned right away, my master," Gordon quickly responded. "And yes, we caught nearly a dozen shifters last night. Since it was a full moon, they were easy pickings," he said with pride and with the hopes of getting back into his master's good graces. He got so excited, he turned to head out of the room and half way to the door, he slipped and fell on his ass again.

"Why do I even try anymore? Humans are so pathetic," Zordic muttered as he shook his head. Embarrassed, Gordon scrambled to his feet and tried to regain his dignity as he walked out the door.

With a wave of Zordic's hand, all the black candles lit up. They gave him a small comfort, but not much. He closed his eyes and used his senses to see if he could detect any kind of threats that could be lurking nearby. The only thing he found was the presence of his prisoners and the humans he had at his command.

Zordic let out a heavy sigh of relief, but in the back of his mind lurked the knowledge that kept creeping out, making him feel more nervous each day.

Chapter Two

Raven Moonrose walked out of her room in Portland's old Costco building, where she lived with Yonuh, Nightshade, and the gremlin, Onyx. She hurried towards a magazine rack that contained an old atlas that had road maps of Oregon and other states. She wanted to check the Portland area first and then expand her search for the demon to include the surrounding cities like Oregon City, Milwaukie, Tigard, and Tualatin.

"His ass is mine if he thinks he's going to drink my Yonuh's blood like a damn Slurpee," she growled.

She was willing to share Yonuh with the necromancer, but a demon had no rights to her *mate*. She now knew that it was high time to prep her ritual items for the coming battle with Zordic. And she knew in her heart that she would give the demon another apocalypse to save her man.

Raven sighed heavily. "Concentrate on the job at hand, Raven," she ordered herself. She remembered she had a charm that was supposed to protect her from demons, but she hadn't bound it to herself yet. Plus, there was a good chance she would need black salt for added protection if she could draw the demon into her circle. Her new athame needed to be cleansed and charged, so it would be more effective in battle. Man, I've been slacking off, Raven thought, but then again we haven't had any real downtime to catch our breaths either.

The witch grabbed the atlas and several road maps and walked briskly to the long customer service counter. She slapped the maps down on the countertop and, one by one, she opened them up in the order she wanted to scry — a method for seeing into the future. She felt a wisp of air behind her and knew it could only be Onyx, which made her smile slightly and wonder what type of mood the gremlin was in today.

"Aww, are you looking for you and Yonuh a newlywed house already?" Onyx smarted off. "How sickening and sweet at the same time; it warms the heart and makes the tummy churn with rotten eggs from the plague!" He put one hand over his heart and the other on his belly, making a sickly look on his dark face.

"You know exactly what I'm doing, you little shit," Raven said and smiled as she half-heartedly swatted at him with her hand. "I'm going to scry for that fucking demon and see if he's still on our plane or retreated back into his own realm."

She glanced at the gremlin. "You seem to be in a good mood. Did you find an extra Dorito bag under your bed or something?"

"Nope and, trust me, I look everyday just to be on the safe side. Can't a gremlin be happy just for the hell of it?"

"If you're happy," the witch said wearily, "it usually means you're up to some sort of mischief. I can smell bullshit. You're up to something."

"Ha! You won't get me to admit to nothing that I may or may not have done!" Onyx shot back with a twinkle in his eye. "So where do you think old sore dick is hiding out?"

"I haven't got a clue, but I plan to search everywhere. He won't stay hidden long!"

Onyx noted the concerned look on Raven's face, and he flew up beside her. Placing his small hand on her shoulder, he said solemnly, "We'll find him, Raven, I promise you. There are only so many places he can hide from us."

Raven smiled at Onyx. She could tell he was being genuinely sincere. "Thanks, I appreciate the confidence you have in me."

"Well, I know for a fact that witches are pretty good at finding people when they scry, so I figure we'll have his demonic balls for breakfast soon."

"Ewww!" Raven exclaimed. "That's just gross! If you want them so badly for breakfast, though, I can serve them to you, coated and baked with your Doritos as a crust on them. I'm sure you would love some Dorito-encrusted balls!"

"BLASPHEMY!" Onyx screamed. With his eyes bulging out in shock and horror, he flew backwards away from Raven, glaring at the witch like she had the plague. "You watch that tongue of yours, carrot top! Never joke about defiling the sacred Doritos, especially with demon balls!" The sound of snickering coming from behind him made Onyx whirl around. Nightshade walked towards him, grinning with Yonuh trailed behind her.

"Now, Raven, you shouldn't tease him like that," Nightshade said with an amused look on her face. "He might run and hide in his room, sucking his thumb." The blonde necromancer chuckled. "I suggest that you go hide your Dorito stash, Onyx, just to be on the safe side."

Onyx glared at Raven and then at Nightshade, thinking hard, and then he flew off shouting, "Don't be surprised, Yonuh, if you wake up and carrot top is bald. She said terrible things about my poor, defenseless Doritos!"

The three of them burst out laughing. As Onyx flew off, he cried out, "Piss off, all of you!"

Nightshade walked over to Raven and gave her a side hug. "Have you found Zordic yet, or are you just now starting?"

"Just getting started," Raven confessed. "Onyx was being a little too nice so be wary around here, girl." She glanced over at Yonuh. "There's my man," she said and smiled. "How did you sleep, sweetheart?"

Yonuh ran his fingers through his long, shiny brown hair and said with a wince, "Okay, I guess, except I kept dreaming of the same thing."

"What are the dreams about?" Nightshade asked him.

"Torture...always torture," the shape-shifter said. "No matter what, I'm being tortured by a demon." Yonuh rubbed his eyes and then stretched his body. Raven and Nightshade looked at each other, concern washing over them like a tsunami.

"How long has this been going on, Yonuh, and why is this the first time I'm hearing of it?" Raven demanded as she tapped her foot. She was clearly scared for the healer.

"The dreams started a few nights ago," Yonuh admitted. "With each one they become more vivid and realistic. It's like I'm actually there, but it's not me who is the victim. It's always someone else, but I'm seeing and experiencing it all through their eyes."

"You say it's a demon torturing you?" Nightshade asked in contemplation. "Hmm, I wonder why you would be seeing these things in the first place."

As Yonuh stepped up beside both Raven and Nightshade, Raven grabbed his hand and squeezed it as she kissed him. "Do you think you're seeing Zordic in these dreams?" Raven asked. "Perhaps we should call them visions?"

Yonuh put his arms around both Nightshade and Raven, making them both close their eyes and soak up his warm, comforting energy that his body always put out. "From what I've seen," he said, "my dreams look like some of the images we found on the P.A.N.E.L. squad's computer. I would have to say that Zordic is indeed the demon doing the torturing."

"So what do you see? Is there anything noticeable about the room or the victims?" Raven asked with heavy lidded eyes, still basking in the healer's warm energy.

"One thing stood out about every single victim," Yonuh said. "They were all shape-shifters, like me. The demon would taste their blood. He seemed very disappointed that it didn't taste a certain way, so he tortured them anyway, just for the pleasure of it. Then, when the demon was ready, he always carved a big inverted triangle from my chest down past my bellybutton—or, rather, *their* chest and bellybutton. It reminded me of the badges that the P.A.N.E.L. squad wore on their uniforms, plus it matched his eyes. The demon had black orbs with a red inverted triangle in the middle for his iris, and he stood nearly seven feet tall. He always stole every victim's life essence, and that wasn't a pleasant experience to feel, even in a dream state."

"Well, that settles it for me," Nightshade said. Like Raven, she was almost in an overwhelmed state from being touched by Yonuh's healing energy. "You're somehow psychically linked to these tortures, and it's safe to say he's hunting for you. For some reason, he loves the taste of your blood. Remember, Derek said he was very interested in having you just for your blood, and he wanted to drink you like a fucking beer. He'll have to keep you alive to satisfy his greed."

"I believe the link is coming from the fact that he's torturing and murdering shape-shifters by the dozens," he said. "Shifters are linked like that, but it only kicks in when those nearby are being hurt in great numbers. Plus, the Great Spirit uses my dreams to show me what may need my attention."

"You bitches will never find my stash now!" Onyx bellowed in triumph as he flew into everyone's view, his arms tightly folded against his chest. "They're safe from your nasty cauldron of baked goods, Raven!"

"Well, at least now I can sleep better knowing your snacks are hidden," Nightshade said, smiling at the gremlin. "Raven, please start your scrying. We've got to find Zordic, so we can take him out."

Raven pulled out her scrying crystal. She took several calming deep breaths and dropped into a meditative state. She held it by its little gold chain and let the scrying crystal freely swirl around in circles over a map of downtown Portland. To help her focus her energy on finding Zordic, Raven closed her eyes and concentrated, using the memory of the demon she had gotten from the young ghost girl, Amanda.

Confusion clouded her mind, and she focused and concentrated harder. Her scrying crystal seemed to go all over the map, getting hits in multiple areas. Raven thought that this was both strange and impossible. How could a demon be in so many places at one time? She decided to experiment and moved the scrying crystal over a different map. Sure enough, she was getting the same kind of reading.

"Crafty little bastard, aren't you?" Raven said with sneer.

"What is it, Raven? Did you find him?" Yonuh asked anxiously.

"Yes, he's everywhere!"

Confused, Yonuh asked, "How is that possible?"

"It's simple, actually," Nightshade spoke up. "All one needs is some small crystals, nothing fancy, and add your own personal energy to them and spread them all over the place. It's a good way to camouflage and deceive anyone hunting for you."

"Sore dick will screw up eventually," Onyx said with grim determination in his voice. "Then, we take him down." He gave Yonuh a long look, studying him. "I'm not going to let him use you as his personal blood bank, Yonuh!"

The healer looked down as he walked away, deep in thought. Nightshade got in front of him to block him from going anywhere and asked wearily, "What are you planning on doing? You've got that look of wanting to go on a suicide mission, Yonuh. If that's the case, then I won't allow it!"

Yonuh sighed. "If it's me Zordic wants, then I should make my presence known to him, so he will stop hurting all these shape-shifters. I can't stand by idly and let people die because of me."

"You don't need to do this, Yonuh. We'll find him!" Onyx insisted as he floated just to the healer's right. "He'll make a mistake, and that's when we'll pounce on him. Sore dick has been around a long time and has learned a lot of cute tricks, like where to hide. As much as this is tearing at you to go into action, patience is the best plan."

Raven curled her arm around the crook of Yonuh's elbow. "You need to know we all love and care about you, Yonuh! We're stronger together than fighting this alone. Now that I have you, I'm sure as shit not giving you up easily! Is the love I have for you not enough for you to want to stay safe?" she asked with tears moistening her eyes.

Yonuh's lips parted as he looked down into Raven's eyes. "I'm so sorry, Raven. I didn't realize I was hurting you. I'm so use to being on my own that I don't consider the feelings of others. I just go into action. I…I've never had anyone to care for or love me like you do." He glanced at the others. "And that goes for all of you too."

"I was about to knock your sexy ass out if you chose to go through with your suicidal plan," Nightshade said. "You've done more for me than you could ever know, and I'm grateful for it. I'm not about to see you die just to save everyone else in some great selfless act! I refuse to let the one person I care about die for me. I would gladly step in front of the worst-of-the-worst spells for you, without even blinking an eye, Yonuh!" Nightshade bit her lip as she felt her rage for the demon boiling over inside her.

Yonuh's shoulders slumped as he felt his face heat up. He needed to protect the other shifters; it was his fault they were being killed. But he also needed to protect his friends. He knew he was never going to win an argument against any of them on this matter.

Onyx cocked his head to the side and said, "Yonuh, do you feel the call of the full moon like the other were-creatures do?"

"Yes, all shifters do. Why do you ask?"

"I imagine the need to shift and run in the wild is strong a day or two before and after the full moon—especially if you haven't changed. Is that correct?" Onyx asked as he rubbed his chin.

Yonuh nodded and smiled. "Indeed, and I sense a plan brewing up in that brilliant mind of yours too."

Raven rolled her eyes. "Don't fill his little head up like that; it's about to burst, already, just from his big ego!"

"Pay no attention to the talking root vegetable over there, Yonuh," the gremlin said. "I say you're due for your monthly run, right?" Yonuh nodded. Onyx turned his attention to the ladies. "I say it's time for a camping trip into the woods with our good friend Yonuh here. We'll be hunting, of course, as we watch over him."

"You want to go camping in the woods that will be teeming with shifters and weres?" Nightshade shrieked. "Have you lost your Doritos-caked brain, Onyx?" The necromancer stood, stunned, with an incredulous look on her face, her mouth gaping open.

Onyx tried to remain patient as he explained, "Yonuh needs this. We can't leave him alone because Zordic is hunting down all shifters, looking for him. I figured, what better way to save some shifters' lives than camping out in the woods as he runs free? If we happen to run across any of sore dick's cronies in the woods, we can kill them and let the other predators eat them. It would cover our tracks better that way too."

Yonuh hugged himself as he rubbed his arms. He could feel his very frustrated beast rumble inside him. The beast liked this idea, and it was in need to be let loose. It had been cooped up too long! The beast needed to hunt and run in the woods. Yonuh closed his eyes and concentrated, trying his best to placate the beast that was now roaring inside him.

As the sweat beaded up on his forehead, Yonuh felt that he was finally winning control, assuring his inner beast they will be free tonight. The healer pulled back into a reality of bickering and arguing. He listened for a moment and then laughed inwardly. It was hard to deal with his beast, but even that paled in comparison to these three when they went on an arguing tangent.

"If he gets hurt or captured, I promise I'll take my fury out on your tiny hide!" Raven hissed.

"Yonuh will be fine, carrot top," the gremlin promised. "He knows the danger, and his beast will be on alert for any kind of trouble too. As long as we watch Teddy Ruxpin's back, we have nothing to worry about."

"Except all the other *weres* and *shifters* in the woods!" Nightshade anxiously chimed in. "They'll not like their cycle run intruded upon by other beings. It's an unwritten rule of thumb to always avoid the woods during the full moon."

"I'm sure they won't mind us being out there tonight," Onyx said, pleading his case. "Yesterday was the actual full moon, so there won't be as many of them out there tonight. We should be fine."

Raven snorted and retorted, "Ha! Easy for you, maybe. You can fly away and be out of danger faster than we can run!"

"Ah, you can easily fly away too," Onyx teased the witch and snickered. "Just pull your broom out of that tight ass of yours—that's where you store your flying broom, isn't it?" He ducked to avoid Raven's swatting hand.

"Yonuh, what do you think about all of this?" Nightshade asked. "I know your inner beast needs this, but would we be safe out there? If the P.A.N.E.L. squad is out hunting for shifters tonight…" the necromancer's voice trailed off as she put a comforting hand on his shoulder.

"I believe I know a way for all of you to be safe," Yonuh answered, "but it's not foolproof. In my bear form, I can mark out an area as my territory, like a base camp where I would bring my kills and store my clothes during my run. I must say, though, if you wish to venture past my territory, I would have to…*mark* you too, except Raven."

"You gotta pee on us?" Onyx squeaked out, sounding rather whiny to everyone. "Oh, but Raven gets a golden shower-free pass? What the fuck makes carrot top so special?"

Yonuh snarled out with a sense of pride and protectiveness, "Raven is my mate; she has my mark upon her to prove it! No other shifter would dare threaten her. She's protected, and you mind your tongue when you speak ill of her. My beast is raring to fight anyone at this time of the month. And threatening or hurting her in any way, is a good reason for a fight, Onyx. So show some restraint and respect, please…I'm having a hard enough time controlling the beast, as it is."

Raven beamed a huge grin and felt a swell of pride as love filled her for the healer. Onyx flew back a few feet with his hands out, "Take it easy, big beast, and you too, Yonuh! So is there any way we can get that same mark as her? I don't like the idea of you peeing on me."

"Well, if you want that mark, you'll have to be my mate." Yonuh smiled mischievously. "That means you'll have to bend over, drop your drawers and let my beast have its way with you while it's biting you. That's what Raven did. So, are you game, Onyx?" Yonuh's smile turned into an evil grin.

Onyx eyes anxiously darted from side to side. Finally, he said, "That's okay, I'll take the golden shower. Like I've said before, I don't swing that way and besides you couldn't handle me in bed."

Yonuh laughed. "Probably so, but it wouldn't be me in the bed with you. It would be my 800 pound grizzly pinning you down, teeth in your neck and ramming your tiny ass!"

Nightshade perked up and told the gremlin, "You would so love it too, Onyx. Take a walk on the wild side!" She smiled seductively at the healer. "I'd be willing to take your mark, Yonuh, since Onyx isn't man enough to do it."

"Hey now!" As jealousy took hold, Raven narrowed her eyes at Nightshade. "That's a special mark for a reason, so don't go making light of it! I don't think his beast goes around marking everyone he fucks..." She frowned and looked at the healer. "Or does it, Yonuh?"

He shrugged. "I've never had it happen until I met you, Raven, but my beast isn't turning down Nightshade's offer either. It likes her too. It's not unheard of for shifters to mark multiple partners, but it isn't the best idea to do either."

"Why is that?" Nightshade asked with a playful smile, ignoring Raven's jealous glare. "I see nothing wrong with being able to walk in the woods with total immunity and that sexy beast-mark on me."

Yonuh pointed at Raven and pleaded, "Look at her, Nightshade, please!"

Nightshade looked over at the witch and noticed her green eyes were blazing brightly, full of malice. Her hand was twitching on her wand, waiting for the fight to begin.

Nightshade was about to reach for her black dagger, but Yonuh stepped between them. "The mark makes the person more possessive," he tried to explain. "Jealousy runs high at times too. Those who have marked multiple mates tend to have no mates after a short period of time. The mates usually end up killing each other. Raven is acting on that instinct right now, and I don't want either of you fighting over me. I'm not worth it."

"NOT WORTH IT?!" Both Nightshade and Raven screamed. Yonuh backed away.

As their eyes flared brightly, Yonuh said, "I meant that I'm not worth you two killing each other over me. I love you both, and it would hurt me to see either of you hurting each other on account of me."

"You damn bitches, stow the hormones already!" the little gremlin shouted. "I, for one, enjoy having a happy-go-lucky Yonuh around here…instead of the dead-to-the-world version. So knock it off—or get naked and wrestle for our entertainment. If you hurt him, I'll end you both."

"ONYX—"Yonuh blurted out.

The gremlin turned and cut him off. "I know I just threatened them, but it was only to make a point, you silly, love-crazed bear! Sometimes you gotta do that, so they will both listen to reason. Common sense leaves the room when they start fighting over you, man!"

Raven walked over to Yonuh and grabbed a handful of his long, black hair. She passionately kissed him. He responded by wrapping his big, strong arms around her tightly, letting one hand grope her ass and explore her body. Raven groaned as Yonuh pressed his lips firmly against hers and let his tongue dart into her mouth.

Nightshade's mouth gaped open. She was about to protest their behavior, but Onyx got in her face. "Let her do this to him. It's instinctual for mates to calm the beast when it's needed, and right now, it's really needed!"

"Oh, that's what she's doing?" the necromancer said sarcastically. "I take it you know this from first-hand experience?"

"Yes, I've been around the block a few times, and I've actually learned some things. They have a bond they share with that mark. If the beast is getting mad and ready to lose its shit—and there's no real need for it to be let loose—the mate can soothe the beast inside the shifter. Does that make sense yet, or do you need flash cards? I can go slower."

Nightshade glared at Onyx. "I may be emotionally challenged, but I'm not an idiot, you little fucktard! I really wish you would treat me with a little more respect."

Onyx laughed as he flew up by her ear and growled, "I will when you start paying attention to your surroundings. Had you interfered with Raven, we both would be dead by Yonuh's deadly-sharp bear claws *and* his powerful jaw! I may not be a great teacher, but I know if you irritate someone long enough, they do take notice, so that's why I do and say the things I do. I'm a student of the world because I look, listen, and remember."

Nightshade looked down for a moment, and then she turned her head towards Onyx, who was pointing at Yonuh and Raven. As she watched the couple, the necromancer did notice a dramatic change in Yonuh. He wasn't showing the outward signs of his beast itching to break loose. His bear claws, which had been poking out, were receding back into his fingers. His hands were becoming a more natural human form. When Yonuh opened his eyes, the golden glow from his beast started to retreat back into its inner soul-cave, and at the forefront were Yonuh's dark brown eyes, faintly glowing from the passion Raven was sharing with him.

The fur that bristled on his arms also began to disappear, showing Yonuh's ruggedly cut muscles and sleek Native American skin that made Nightshade smile and want to touch him. The necromancer looked over at Onyx, who gave her a respectful nod of approval. "The more you observe, the longer you will live. Gremlins are great at hiding, so it makes it easy for us to observe our surroundings. You've been taught many things, but this lesson is simple and a lifesaver too."

"I see that," she agreed. "I love using the darkness for most of my observations, but lately, especially after the plague, things have been different. There's no longer a natural order of things that go on during the day or even bump in the night. I haven't had the chance to sit back and observe, like I used to do, mainly because I've been going through the motions of staying alive."

"When we go out into the woods tonight," Onyx told her, "you ought to go back into the shadows again and observe. Hell, we'll all be doing that if Yonuh gets to have his run, so you might as well take advantage of the situation."

Nightshade smiled as she approved of Onyx's reasoning. She reached out and put her hand on his small shoulder. "You're a good person, Onyx. You've got a caring heart too. You may be gruff and talk all nasty and mean, but deep down, I can see the true you."

"Oh knock it off!" the gremlin grumped with a hint of a blush. "I don't want you going all Nicholas Sparks on me! Sheesh, you're about to see me regurgitate my Doritos!"

"Are they not better the second time around?" Nightshade teased as she rubbed Onyx's little belly. "I thought you loved them so much that you would do that regularly."

"You're one sick, twisted bitch; you know that, right? I guess that's why I manage to tolerate being around you. Just for the record, no they don't taste better the second time around. They taste like your ass — nasty and rotten!"

Nightshade laughed as Onyx made a sickly face, sticking his tongue out and acting like he was heaving. A soft moan behind them caught their attention. Yonuh had finally released Raven from his vise-lips and was just holding her next to him. A look of happiness stretched across his face as he smiled contentedly. Raven's eyes were closed as she cuddled as close as she could to the healer, taking deep breaths and inhaling his scent.

"Feeling better, Yonuh?" Onyx asked with a grin and a wink.

"How could I not? I have my mate in my arms, and I'm surrounded by my friends."

"Ah hell! This mushy shit is becoming contagious. Maybe I should leave before I start spouting poetry!"

Nightshade walked over and gave both Raven and Yonuh a hug, saying over her shoulder to the gremlin, as she did, "Onyx, come and join the dark side of love."

Onyx crossed his arms and hovered beside them. "Maybe later. Right now, I'm going to pack a few essentials for our little excursion into the woods tonight. You all should do the same after you're finished with your little orgy—HEY! LET GO, DAMNIT!"

Nightshade snaked her arm out and snatched Onyx's leg, bringing him into the group kicking and screaming. He was pinned by Yonuh, Raven, and Nightshade's arms as they all laughed at his reaction.

"I swear I'll bite the shit out of all of you if you don't let me go! Fucking hippie, bastard bitches! I don't want a hug! Ah man, I feel dirty and violated!"

Yonuh looked down at the squirming gremlin and said in his most gruff voice, "That's the point, Onyx. You'll feel the love whether you like it or not!"

"Now that you have us all gathered around your furry ass," Onyx spat out, "is this where you pee on all of us?"

"Pee on you? Who said anything about being peed on?" Yonuh asked, forcing an innocent look on his face.

"YOU DID!" Onyx screamed in frustration, still kicking, trying to get away. "You said if we wanted to venture out past your damn camp, you had to mark us with your pee."

"But I never said that, Onyx," Yonuh insisted. "I said I would have to mark you, but I didn't say I would have to pee on you." He grinned at the squirming gremlin. "Hmm, sounds like someone is still jumping to conclusions before he knows the full story. You still have much to learn, oh student of the world. All you need is a cloth bag with my urine scent on it. You can wear it around your neck. If you want, you can put other things in the bag to cut down on the pee odor. Other creatures will still be able to smell my scent."

Onyx looked Yonuh in his eyes, and he knew the healer was being honest. It made him feel like an idiot. Nightshade looked down at the little gremlin and asked, with a teasing smile, "Does that make sense yet, or do you need flash cards? Perhaps Yonuh can go slower, so you can keep up?"

Chapter Three

One of the escapees from his jail was a necromancer, and they were not the sort of beings Zordic took lightly. He knew they primarily worked alone and rarely banded together with others. But if they did, it was with their *own kind*. This necromancer had the skills to actually get his name from any one of his dead followers, but would she act on that information?

Of course she would! That's what her ilk does. He growled savagely in a low, vicious tone and swore he'd never find himself a slave to the necromancers again! A most cruel lot, he remembered. They forced me to do things to help them gain edges in their battles or to make their spells more powerful. He shivered, thinking about them.

Enslaved, Zordic vowed he would learn and study everything he came across or witnessed, and in the end, it all paid off. Ignorance is bliss as the humans would say, but to play ignorant around skilled practitioners of the dark arts took skills that most couldn't have pulled off.

Zordic smiled as he felt a great deal of pride knowing he had outwitted, deceived, and learned the ways of the necromancers. Those skills were benefiting him now, and all under their very noses. They had "volunteered" him to aid them in sending a deadly serial killer who was an energy vampire into the void. Most of their magic wasn't working on the vampire because he kept feeding off that magic, along with whichever necromancer got caught in his path.

After they had traveled a long way, Zordic knew that his time to break free of their control had come, and he wanted to make it a permanent break.

For weeks, Zordic had planted the seeds of suspicion in the necromancers' collective unconscious. They come to believe that he knew of a demonic way to fend off the energy vampire during an attack. Once they reached the outskirts of Paris, the necromancers commanded him to tweak the casting spells so they would be more difficult for the energy vampire to absorb.

Zordic gave them a small list of demonic sigils that they had to have in place wherever they planned on fighting the energy vampire. The sigils had to be drawn in their own blood, he told them. For these energy castings to work, each necromancer going into battle had to have a certain mark upon their skin. The demon explained that when he breathed life into his blood magic, the sigils would activate and would act as a kind of shield for them against the energy vampire's physical attack.

Not surprisingly, the necromancers were wary of this plan, but Zordic reinforced in their minds that all who went up against this vampire had failed. Even melee combat wouldn't work because it would leave a person exposed to a simple grab and, in turn, be bitten and drained completely.

In the end, the necromancers agreed to do this. Zordic had them all bare their chests so he could put his mark upon them—an inverted triangle that went from nipple to nipple and traveled downwards to a point, just past the navel. He told them it had to be big since it was a shield and apologized that he had to carve it into their skin. "With it here on your chest," he told them, "it will be concealed from the energy vampire. He won't know what's going on until it's too late."

Each necromancer took turns cutting their hands and letting their blood pool into a bucket, so Zordic could mix and use it for the demonic sigils. He explained that once the sigils were in place and activated, the necromancers would still be in danger. He needed to place them when the battle began, so he could hang back and do his incantation.

The necromancers seemed to have complete faith in him, and none of them bothered questioning him further. He had been amazed that not one of them had asked what the individual demonic sigils meant or how he knew so much about blood magic.

It didn't take long for them to draw the energy vampire out, mainly because he wasn't intimidated by them, and he loved feeding on necromancers. Zordic teleported to several different spots as the battle ensued and quickly put the sigils in the right order. By the time he finished, two necromancers had died.

The lead necromancer cried out, "Zordic, do it now!" This surprised and scared him at the same time. The vampire heard the man and glanced around. He saw Zordic, which meant he put a name to a demon's face.

Irritated beyond measure, Zordic cringed. He didn't like that this energy vampire now knew his name. Having your name known was dangerous for a demon. He tried to push this setback out of his mind as he concentrated and chanted in his demonic language.

Suddenly, all the sigils flared to life, and immediately the necromancers noticed their attacks were beginning to have an effect. The sigils kept the energy vampire at bay while one of their own harried him. A portal opened, and the necromancers forced the vampire towards it.

"ZORDIC, YOU BASTARD!" the vampire screamed in rage when he saw the portal. He realized what the opening meant for him, and he desperately tried to keep away from it. His efforts were useless. "You helped the enemy! I'm Drexel, and I promise to return for your head!"

Once the energy vampire was pushed into the portal, it immediately sealed and dispersed. The remaining necromancers let out cries of victory and patted each other on the backs.

As they all gathered around Zordic, they noticed he was still chanting. The leader of the necromancers called out to him, saying, "Zordic, you may cease the incantations, my friend. The battle is over, and the day is won...by us!" They all laughed.

At that moment, he knew all their guards were down. With a quick thrust, Zordic extended his arms, his clawed-hands open. His incantation reached a feverous pitch as his eyes opened, revealing two black, glowing orbs. One by one, each necromancer fell to the ground convulsing like they were having seizures.

Working in tandem, the blood sigils and then his mark on their chests helped him steal the life essence from a dozen necromancers. Zordic stood over them and watched as they died, one by one. Just before the lead necromancer died, he choked out the words, "Why? Why this...betrayal? Why, Zordic?"

Zordic knelt down and, with an icy cold calm, said, "I'm a demon. What did you expect? I've been waiting for this moment for a long time, and now I'm free. You can now die knowing you taught me about your ilk and your ways. I'm sure it will come in handy some day."

With a toothy grin, he yanked the last bit of life essence from the necromancers' leader and stored it all in an ethereal globe he had just summoned.

He realized even back then that life essences could not only give one more power, but they could be traded to others for payment of services, so he saved them and stored them for centuries. He felt he would instinctively know when he would need them the most, and it seemed to him now that the time was drawing near.

On the open market of black arts, life essences were worth more than human souls. The essences were easier to trade to others, plus most entities didn't like dealing with the souls, period.

The sound of a door opening caused Zordic to snap out of his reminiscing and back to reality. A small group of his followers had come pouring in, with Gordon bringing up the rear. The man was pointing out where to clean and designating several of the others to remove "the garbage" from the master's table. The group charged with body disposal walked out of the room, leaving Gordon and the others to sweep up chunks of flesh and place them into an old, fifty-five gallon trash can on wheels. The body disposal group returned with a water hose and a long, gray garbage cart.

The men pulled the garbage cart over to the steel table and scurried around, trying to pick up the remains of the flayed shape-shifter. The shifter's blood seemed to act like glue, and the loose skin on his back was sticky and stringy. It took a few tugs, but they managed to peel him off the table. The body was tumbled into the garbage cart, which already had its own brown and crimson colors on the inside. The cart was pushed out of the room.

"Take it to the furnace in the basement, my children," Zordic said with a benevolent smile. "We don't need that filth stinking up our home now, do we?"

Gordon walked across the room and over to a sink that had been retro-fitted with a brass hose bibb valve.

As he screwed on the hose, Zordic calmly called out, "Make sure you don't get any water on my sigils, or you'll be next on the cleanup list, Gordon."

Gordon's heart sank. "I understand, my master. I'll be careful," he replied in a shaky voice as he turned on the water. He hosed down the floor, pushing the crimson lake towards a water drain in the floor. The other men had push brooms. It was their job to scrub up any thick, bloody chunks that was stuck to the floor. They also helped guide the water to the drain.

Feeling much trepidation, Gordon slowly walked towards the steel table, knowing he had to rinse it off. The master's blood sigils were nearby. He didn't dare put his thumb over the water nozzle here. Instead, he let a narrow stream of water flow smoothly over the table, rinsing it. He was grateful the table had holes in it which made the cleanup easier. Several other men scrubbed away the skin patches and other blood remnants stuck to the table.

As the steel table got fully cleaned, Gordon pinched the hose and walked back to the sink and shut off the water. He set the hose end in the sink and let go of it, releasing the last bit of trapped water. He turned and noticed Zordic was looking around the room, inspecting the sigils. A cold sweat broke out all over Gordon's body as he began to fear for his life. He closed his eyes, trying to recall if the water spray could have hit any of the sigils. As his heart raced, waiting for Zordic's judgment, his anxiety level shot through the roof. He shook so hard, he thought he might actually collapse.

"Ah, my children, you've done well in cleaning up what that filth left behind." He glanced at Gordon and gave him an evil grin. "You may relax now, Gordon. The sigils are untouched."

The man let out a huge pent up breath as he wiped his brow with the back of his forearm. Zordic finished his examination of the room and was very pleased. Now it was time to go back to work. He looked directly at Gordon. "Take several of my children down to the holding area and fetch me another shape-shifter to interrogate."

"Yes, Master, right away!" As Gordon ran out of the room, Zordic could hear him yell out, "Carl! Jack! Tom! Come help me fetch another shifter for the master's table!"

Zordic looked down lovingly at his steel table and spoke barely above a whisper, "Where are you, my little shape-shifter? I so wish to meet you and partake of that exotic, intoxicating blood of yours. Why must you hide from me? We could be great friends with benefits — where I drink your blood and reap the benefits of it!" He ran his clawed finger along the steel as if it was a lover. The table had, after all, given him a great deal of pleasure over the years.

A tingling sensation made him flinch as he felt the use of magic somewhere. Zordic anxiously twisted the protection ring on his finger as he felt the tell-tale signature of someone scrying for him. That damn redheaded witch! It had to be her. Who else could it be? No one else was left alive who knew his true name, let alone that he existed and walked freely on the Earth.

He concentrated hard, putting up magical barriers of his own and sent out his energy signature to different areas where he had been recently. He had meticulously buried crystals with his imprint on them to further confuse and frustrate the witch. Surely, she wouldn't be able to find him.

Zordic felt a small sense of satisfaction as the scrying energy went away, and he noticed he was grinning from ear to ear. The bitch is stumped, and now I'm once again the master of my own freedom.

But that happiness was short-lived because of the creeping voice in the back of his head, reminding him that if she could do this, it was only a matter of time before she discovered a new way to find him.

Hell, she could be part of a coven, he thought. With that kind of power at her disposal, there'll be nowhere for the demon to hide. Anger took hold of Zordic as he thought first of this witch scrying for him and then about his enslavement at the hands of the necromancers. Why can't they leave me alone? I just want to live in peace and rule over humanity. Is that so wrong?

From the open door, Zordic could hear the familiar sound of heavy combat boots marching down the hall towards him. No more time for anger, Zordic thought. It's time to introduce my new friend to my table.

Zordic centered his mind and body, trying to shake off any visible signs of distress that his followers might see. I must maintain control. If my followers perceive me as weak in any way, I could lose all of them.

Through the open door, Gordon and three other men marched in, weapons drawn. In the middle of the group was a young woman who Zordic thought was in her early twenties. Around her neck, the men had placed a neuron disruptor which kept supernatural beings from using their powers when being escorted. It also fed off the wearer's natural energy, helping it to keep powered.

Standing slightly over five feet tall, the petite prisoner had barely any muscle or fat on her slight frame. As Zordic looked her up and down, the shape-shifter said with annoyance, "So you drag me all the way over here so you can ogle me? If I'd wanted that, I'd have gone downtown where the good looking pervs live."

Zordic smiled. He liked her attitude and was hoping she had the special blood he craved so he could teach her what a real perv was like.

The demon looked her squarely in the eyes and then ordered, "Strip her down now, my children. I must interrogate this one slowly."

Eyes wide, a look of horror spread over her pretty, heart-shaped face. The shape-shifter felt hands moving over her entire body and heard the awful sound of her clothes tearing in places. She did what she could to defend herself, but the neuron disruptor had weakened her to the point of almost collapsing just from the struggle.

As much as the men were disgusted by her true supernatural character, they were men, nonetheless, and they pawed and groped her anywhere they could.

She felt something at her feet and glanced down. Her shredded clothes were in a pile on the floor. Tears flowed down her face as she felt the coldness of the room invade her naked body.

"Now would you be so kind and help the lady up on the table," Zordic said, "and make sure she's restrained."

The men lifted up the shape-shifter like she weighed no more than a feather. Squirming and struggling in their vise-like grips, she realized to her horror that she could barely move. She felt her energy being sucked out of her body by the collar around her neck.

As the men placed her limp body on the steel table, her head lolled from side to side like she was in a daze. Her wrists and ankles were bound tightly and securely locked in the magically-spelled and imbued restraint cuffs. Gordon leaned over the female and unlocked and removed the neuron disruptor from around her neck and then spat in her face.

"Ah, nicely done, my children. You may go down to the cafeteria where there is music, women in waiting, whether they like it or not, with all sorts of food and drink.

Enjoy your rewards for serving me. Oh, Gordon, do be a good son and pass along that all witches and necromancers are to be killed on sight, with extreme prejudice," Zordic said with a toothy, malevolent grin.

The men left the room in a jovial mood, laughing and patting each other on the back. Zordic looked down on the shape-shifter's naked body and felt it would be best to test her blood now. No sense mutilating this little body, especially if her blood had what he so dearly craved. He grabbed her arm and pierced the palm of her hand with his black thumb claw, making her yelp in pain.

"What are you doing, you sick fuck? Is this how you get your kicks? Strapping down, torturing and then raping women? You're a pathetic excuse of a demon!"

Zordic ignored the shape-shifter's rant as he closed his eyes and slid his thumb into his mouth, suckling all the blood off. As the characteristics of her blood flooded over his taste buds, his heart sank with disappointment. This little one wasn't his special prize, but that wasn't going to stop him from claiming her life essence.

"Thirsty are ya, big boy? I guess you're nothing more than a fucking leech! OUCH! HEY! WHAT THE FUCK! STOP THAT!" Zordic cut her rant off once he started carving his inverted triangle from nipple to nipple, all the way down just past her navel and back up again.

"Unfortunately for you, my little friend, you're not the one I'm looking for —"

"Good! Untie me, get me some clothes and we can just call this a big misunderstanding."

"I'm afraid it's not that simple. If you were the one I wanted, your life would have been spared. You'd still be my prisoner, of course, but your blood would be mine to drink.

Since your blood is normal, I'll take your life essence as payment for not being the one I wanted. I would apologize to you, but I don't care. The world will now have one less supernatural being in it."

The shape-shifter thrashed and yanked at her restraints. She had a fierce, determined look on her face, straining to unleash her beast.

Zordic put his hand on her chest and said coldly, "Relax, my friend, the restraints have been spelled and imbued with powerful magic, so there will be no shifting coming from you.
You might as well get comfortable because your pretty, bony ass isn't going anywhere — except, to the other side." He rubbed his hand over her breasts and said out loud, "Hmm, do I torture this lovely, little body, or should I just kill you now? Decisions, decisions, indeed!"

"I'd rather die than be soiled by you!" the shape-shifter hissed.

"You don't get a say in this, so I might as well have some fun…as I kill you and take your life essence." As he gazed down into her eyes, thoughts of the witch who had been scrying for him earlier flooded his mind. "Time to cash in on some of my stored life essences and put an end to this bothersome witch," he mused.

"Huh?" the little shape-shifter asked and swallowed hard.

An evil smile creased Zordic's lips. "Just thinking out loud, my dear."

And he knew exactly what to send after the witch.

Chapter Four

The sky grew darker with each passing minute, and clouds overhead released a light drizzle. The damp wetness made everything in the woods smell freshly cleansed and alive. The moistened grass glistened with what little natural light remained, and the soil teemed with night crawlers under the felled leaves and tree stumps. As trees swayed in the breeze, the sound of barn owls screeching could be heard off in the distance.

Yonuh pulled off the road and into a small area near the edge of the woods that was encroached by thick sticker bushes. As he stepped out of the white van, he took a deep breath, inhaling the freedom of the night and feeling an immediate rush of euphoria. His beast was urging him on to mark their territory. It wanted loose for the night.

Raven slipped up next to him and took his hand as she leaned on him. "It's so peaceful and beautiful out here. If it wasn't for the fact we have to watch out for the P.A.N.E.L. squad, I would be dancing skyclad by fire light." She was rewarded by Yonuh's low growl of approval as he squeezed her hand firmly.

"No time for romance out here," Onyx said as he held his modified impact gun, inspecting it while scanning the area for trouble. "We have a job to do and assholes to kill!"

"So how far is it to your camp area, Yonuh?" Nightshade asked as she looked up and down the road, making sure they hadn't been followed.

"Roughly a mile ahead of us," the healer told her. "Just be careful because there's a small creek that's concealed by ferns and sticker bushes. You could easily fall off the edge without warning. I know because I've done it too many times to count," he said and giggled. Both Raven and Nightshade smiled. For reasons they couldn't explain, they loved his giggle.

"I said no time for romance," Onyx grumped in a reprimanding tone. "I guess I should have included tussles in the bushes, judging from the odor you two ladies are putting out."

"You're a real buzz kill," Raven said and blushed. "I can't help it if nature makes me feel so alive and free. To have Yonuh out here…" she sighed contentedly. "Well, I just can't help that my natural needs are in overdrive at this moment."

"The night is my companion," Nightshade told them. "The sooner we make it to your camp, the faster I can get reacquainted with her once again. It's been way too long, and I want to stalk the night too."

"Is that what's making you lustier than a virgin succubus in a dildo factory?" Onyx asked with a raised eyebrow.

A mischievous grin washed across the necromancer's face. "I was just thinking of you, Onyx, and how fun it would be to track you down and have my way with you."

"Ha! In your dark, wet dreams…maybe! You couldn't handle what I have anyways."

"Is that a fact? What makes you so sure of that, little big man?"

"I'm alive, so I'm not your type!" Onyx cackled as he dodged a volley of rocks thrown by Nightshade.

Onyx darted off into the woods and out of sight. Nightshade searched, using her natural night vision, but she still couldn't see him. As she started to walk ahead, she stumbled forward and felt something to the right of her tug on her cloak. The necromancer found she was sliding down a wet, muddy embankment. Suddenly, she splashed face first into a stream of water.

"Watch your step, guys. Nightshade just found the creek Yonuh was talking about," Onyx hollered out as he hovered above the water with a huge grin on his small, dark face.

Yonuh and Raven looked over the edge just in time to see Nightshade slowly rise out of the creek. She spewed water out of her mouth and coughed. Her silver, almond-shaped eyes glowed brightly from anger and frustration. Furiously, she unsheathed her black dagger as she looked up at the gremlin with a mud-caked scowl.

"You little prick! You tripped me! You yanked me by my cloak, so I'd go over the edge!"

"What? Me? I'm shocked and appalled you believe I would do such a mean thing!" Onyx exclaimed. He forced an innocent look on his face, while making over-exaggerated gestures with his hands. "I'm here trying to look out for Yonuh's safety, as well as the rest of you. I can't do my job if you plan on being a clumsy twit who wants to play in the water all night. Would you like me to help you out of there, or—"

Nightshade seemed to relax. A smile crossed her lips as she stared up at Onyx, who seemed dumbfounded by her reaction.

"To our left is an easier way to cross the creek," Yonuh called out, pointing toward the spot. He couldn't help noticing a change in the energy around Onyx. As he walked in front of Raven to help usher her down the bank safely, he kept an eye on the gremlin.

Onyx shrugged his shoulders, figuring Nightshade was taking his latest prank in good stride. He turned around to see which way Yonuh and Raven were going. As he did, Onyx got a look of pure horror on his face and flew backwards extremely fast, yelling out, "HOLY FUCK! Guys, run! We gotta—OOF!" Onyx turned around just in time. He slammed into a huge oak tree, where he dropped from the air like a sack of potatoes.

Yonuh and Raven ran over to see if Onyx was okay. Yonuh stood guard, looking in the general direction where the gremlin had been before he flew into the tree. He couldn't see anything scarier than an opossum family hanging upside down on a nearby branch.

Raven dropped to her knees, looking the little guy over. The gremlin had a small gash on his forehead but, other than that, he seemed okay. He slowly opened his eyes, looking dazed, and glanced around. "What happ…?" he said weakly. Suddenly, his eyes grew wide, and he began squirming, trying to get up. Raven grabbed hold of him and firmly held him down.

"LET ME GO, DAMMIT!" Onyx screamed as he struggled to break free of the witch's hold. "We have to leave," he pleaded. "I can't be here anymore. We're surrounded by…oh, it's sooo BAD!"

Yonuh looked down at the little gremlin, who still struggled to get free, and then he turned his head in Nightshade's direction. She was casually washing mud off her face and clothes. He walked over to her and asked with a smirk, "I gotta know what you did to Onyx?"

"Moi?" she said, feigning innocence. "What makes you think I did something to him?" The necromancer batted her eyes at Yonuh.

"I sensed the change of energy around him just before he went all kamikaze into that tree and—"

"Oh that? You believe I had something to do with that?" She pointed in Onyx's direction, where he was still hollering in terror as Raven sat on him. "You know the safety of everyone here is my top priority. Those petty games he likes to play is so beneath me."

"Belladonna!" Yonuh impatiently growled as low as he could.

"Oh fine, I did it, but he pissed me off! I just wanted to scare him, you know. Teach him a lesson not to mess with me. I didn't expect him to go all ape-shit into that tree."

"Come on," Yonuh urged her. As he turned and walked back toward Onyx, Nightshade sighed and followed him.

Raven looked over her shoulder and hissed, "I could use a little help holding him down!"

The healer dropped to his knees and grabbed hold of Onyx's little shoulders. Raven scooted down and held his ankles. When Nightshade walked up, she looked down at Onyx. A big smile swept across her lips.

"Why the hell are you so damn happy?" Raven growled. "He's hurt and—"She studied the necromancer for a moment. "You did this to him, didn't you?" She wanted to let go of Onyx to throttle her, but she couldn't.

"Guilty as charged," Nightshade said as she beamed a smile at her. "I didn't think he would head ram an oak tree but, then again, I had no idea what he saw when I cast my *Terrify* spell on him."

"Take it off him now!" Raven demanded. "I don't want him to hurt himself again, you fucking bitch!"

"I can't; it has to run its course. That's why it works so well. It's good for when one is surrounded and in need of an escape."

"Oh wonderful!" the witch growled sarcastically. "Now Yonuh won't have his opportunity to run, and it's all because YOU can't take a joke! I'm going to kill you—"

"Raven, my love, calm down," Yonuh ordered. "I'll be able to run tonight. I believe I can extract her curse from Onyx. I just need you both to work together at holding him down, so I can do it. Will you please both do that for me?" he asked in a demanding tone but gave them a small, pleading smile as he did.

Raven's anger seemed to ebb a little as she smiled back at him. "How's a girl supposed to resist that smile of yours?" she said coyly. "Only for you…I'll behave." She glanced over at Nightshade and scowled. "We'll be having words later!"

Nightshade ignored her and dropped to her knees. "I'm curious to see if you can actually do this, Yonuh." She placed her hands on the squirming gremlin, making sure Yonuh got a good view of her cleavage.

The healer let out a soft groan as he shifted his gaze away from her. He began rubbing his hands together in a circular motion, heating them up. He put one of his hands on Onyx's forehead, and immediately the gash began to mend.

Onyx closed his eyes and seemed to enjoy the warm comfort coming from Yonuh. He gave out a small sigh.

Yonuh moved his hand down Onyx's chest, still wanting to give him comfort. He held his other hand just a few inches above the gremlin's little head. The healer's hand looked like it was waiting to catch something as he began chanting in his native tongue of Cherokee.

Yonuh's face showed both strain and anger at the same time, which made Raven and Nightshade look at each other with worried concern that this might be more than he could handle. The healer made a circular motion with his hand, swirling the energy around Onyx's head. Before long, a dull red glow appeared to be dancing in Yonuh's hand. It seemed alive, trying to escape his grip on it. He chanted louder and faster, forcing more of the curse out of the gremlin.

Yonuh eased his chant slightly as he pulled his hand away slowly. He took his other hand off Onyx's chest and made a circular motion around the curse energy, creating a bubble around it. When he was satisfied with it, he put his hand on the ground and forced the curse energy to flow into the earth. Yonuh sat quietly with his eyes closed for a moment, regaining his senses. As he opened them, he noticed that both Raven and Nightshade had a look of awe on their faces.

"I...I can't believe you were able to do that. That was amazing!" Nightshade exclaimed with glowing, disbelieving eyes.

"Are you okay, Yonuh? I was worried because it looked like you were hurting from it," Raven said sympathetically as she stroked his arm.

"I'm fine, but the curse did put up a fight." He glanced at the necromancer. "Quite the nasty energy you put on him, Nightshade. Please don't do it again."

"I'll try not to, but there are no guarantees. If he can't behave himself, then maybe I'll not be able to control myself. Onyx is very good at bringing out my nastier side."

The gremlin shook his head, ridding himself of the last bit of fog left by the curse. When he noticed everyone was hovering around him, holding him down, he politely screamed, "GET YOUR DAMN HANDS OFF ME! I DON'T LIKE BEING MAN-HANDLED!"

Raven and Nightshade let go of him, and he immediately took to the air, searching all around. Seeing nothing, he looked down and asked, "Is it gone? Did you guys defeat it? What the hell happened?"

"Nothing's there, Onyx," Yonuh explained. "As retribution for knocking her in the creek, Nightshade slapped a *Terrify* curse on you, making your mind see terrifying things that appear to you as real."

"YOU DID THAT TO ME?" Onyx screamed. "YOU FUCKING BITCH, I'LL KILL YOU THREE WAYS TO THE FUCKING MOON!" He flew straight at Nightshade. Yonuh stepped in between the gremlin and his target. Onyx ended up in Yonuh's waiting arms, and the healer took the brunt of the little guy's attack. He quickly pinned Onyx to the ground.

Yonuh held him tightly and let his soothing, calming energy slip into the gremlin's body. "Enough of this bullshit!" the healer growled. "You fucked with her, and she returned the favor by cursing you. So now you're both even. We came out here together with the agreement to watch each other's back, not to play pranks and kill each other. If that's how you two want to act, then leave! I'm having a hard enough time as it is without having to play referee. I can do this on my own if all of you want to fight!"

Onyx grunted as he stared up at Yonuh's face and knew he was being serious. "It's too dangerous for you to be out here by yourself," the gremlin whined. "You know I'm not going to leave you, so...I'll stop being so...'*me*' and behave." He glanced at Nightshade. "No more spelling me! You hear me, you albino corpse fucker?"

Nightshade ignored Onyx's rant as she put her hand on Yonuh's shoulder. She shuddered from the energy he was putting out and said, "I'm sorry too, Yonuh. I promised myself that I would keep you safe and protect you from harm. It's an oath I don't want to break." She dropped her shoulders and hung her head low. "I love you, and I refuse to let my pettiness get the best of me again. Raven's lucky to have you as her mate, and I'll see to it she gets to keep you all in one piece."

Raven crawled over to Yonuh. "You're stuck with me, and you can't get rid of me that easily. I plan on having words with her but not now, my love. Your run and safety is more important right now, so let's get back on track and let that sexy bear have some fun tonight!"

Yonuh's dark brown eyes flared as his beast's golden eyes showed through in total agreement with her. He looked down at Onyx. "Just out of curiosity, what did you see that scared you so badly?"

"Ask her, she's the one who did it to me!" Onyx hissed at Nightshade.

"I only control the curse; I don't choose what you see because I don't know what would scare you."

Onyx eyed her suspiciously but finally said, "It was a horrible beast with no face, green and slimy, and it was covered in plague chutes all over its body. It was probably twenty-five feet tall too!"

"Wow, that does sound scary!" Raven said with wide eyes, picturing the beast in her mind.

"But that's not the worst of it. This thing was throwing Doritos everywhere. Corrupted with the plague, it was singing that fucking song "My heart will go on" as it defiled my beloved Doritos! The horror of it all…" Onyx shuddered.

"That was the worst part of it all?" Nightshade snorted and laughed. "Singing the Titanic song and ruining Doritos? I thought it would be worse than that."

Yonuh let go of Onyx and stood up, dusting grass and dirt off his clothes. He noticed his shirt had new holes in it and blood stains too.

He looked down at Onyx, who shrugged his shoulders. "What can I say?" the gremlin said, grinning sheepishly. "Those were meant for the necrophiliac over there. I wasn't intending on impaling you."

Yonuh put his hands over his injuries and softly chanted. Before long, the puncture wounds from Onyx's claws were healed over, and new skin had grown over them. He let out a heavy breath and said, while pointing past everyone, "My camp area isn't far from here. Let's stop the squabbling and get a move on."

Yonuh walked past everyone with an irritated look on his face. He felt like it would have been better if he had just snuck off and left everyone back at the Costco. He knew being alone made things like this easier, but he hated the loneliness—although, at times like tonight, he yearned for the solo life. He shook his head as he mentally slapped himself. No way will I give up on this new life, he thought. He had friends who cared about him and not just the energy he put out. His energy had made most of his social relationships all one-sided.

He found his one true love and mate in Raven Moonrose, and he would rather die than lose her. The beautiful Nightshade was a scarred and confused lady, with a cold heart; however, she was now warming up, and he wouldn't have her any other way. He liked that about her — her willingness to change and improve. Onyx, on the other hand, was a small pain in the ass with a mouth and an attitude bigger than the galaxy. He was quirky and rude, but Yonuh enjoyed the gremlin's company, and he made everyday life interesting.

The healer smiled as he mentally thanked the Great Spirit for the path he was on. He also gave thanks for his new companions who showed him their loyalty, love, and concern for his wellbeing. He felt a sense of pride and happiness he never thought he would experience in his lifetime. He had a huge, goofy grin on his face as Raven caught up with him. Slipping her arm around his, she sighed and said, "So what's got you grinning like a Cheshire cat?"

"My life as it is right now. I wouldn't have it any other way. I'm happy and grateful to have all of you, especially you, Raven."

Raven blushed as she squeezed Yonuh's arm tighter. "I didn't know love could be like this. It seems my love for you grows with every second I'm around you.
And…well, it's more than I expected, that's for sure. I'm definitely going to enjoy this ride and you too, my sexy bear!"

"Mom! Dad! Are we there yet?" Onyx cried out as he flew beside Nightshade. The necromancer was walking backwards, keeping her eyes open, so no one could sneak up on them.

"Don't make me turn this car around," Yonuh said, playing the gremlin's game. "If I have to, you won't get any Doritos for a whole week!"

"NO!" Onyx shot ahead of Raven and Yonuh. He flipped over and flew backwards, with his hands clasped together in a praying motion. "I'm sorry. I'll be a good, little gremlin, I swear! Don't take away my precioussssss Doritos!"

"Wow, now that's the most pathetic groveling I've ever seen," Raven said as she snorted. "Doritos is his weakness; how sad it must be for his life to revolve around those cheese-dusted chips."

Onyx pulled a bag of Doritos from his satchel and rubbed on it like it was a pet. "Don't listen to her," he said softly, "you hear me? She knows not of what she speaks because she hasn't been educated in your wonderful ways of goodness." He glared at Raven. "Heathens, all of you!"

"What will you do when the last of the Doritos are gone because, you know, one day it will happen?" Raven asked with a smirk.

"I'd die of a broken heart and then throw myself off the St. John's Bridge! The world would no longer be suitable for me to live in!" Onyx said with a pouting face.

"That ego and big head of yours would save your scrawny ass. Besides, you'd probably bounce off the water to safety, skipping down the river like a rock," Raven said, teasing him.

"No, that wouldn't happen to me. That would happen if you jumped off." Onyx flew above her and patted her hair repeatedly, "That mass of curly red hair would bounce your ass like a beach ball!"

"Damn, I knew I forgot my fly swatter! It would come in handy right about now," Raven irritably said as she swatted her hand above her head, just missing Onyx.

"All clear in the rear back there, pale tits?" Onyx hollered back at Nightshade, who was still walking backwards.

"I believe so, but I'll go ask your green, slimy giant friend to confirm this for me," the necromancer replied as she gave him the middle finger.

The brush gave way to a small, circular clearing surrounded by trees. Towards the middle was a rock circle that had black ash and charred wood — remnants of an old fire pit. The grass in the clearing had been trampled down, making the ground into a soft padded nest to lie on. Yonuh turned around to the others and said, "It isn't much, but this is my campsite. Over there in that thicket is a small lockbox that has matches, lighters, and a fire starter puck, with plenty of firewood next to it."

As Nightshade gathered the firewood, Onyx flew over and grabbed a box of matches and a fire starter puck. "Matches and a fire starter puck? I was expecting a pointy stick and kindling. You know, like your people used back in the day," the gremlin snickered.

"What can I say?" Yonuh said. "This is much quicker and easier. If you want to be more traditional and rub sticks together, then go for it. There's also a pocketknife in the box to whittle your own sticks."

"Naw, that's okay. I can use these. Besides, Raven might get jealous if we rubbed our sticks together." Onyx cackled at his own double entendre.

While Onyx set the fire starter puck in place under the stack of firewood, Nightshade set up the fire pit. The gremlin struck a match and set it on the fire starter puck. Before long, they had a nice, cozy fire burning.

Nightshade sat near the fire, so she could let the heat dry her clothes. She glared at Onyx as she remembered why she was soaking wet.

Yonuh gave Raven a long hug and kiss, and then he gently ushered her to a seat by the fire. She looked up at him and gave him a reluctant, pouty face. "No fair, I want to sit with you by the fire some more. I promise not to get too greedy or selfish tonight." Standing perfectly still and ignoring everything else, love murmurings passed between them as they stroked each other's face and hair.

Suddenly, a noise caused them to turn their heads and look toward the woods. "Is someone throwing up?" Raven asked, looking bewildered.

Onyx flew over a nearby thicket and back towards the fire, wiping his mouth with the back of his hand. "All this mushy crap from you two is making me sick! I think I threw up my own spleen. Enough with the lovey-dovey junk," he growled. "Or get a cave!"

"Admit it, Onyx," Nightshade replied. "You're actually happy they're together and in love. You're just putting on a show to pick on them. I seriously doubt you're that sick. Hmm, I shall remember to do that later."

"Do what later?" Onyx narrowed his eyes as he looked at her warily.

Nightshade shrugged her shoulders and gave him an evil grin. "In due time, you'll find out soon enough."

Yonuh backed away from the fire pit and pulled out two leather pouches, each cinched together by a leather cord. He smiled at the others as he held them up. "I'll be right back. I just gotta fix these for you guys."

"Oh goody," Onyx said sarcastically. "I can't wait to be sniffing-buddies with your piss all night!"

"Since you're so thrilled by this," Yonuh shot back, "I'll super soak yours!"

Raven and Nightshade both doubled over laughing while ignoring Onyx's irritable glare. After a short while, Yonuh walked back into the clearing sporting two pouches, each dripping wet with his urine. He grinned as he walked over to Onyx and handed him one.

"Thanks dad!" Onyx wrinkled his nose as he slipped the leather cord over his head, letting the pouch drop into place. It made a wet, squishing sound as it hit against his chest. "It's just what I always wanted, *Eau De Ruxpin* cologne!"

Yonuh giggled as he handed the other piss-soaked pouch to Nightshade and noticed she was smiling at him. He also noticed Raven wore the same expression, but he figured the two ladies were merely amused by Onyx's drama show. Nightshade tied the necklace to a belt loop on her pants.

Onyx took noticed and whined to Yonuh, "Hey! Why does she get to do that? You never said we could wear it on other places!"

"You're right, Onyx, but I never said it had to go around your neck either," he said grinning. "Remember, as long as you're wearing the pouch, my scent will deter other shifters and *weres* from attacking you." When he saw the gremlin scowling, he reminded him, "You could have asked me where you should wear it, Onyx. It's not my fault that you once again assumed wrongly."

The gremlin looked at Nightshade, who was smirking. When she opened her mouth to speak, Onyx cut her off. "Don't you dare say anything about flash cards," he growled, "or I swear I'll tea bag you in the face with this piss bag!" Nightshade promptly closed her mouth but gave him a knowing smile.

Raven chuckled. "I'm glad Yonuh marked me as his mate. As much as I love him, I wouldn't want to wear one of his piss bags all night."

Yonuh laughed and ran his hand over Raven's hair as he lovingly looked down at her. "It's time for me to go, my sweet Raven." He glanced at the others. "Everyone make a big effort to be safe tonight, especially if you see any of Zordic's cronies out here."

"We will, but I'm curious about something, and I want to try it with you tonight," Raven told him.

"What might that be?"

"I'm curious to know if you can hear us telepathically as a bear, and if so, can you reply back?"

"Huh?" he exclaimed with surprise. "Now that you mention it, I too would like to know that as well." Yonuh leaned down and firmly kissed Raven on her lips. Slowly, he backed away, leaving her wanting more from him.

He grabbed the hem of his shirt and slowly tugged it over his head. Nightshade leaned against Raven and said, "Mm, this has to be the best part of coming out here. I'm thoroughly going to enjoy this show. I think we should have brought some popcorn, don't you agree, my redheaded hooker?"

Raven giggled like a schoolgirl and replied, "You know it, you dark and mysterious slut! I could never get enough of this eye candy. I'd watch him all night!"

"The hell with watching," Nightshade declared. "I'd tackle and ride his ass for as long as I could! I'm sure you would agree that is way better of the two choices." Raven smiled as she nodded in agreement.

Onyx sniffed around and then asked Yonuh, "Is there a particular reason you chose this spot as your favorite campsite? It definitely has some interesting odors, all mixing and meshing together."

Yonuh kicked his shoes off and began unbuckling his belt. "This happens to be where I met Fruxendall—you know, Bigfoot. Well, more like this is where I found him. He was in a bad predicament; his leg had gotten caught in a huge bear trap set by a couple of drunken human hunters."

"So do tell the class what happened," Onyx urged as he stuffed a couple of Doritos into his mouth. "I can imagine he wasn't in the best of moods."

"Fruxendall had traveled from his dimension and landed here on the trap. It snapped around his leg, which tripped him. As he fell, his leg broke. He started screaming—a sound so horrible it would have sent most creatures and beings running, if they had a lick of sense about them. I was close by and had seen it happen, so I moved towards him to help him out. Only, as I neared him, the hunters excitedly ran over to him. I stopped and watched them for a few minutes, hoping they would help him. No such luck! Shotgun in one hand and a beer bottle in the other, the hunters stood over Fruxendall, taunting him. One of the men had the nerve to piss on him!"

"Well that explains the odor," Onyx mused. "Wet hair and piss, all mixed with sulfur!"

"I couldn't stand it any longer, so I crept to the nearest tree and shifted. I stood behind both hunters, who were ready to shoot poor Fruxendall, and let out a roar that made them both jump. They stumbled as they whirled around, and both of them fell." Yonuh began to unbutton his pants.

"I killed one while Fruxendall snatched the other hunter and crushed his head like a grape. I shifted back in front of him and told him that I meant him no harm. I also explained that I would free him and heal his leg. He was in great pain, but he was also still leery of me. That didn't stop me, though, from opening the bear trap.

"He howled in pain as he removed his leg from the trap. I gently touched where it had broken, and immediately he calmed down, feeling my soothing energy. I chanted and mended his leg to the point that it showed no damage, just bloody fur. Fruxendall opened the psychic communication pathways in my head, and we spoke to each other and became allies."

As Yonuh kicked his feet out from his pants, he picked them up and placed them with the rest of his clothes, earning several moans of approval from Nightshade and Raven. Looking at Raven, he dropped to his hands and knees. He winked and blew a kiss at her as he began to shift.

Yonuh's eyes went from a dark brown to a glowing gold, almost amber color. As his size grew, fur rapidly sprouted all over his massive body. Raven stood up and strolled over to Yonuh, running her fingers through the fur around his head. So soft, she thought, as she hugged him and kissed his massive forehead.

"Okay, my sexy beast, let's see if we can chat telepathically." Raven smiled as Yonuh licked her face.

"*Yonuh, can you hear me, my love?*"

The bear's head bobbed up and down.

"*Good, now you try,*" Raven said as she backed away.

Yonuh stared at her for the longest time before she heard his voice inside her head. "*Raven…hard to control…working…talk…*"

"*I see. It's very garbled, so let's have you say the word 'help' if you need us. Simple words may get through easier for you, sweetheart. Now go play and have fun, just don't bring any stray bears back with you!*"

Yonuh let out a growl as he turned around and ran off into the woods at full speed. Raven felt a hand on her shoulder and looked around. Nightshade leaned in and kissed her softly on her cheek and said psychically, *"Now it's our time to keep watch over him. I'm going to move around along the creek as I dust off my nighttime stealth. If you two need me, you know how to contact me. Be safe, both of you. Something feels off tonight, and I'm not sure why."* Nightshade slowly backed away and melded into the darkness.

She crept in the shadows and seemed to be one with the darkness. A sense of calm washed over her, something she hadn't felt in a long time. She knew this feeling came over her anytime she stalked the night. This was her playground, and tonight she felt there would be plenty of playmates.

Nightshade smiled as she slipped through the shadows like a panther. She pulled out her black dagger and prepared it by charging it up with energy in case someone actually spotted her. The black dagger glowed slightly, and it seemed to hum with energy. She made her way to the creek and found a spot where a felled tree crossed over the water, making it easier to move to the other side quietly. As she crept low, along the tree, Nightshade could barely make out voices coming from upstream. She smiled.

"If you see anything, check in," Raven ordered psychically. *"Check in even if you don't see anything."*

"Yes, Mom! We'll call and check in with each other in, say, twenty minute intervals? I'm going to be in the tree tops, watching everything from above," Onyx said as he flew up and away.

"I'll head in the opposite direction of Nightshade and wander through the woods," Raven said. *"If the P.A.N.E.L. squad is out here tonight, it'll be one way to draw them out into the open and take them out."*

As Raven walked away from the camp, she looked down at Yonuh's pile of clothes strewn on the ground. She felt puzzled as she stared at them. She distinctly remembered he had left his clothes stacked neatly together. Now, though, they were toppled over. Even more disturbing was that Yonuh's blood-stained shirt was now missing!

Raven narrowed her glowing green eyes as she walked through the thicket and into the woods. She psychically called to the others, *"The squad's definitely here, guys — be ready for anything!"*

Chapter Five

Gordon slinked away from the enemies' campsite undetected. He felt a sense of pride at being able to not only snatch the shape-shifter's bloody shirt but also for learning each of the enemies' names. He had taken a few pictures of them also. Gordon reasoned that if they got away tonight, his master would have a face and a name to put with the blood he seemed so obsessed over.

He was surprised he had gotten so close to these vermin. They hadn't even noticed him. He felt a swell of luck around him and knew the divine savior was with him and his team tonight. Our goal will be achieved, he thought. My master will reward me well with what I've discovered, and if my crew captures this shape-shifter named Yonuh, I won't have to worry about being placed on that cold, steel table.

Gordon shuddered at the mere thought of that table. He didn't mind strapping these damn supernatural creatures down on it, but Gordon also knew that Master Zordic would place any one of his followers on it for incompetence or not finishing certain tasks that he demanded be done.

He made a dash for a large uprooted tree nearby and slid down into the hole left by its upheaval. He leaned back against the dead roots, hoping no one had seen him. When satisfied he was safe, he pulled off his backpack. Stuffing the bloody shirt into it, he snatched out a radio headset with a small microphone at the end and slipped it onto his head. Gordon pulled out a camouflage canopy and carefully placed it around the stump to give him more cover. Here, he could stay out of harm's way and coordinate the capture of the shape-shifter and the elimination of the other vermin.

Gordon slid the stakes into the soft, muddy ground, thanking the divine savior that he didn't have to hammer them in. That would give away his position to the enemy. Once he got the canopy up and situated, he prodded the headset with his fingers and turned it on. Gordon looked around; he could see the witch wandering off into the woods but didn't see any of the other filthy scum. They had to be at the camp or splitting up.

As he whispered into his radio's microphone, he heard drops a rain gently land on the canopy. "Jered, what's your location?"

"We're near the creek, watching a lot of movement out here."

"The master's prize is out here tonight!"

"Are you positive? How do you know?"

"I found a campsite that had all four of the vermin that matched the ones who broke out of the master's jail. I saw a witch, a necromancer, a gremlin, and a shape-shifter who, by the way, shifts into a grizzly bear. The bear's out running as we speak. Plus, I got pictures of each of them. I'll send them to you now." Gordon pulled his phone out of his pocket and opened it. As he forwarded all the pictures to his team, he silently thanked the master's magic for these kinds of luxuries. No one else had phones these days.

"What are your orders? Where do you want us?" Jered asked excitedly.

Gordon looked over his map of the area, using his phone as a light source. "You and four others stay put by the creek in case the bear gets thirsty; Donnie, you will take six others to the north about three miles where it's a valley that has a lot of fruit trees and berry bushes that the bear might eat when it gets hungry;

Lee, you'll take the remaining five men to the west for three miles where there's a high-rise of hills. You guys can watch out for the grizzly and hopefully tranquilize him there. If you see any of his companions that are in the pictures I just sent everyone, kill them on sight. But under no circumstances do you hurt that bear!"

"Copy that, Gordon, and where will you be?" Lee asked with irritation in his voice.

"I'm watching over their campsite under the cover of a felled tree. If any come back this way, they're dead and don't even realize it."

"So basically, you're hiding while we do the grunt work as usual?" Lee hissed.

"Knock it off, Lee," Gordon growled. "Do your job or —
"

"Or what?" Lee angrily shouted into the radio. "You'll come out of your hole? That would mean you might get your hands dirty!"

Gordon tried hard to control his building rage. How dare this malcontent speak to him this way! He took a deep breath and said in an icy calm voice, "The master placed me in charge of bringing his shape-shifter back to him. Whoever gives me trouble is endangering the master's mission. I have my sat phone with me; it'll only take a few seconds to call him. He's been looking for this shifter well over a month now. Do you really want to tell the master you're not happy with his plan to recapture his coveted prize?" He waited for a moment. When Lee didn't answer, he goaded the man. "Well, do you, Lee?"

Dead silence for thirty seconds and then Lee snarled, "You bastard! No one likes a little snitch. Just remember, Gordon, they always get taken care of in the end!"

"That's good to know, Lee. Now everyone get into position and keep radio chatter to a minimum from here on out."

Gordon rolled his eyes as the rain came down in a steadier pace. Lee's bad tempered, Gordon thought. He's jealous of anyone who's in charge. He can't get it through his thick skull that the master wants smart, level-headed people running his operations. Lee's a hothead. Gordon smiled. Hotheads do stupid things. They don't think things out. They die! Gordon's smile widened. Lee could die tonight. That would be a great burden lifted off my shoulders, he mused. What if I put him in the line of fire every time? A good general always commands far away in safety while his troops follow the battle plan.

Lee is nothing more than fodder in this supernatural hunt, and with his temper and missteps it'll be only a matter of time before I get my wish. Gordon smiled again at this thought and looked around with his night-vision binoculars. He spotted the witch still roaming the woods, heading in Lee's direction. As much as he despised what she was, Gordon couldn't help checking her out. If she's human, he thought, I'd have her whether she wanted me or not. Knowing she was a witch, most men in the squad would have no problem raping and killing a fair beauty like her.

"She has a nice, lovely form…hmm," he said lustfully. "Maybe that's how she got the other squad members to fail in their mission. She would make for a good distraction while someone came up behind you and slit your throat."

Gordon decided not to inform Lee that the witch was heading straight for them, hoping that she would kill him before the rest of his group killed her. Two birds with one stone! Be my stone, witch, as I throw you into the fire to burn from wince you came! My men will end you for sure, and we humans will be one step closer to restoring humanity to the way it was before your kind came out of the shadows.

"Gordon, this is Donnie; we're in position."

"Copy that and stay sharp."

"This is Jered; my group is in position — what was that?"

"Do you see the bear, Jered? Report!"

"I don't know yet, Gordon, but I'll contact you shortly when I do know."

Dead silence. Nothing to do now but wait, Gordon anxiously thought. He didn't like this. It didn't seem right. It was too soon for the bear to go to the creek for water. It had to be one of the shape-shifter's companions. Suddenly, a thought hit him. It might be another shifter or *were*-creature running out here tonight. Everyone knows these woods are crammed with them during a full moon. Gordon felt his gut twist in a bad way, sensing his hunt was about to go to hell in a hand basket. Feeling nervous, Gordon radioed, "Jered, what's happening out there?"

Silence!

Gordon looked in the direction of the witch and saw — nothing! How could that be possible? The witch couldn't have run off that quickly. No one has that kind of speed on two legs. As sweat beaded across his forehead, he felt his heart race. He turned and looked at the campsite. It was dark now; the campfire had been extinguished by the rain, which was now a downpour. The only movement from the campsite was smoke trailing upward from the last of the embers.

"We got them on the run!" Donnie called out over the radio. "Lee, we need you to cut off their flank, so we can surround them!"

"Copy that!" Lee excitedly radioed back. "Move out, men. They're at the creek. Let's end this hunt now!"

"Seal off any escape routes," Gordon commanded. When Jered didn't respond, he anxiously radioed the man, "Do you read me, Jered?"

Silence!

He tried again. Nothing! This was bad. He knew it. "Jered, what's happening? Jered, answer me!"

"I'm sorry, but Jered can't come to the phone right now," a woman's icy voice replied. "He and his little buddies are floating face down in the creek mud. If you leave me your name and number, I'll gladly help you join them!"

The hairs on the back of Gordon's neck stood on end, and the urge to run away tried to take hold of him. This must have been the necromancer. She had just wiped out Jered's hunting party all by herself. He knew they were deadly creatures of the shadows, and one practitioner was very capable of taking out a group much larger than Jered's.

"Who are you, and why are you on this frequency?" Gordon demanded with a hint of trepidation in his voice.

"I'm the bringer of death, and you're my top priority for the night. You don't dare threaten my friends and get to live to tell the tale to your boss, Zordic! Hmm, maybe I should add you to my new collection of shades. I'm sure you'd fit in nicely. One of your friends—what's his name? Oh yes, Derek. You two would get along great! Like Derek, you'd never be fully at rest and always at my command. Doesn't that sound like fun, Gordon?"

"You did that to Derek?! You evil witch! You'll never find me, let alone add me to your sick and twisted collection!"

"I'm not a witch. I'm a necromancer, so get it right! When I find you, I'll show you the difference between the two."

Gordon felt a cold chill flowing through his veins when she used the word, "necromancer." He had helped capture a few in the past, and each one seemed more cunning and deadlier than the previous. Gordon had seen with his own eyes what these creatures were capable of doing: they used spells to drive men to the verge of insanity; they made men temporarily blind; they turned friends against each other which tended to lead to death. These creatures were all about death and carnage. They loved death!

Now a necromancer was after him!

Gordon reached into his backpack and pulled out a silver dagger and strapped it to his left combat boot. He closed the backpack up again and slung it over his shoulders. Over the headset radio, Gordon could hear Lee swearing, "GOD DAMN FUCKING FREAKS! DONNIE, GET YOUR HEAD OUT OF YOUR ASS AND CUT THEM OFF!"

"It seems your troops are having a bit of difficulty out here," Nightshade mocked. "Maybe you should coordinate with them better if you want them to survive the night."

"Donnie, LEE! What's happening out there? Report!" Gordon's heart pounded in his chest.

"Here's my report: FUCK OFF, COWARD!" Lee screamed into his radio. "I'M BUSY!"

"We're closing in on the shape-shifter. He's a bear, all right! He's got the witch riding on his back. The gremlin is just ahead of them. I do believe that—ACK! KILL THAT BITCH!"

"Stay on them, Donnie!" Gordon ordered. "We can't fail when we're this close to fulfilling our master's wish. Remember our much deserved rewards!"

"The only reward I want is to bury your spineless ass in the ground!" Lee hissed out his rage.

"Lee, why not take your anger out on that scum that's in front of you?" Gordon growled in frustration. "Are you really that dense that you have to blame all your problems on me? Get over yourself and do your damn job right—for a change!" Gordon barked out, feeling as much rage as Lee.

"There's a huge, fast-flowing river ahead," Donnie radioed. "It's too dangerous for them to cross. They're blocked! We'll have them in minutes," he said with an air of confidence.

"Where's this river? I don't see shit!" Lee roared over the radio.

"Lee, we've been hunting out here for the past few nights; I know where we are. Trust me when I say, we have them right where we want them!"

"Grrr....copy that!" Lee muttered out.

Even with hearing this new information on how the chase was going, Gordon still felt something wasn't right. This wasn't going to go as smoothly as Donnie believed. A snap of a branch brought Gordon back to reality, and he turned quickly in that direction. Pulling out his 9mm that was loaded with silver bullets, he held it close to his chest. Anticipating an attack at any moment, Gordon's heart was racing; his breaths were quick and short.

"Targets have halted at river's edge and appear to be making a stand," Donnie reported. "The gremlin is...taunting us. Proceeding with caution. Lee, be ready for anything."

"Copy that. Just don't break ranks. We'll have the shape-shifter, along with a couple of extra trophy heads for my wall," Lee replied as he calmed and focused.

Gordon couldn't shake the feeling he was being watched. As he turned to look at the campsite, a red beam of pure energy struck the tree and would have hit him directly in the heart. Gordon had no doubts in his mind that the necromancer had found him. She confirmed it with a maniacal laugh. "Are you ready to join my army of the unwillingly dead, Gordon?"

"Fuck this and fuck you, bitch!" Gordon scurried out of the hole and took off running while firing his gun in the general direction of the necromancer's evil voice. He ducked behind an oak tree as another blast of red energy hit the trunk. Breathing heavily, he felt fear gripping his heart and mind. Gordon used the massive oak to cover him as he ran ahead, hoping to stay out of her sight.

Before he made it through the thicket, he turned and fired his gun wildly, earning him a female grunt of pain, which was sweet music to his ears. He pushed forward but lost his footing and slid down a rather steep embankment and into the creek.

***

"I sure hope your secret plan works, Onyx," Yonuh said as he moved between the approaching guards and the river, trying to protect Raven. "Because we've got company..."

Raven looked around him and saw both groups were slowly advancing on them. She glanced over at Onyx's little mud-caked leaves that lay on a carpet of pine needles. Only, there were no pine trees nearby. Frowning, she had no idea what was going to happen. Something spectacular had better happen, though, because she and Yonuh were trapped between the men and the river.

Onyx took a few steps towards the men. He had taunted them several times tonight. And he liked it! The gremlin yelled out, "Want to know how I can fly?" he promptly dropped his pants and grabbed hold of his long member, quickly twirling it at them. "I'm a fucking helicopter! Too bad yours are so small or you could fly too!"

Raven had a hard time controlling her laugher, but then a few bullets came whizzing by. Someone didn't find Onyx so amusing.

Onyx dropped to the ground as he pulled his pants up and said psychically to the others, "*Almost...almost, NOW RAVEN!*"

As she had been instructed to do by Onyx, Raven aimed and fired at each of the gremlin's mud-caked leaves. As each leaf exploded, rocks shot out from the pine needles and flew upwards. Gravity grabbed them and pulled them back down. They pelted the head's of the P.A.N.E.L. squad.

Only, when the rocks hit the pine needle-covered ground, a lot of loud, horrible popping sounded out. The witch was confused. The popping had an eerily familiar sound to it that she couldn't quite place. It hit a chord in her soul. What the hell was under those pine needles? She immediately got her answer as one of the men screamed out in terror.

"PLAGUE!"

"Oh shit!" she cried out frantically.

That popping noise was the sound of spores bursting out of the dead and bloated corpses of plague victims. The pine needles were hiding a death pocket—a place where plague victims were buried in a hurry—and Onyx had led the P.A.N.E.L. squad to their deaths...as well as her, Onyx, and Yonuh!

There was nowhere to go, except the river. Onyx took to the sky as he screamed, "GET YOUR ASSES IN THE RIVER NOW! SWIM FOR YOUR LIVES!"

Without thinking, Yonuh grabbed Raven around her waist and held her tightly to his body as he made a mad dash for the river. Raven looked over Yonuh's shoulder and could see all the members of the P.A.N.E.L. squad screaming in agony and falling down, triggering more erupting spores.

And those erupting spores were heading towards them!

As Yonuh ran as fast as he could, Raven felt like she was flying for a moment and then felt a huge splash of water cover her as they hit the cold river which swept them away from the danger of the spores. Only now, though, she worried, will we survive this horribly swift water?

***

Gordon had heard his men screaming over the radio. He tried several times to connect with any of them. But when he had heard the word "plague" he stopped trying. He waited. Now there was nothing from his radio but eerie silence.

It was then that Gordon realized this hunt was a complete debacle. If he made it out of here alive, he would certainly face a fate worse than what the necromancer had offered him.

Gordon pressed a button on the headset which made it squeal as he chucked it to his left, hoping the noise would distract the necromancer enough to get away. He would present his findings to the master and pray he spared his life.

He quickly darted across the creek over the downed tree, splashing water and making enough noise to wake the dead, he eerily thought. From his map, he knew where the river was…and his dying men, so he went in the opposite direction.

Crawling up a small embankment, he rolled through the heavy brush in time to see the necromancer. He froze momentarily, but then he slowly belly-crawled backwards. She had taken down several of his men at the same time with her magic, and he didn't want to tackle her alone.

She hadn't seen him. Good, Gordon thought, I'll deal with her another time.

Chapter Six

Fearing she would slip away and possibly drown, Yonuh held Raven as tightly as he could. The water was icy cold, and he could feel her shivering terribly. He wasn't sure how good of a swimmer she was, and he sure didn't want to find out tonight, especially in this kind of river. Onyx's plan had worked great in that they had gotten rid of all the P.A.N.E.L. squad, but now he wondered if the little gremlin had thought farther ahead or was *jump in the river* as far as he went.

Yonuh had no problem floating on his back with the current since he was strong and heavy enough, so he used his body as a life preserver for Raven. Again, he felt her violently shiver from the icy water. Using what little supernatural energy he had left, Yonuh melded it with the energy of the heavy flowing river. Friction between the two energies heated up just barely enough to keep them both warm and to regenerate his own nearly-depleted energy that he had spent while running in his bear form.

Raven squeezed her body closer to him, enjoying the heat which made Yonuh happy. He winced as he felt something sharp under the water scrape his back. He shifted slightly to make sure Raven didn't come to any harm, and he used his body to shield her from the debris beneath them.

Onyx hovered over them as they were swept along by the river. He folded his arms across his chest and proudly called down to them, "Those pricks didn't see that coming, now did they? Damn, I'm so good at being so bad!"

"True, but how do we get out of this fucking river, or did you not think of that?" Raven yelled up at him.

Onyx scratched the back of his little, dark head and hollered down, "Would you be too mad if I said that I had hoped you two would be on a bank by now?"

"What? Some plan. Kill the bad guys and hope for the best for us!" Raven furiously shouted.

"Well when you say it like that, of course it's going to come off sounding rather…incomplete. But hey, at least you're both alive and in each other's arms. Aw, how romantic!"

"ONYX—"

"Pipe down and keep your panties on! I'm waiting for the right spot to get you both out of there. I see a downed tree that's partially in the water. I'm going to steer you to it. Does that make you happy, carrot top, or should I rethink my master plan?"

Raven only glared up at the grinning gremlin and was wishing she could reach him so she could drown his ass. She felt Yonuh kiss the top of her head, but she also felt his body getting jarred around too. Raven looked up at Yonuh's face and saw pain. He shifted her body more onto his. It was obvious what he was doing. She sighed. It was hard to like the gesture when it was causing him more suffering just to keep her safe from the unknown obstructions in the river.

Onyx flew down by Yonuh's head. "I'm going to turn you around now, and I'll steer you by using your feet. It's going to hurt when you run into the tree, but it'll be easier to grab hold of it. Nightshade is over there waiting to help get you out."

"I…I understand, d…do what you must. I trust you, Onyx. OUCH!" Yonuh couldn't hold back the pain any longer because as Onyx turned Yonuh's body, something sharp and jagged in the river cut him up.

The gremlin hovered down at Yonuh's feet. As he grabbed hold of them, he shrugged his shoulders and said, "Sorry about that, Yonuh."

"It…it can't be helped," Yonuh said in pain and grimaced.

"Please, Onyx, are we getting close to the tree?" Raven asked with concern for the healer on her face.

"It's just around this bend." The gremlin shifted Yonuh to guide them safely. "Hey, check it out! I'm driving the Yonuh Express down the river! Just call me Captain Onyx! On your left, you will see trees and more death pockets. To your right, you will spot a pale, grumpy lady that looks like a drowned rat."

Raven rolled her eyes as she prepared her body for the coming impact. She leaned against Yonuh's body the best she could and was thankful for the warm heat he was putting out. Raven didn't particularly like the cold because it tended to make her body hurt more. In Yonuh's arms, though, it was tolerable, and she felt grateful to be with him right now. The healer closed his eyes and meditated, so he could block out the pain, but it wasn't working very well.

"Tree's coming," Onyx called out. "Nightshade, get ready because I don't want to lose either one of them!"

Yonuh felt Onyx tug on his feet, trying his best to minimize the impact against the tree. Yonuh pulled Raven up on top of his naked body just as they hit the tree. Nightshade immediately grabbed Raven's arms and yanked her up on the bank. Yonuh grabbed the tree and let Onyx push his legs up on the bank. As soon as Nightshade and Raven grabbed Yonuh's ankles, Onyx flew up and grabbed the healer by his wrists and ordered, "Let go Yonuh. Pull ladies!"

With one mighty heave, Yonuh was up and out of the river. Onyx gently guided him down on the ground, face down. Raven and Nightshade both gasped when they saw his back. It was a mess of scratches, cuts and a lot of gashes, and it was bleeding all over. Onyx walked over to him. "Damn, Yonuh! What were you doing in the river fighting with Freddy Kruger?"

"Protecting Raven...the only way...I knew how," Yonuh said breathlessly.

Nightshade pulled off her cloak and draped it over Yonuh's body. He flinched but managed to say, "Thank you," before he passed out. Raven looked over and saw that Nightshade had the presence of mind to bring his clothes. Only, it was raining, and with him fresh out of the river, it would be pointless to get him dressed now. So Raven gently patted Yonuh down, using the cloak to dry him off the best she could. She looked up at Nightshade and saw she was wincing and favoring her left side.

"Are you okay? Oh gods, you're bleeding!"

"I'm fine. A bullet grazed my temple which made me slip and fall on a rock. The little bastard was scared out of his mind and was firing his gun wildly. I'm surprised a bullet actually hit me. Unfortunately, he got away. The prick was hiding near our campsite."

"I knew it! I bet he's the one who stole Yonuh's shirt—creepy little fucker! That's how I knew the P.A.N.E.L. squad was here. Someone snagged his blood-stained shirt and knocked over his clothes. I imagine he's going to give it to his master as a fucking gift!"

"It's a good bet that if he was nearby, he may know our names too," Onyx said as he helped pat down Yonuh.

"So what if they know our names?" Raven growled. "We know their master's name. Sooner or later, he'll slip up, and we can track him down." She hissed out the words angrily as she patted down Yonuh harder, earning a grunt of pain from him. She immediately stopped. "Sorry."

"It makes it easier for him to find us and send more of his goons after us," Onyx explained. "He could have someone going around looking for us and offering a reward for our whereabouts."

"You have a valid concern there, Onyx," Nightshade interjected.
"Just to be on the side of caution, I think we should put up our own wards and protections on the old Costco. In case Zordic decides to use someone other than humans to come after us."

"Well, I'm glad I stocked up on my supplies," Raven told them. "It's going to take a lot of incense to cleanse Yonuh's place, but I want to ask him first before I do it, since it's his place. Oh damn, he's hot!"

"I don't need you to tell me that," Nightshade giggled. "I already knew he was hot and sexy!"

Raven shook her head. "No, he's really hot to the touch, like he's burning up with fever! Can't you feel it, Nightshade?"

"Yes, now that you mention it, but I thought it was just his dual nature making him so hot."

Raven gently pulled back the cloak. A sauna of heat flew up from Yonuh's body and greeted her in the face. To their amazement, Yonuh's wounds were almost healed, and many of them mended as they watched.

Onyx hovered above them. "That's why he's burning up" the gremlin declared. "It's because he's healing his body as he's resting." He grinned. "How cool is that, or should I say how hot?"

Raven watched as Yonuh moved his lips slightly in his sleep, chanting and healing his body.

"I think when we get back home," Nightshade offered, "I should ask our old friend Derek more about the compound where the P.A.N.E.L. squad does their training."

"Why? You looking for a date?" Onyx snickered as he shot away from Nightshade's hand.

"If they know our names," Raven growled, "we might as well take the fight to them. Take out as many of those pricks as we can. That compound sounds like a great starting point, plus it could cripple the P.A.N.E.L. squad's numbers."

"I don't know if we can cripple them or not," Nightshade said as an evil grin washed across her lips. "I do believe, though, that their training compound needs to be burned to the ground."

"Great! She's been listening to Def Leppard again and now look at her. She's a pyromaniac!" Onyx howled out a belly laugh.

A low growl made everyone look down. Yonuh was waking up. He gave his body a long, satisfying stretch. Rolling over, he exposed his naked body to both Raven and Nightshade. They stared at him intently, giving his body the *elevator eyes* before he realized he was still skyclad. He blushed as he ran his fingers through his hair and asked, "Does anyone know where my clothes are? Are they still at the campsite?"

"Why do you need them?" Nightshade said with a sultry breath. "You look fine the way you are!"

Raven smiled as she ran her fingers up and down Yonuh chest. "Yes he does…and sexy too."

"A little help here would be nice, Onyx," Yonuh called out with a pleading voice.

Onyx laughed and put his hands out. "Oh, hell no! You're on your own. Giving you clothes would be suicide for me. Just look at them — two ravenous wolves eyeing the last piece of meat. I'm not getting between them. I may be small, but I'm not stupid."

Yonuh looked at each of them. Sure enough, they were eyeing him like the last cookie in the jar. He noticed dried blood was caked on Nightshade's left temple. This ought to change the subject and get their hunger off me…maybe. He scrambled to his feet and perused Nightshade's wound. "How did you get hurt?"

"A bullet grazed me, but I'm okay. You don't need to — whoa!" Lightheadedness from the energy Yonuh was pumping into her caused her to start swaying. With Raven's help, the healer guided her down to the ground and continued to chant. Nightshade's eyes rolled back, and her eyelids fluttered as she enjoyed feeling not only the warm, comforting energy, but his physical touch as well.

Yonuh ceased his chanting as he removed his hand from her head. He took a deep breath to center himself. Nightshade touched her temple and only felt her blood-caked hair. No wound! She smiled. "Thank you twice, Yonuh."

"Twice?"

"Once is for the healing." Nightshade's eyes looked directly between Yonuh's legs. "Twice is for the lovely view down here."

Yonuh shot up and covered his body with Nightshade's cloak. He hurried over and found his pile of clothing. He immediately jabbed his legs into his pants and pulled them up, much to the dismay of Raven and Nightshade. He turned around and asked, "Where's my shirt at? I can't find it anywhere."

"The one that got away tonight stole your shirt," Onyx explained as he landed beside Yonuh.

"Uh...okay, that's creepy. Why the hell would he do that?"

"We think it has to do with your blood being on it," Raven said as she stood up and walked over to be with Yonuh. "He snatched it to take it back to Zordic. It's like a junkie getting a score, except he's giving it to his master to enjoy."

Yonuh shook his head. "I don't understand what's so great about my blood that he wants it so damn badly. As far as I know, it's just like me — not that special nor great."

"Well Count Dracula seems to see it differently than you do," Onyx said. "That makes it even worse that the little weasel got away."

As Nightshade walked over to him, he slipped his shoes on and handed her cloak back to her. She draped it over her shoulders and said in her sultry voice, "You're more precious and special than you know, so don't be selling yourself so short. I see you as the savior of my mind, body, and heart." She glanced at Raven. "Girl, how many men do you know who could do something like that and not be special?"

"Men like that were a rare find before the plague," Raven answered. She hugged Yonuh and looked up into his big, brown eyes. "I would have said they were all extinct until you came into our lives, Yonuh. You touch more people's lives than you realize, just by being you. So if you say you're not special, I will spank your cute ass until you get it in your head that you *are* special!"

"I think if you did that, Raven," Onyx said with a snicker, "he might enjoy it. One of his heads might pop up and show you that it's got it, all right!"

Yonuh rubbed his face with both of his hand as he blushed even more. He felt he was the center of everyone's attraction, including a demon, and it made him feel uncomfortable. He wasn't use to this and never sought it out. He preferred living a simple, mundane life. If someone needed help, he offered without thinking twice because that's how it was growing up and learning his Native American ways. Yonuh always felt a heavy responsibility in his heart to help people. Now he had his new dysfunctional family, and it seemed to weigh him down farther because he felt they were in his care, and it was up to him to keep them all safe.

"All right, this has been a lot of fun," he told them, "but I'm worn out from tonight's excitement, and I could use a good night's sleep. So, if there're no objections, let's go home."

Raven snaked her arm around his elbow and said, "You're right. We should all go back. I, for one, could go in for a long, hot shower after Onyx's great rafting idea." She glared at the gremlin. "You could have given us a better heads up about your plan other than jump in the river after exploding the plague bodies."

"Ah, but what's the fun in that if there's no surprise for everyone?" Onyx said and grinned. "It was priceless to see the looks on their faces once they realized what was happening. Damn, I wish I had brought a camera. The look on your face was picture perfect too; it said, 'Oh shit, we are so fucked!' — all in one facial expression."

"Dammit, that's my point, you little shit!" Raven growled. "You could have gotten us killed! I trusted you, and that's how you repay me by not letting us know a crucial part of your plan was using plague bodies? I'm so going to kill you!"

"All part of the show, carrot top. Had you known about that, would you have really followed me all that way into the woods?" Raven only scowled, so Onyx continued on, "Didn't think so. It was our best chance to wipe them all out in one shot. Would you rather still be on the run right now? Getting shot at and having to be on edge with each step you take out here? If you ask me, you *owe* me not only your lives but a whole bunch of family-sized Doritos bags."

Raven stomped past Onyx who had a smug look on his tiny, dark face, dragging Yonuh along in her wake. Nightshade smacked Onyx on the back of his head as she walked by him. Onyx rubbed the back of his head and yelled out, "What the hell was that for, you pasty bitch?"

"I'm just doing what Raven wanted to do, but she knew she couldn't, so she asked me to give that to you as a present," Nightshade called back over her shoulder.

"Now I remember why I prefer my bachelorhood; it has less drama and no sneaky, conniving women plotting behind my back."

"Wow, so you can dish it out, but you can't take it…even from your own kind? Kind of ironic if you think about it."

Onyx flew up in front of Nightshade with an angry scowl on his face, stopping her dead in her tracks. "What the fuck is that supposed to mean?" he hissed.

Nightshade irritated him further by patting him on top of his head as she moved around him. "For someone who excels in mischief and pranks, you sure do hate it when others turn the table back on you. Tsk, tsk, Onyx, you're the embodiment of hypocrisy."

All Onyx could do was hover. He angrily clenched his hands repeatedly, considering whether he should kick her ass or not. It irritated him even more because he knew she was right. He never enjoyed being pranked or getting bested by his kind, so he prided himself at being a master of mischief. Anyone pranking him, other than another gremlin, really bruised his world-sized ego, so he tended to opt for violence.

This trait was exactly what got him caught by the P.A.N.E.L. squad in the first place. A human in a crimson uniform walked right up to him, handed him an egg, and told him that there was no way he could break it. Then the man stepped back and watched.

Onyx puffed out his chest and grinned confidently as he clapped his hands together hard and felt the satisfaction of the egg immediately breaking in his hand. He tried pulling his hands apart and saw that there was a sticky, tarry substance on the egg, gumming up his hands, making it difficult to pull them apart. Onyx saw the man in the crimson uniform had doubled over and was laughing his ass off, saying "Oh man, you are sooo gullible! That's the oldest trick in the book. You prank so easily!"

Onyx flew at the guy and went full-on gremlin, losing his glamour. With his magick lifted, Onyx morphed into a creature with thick, dark, leathery skin. He had razor-sharp claws and small, serrated teeth. Onyx shoved his sticky, tarry hands as best he could on the man's mouth, wanting to shut the human's laughter up and maybe even make him eat it.

In his rage, the gremlin felt several sharp, stabbing pains in his back that seemed like bee stings. He instantly felt woozy and toppled over. As he passed out, he heard cheers, and someone bragged, "Now that's how you catch a fucking gremlin, boys!" The next thing he knew, Onyx was trying to kill Yonuh in their jail cell.

Onyx let out a quick huff of breath and decided it wasn't worth it to lose his cool over Nightshade's comment, but he wasn't going to let her get away with throwing the ugly truth in his face like that either. He spun around and flew straight at Nightshade's back. He quickly flipped her cloak over her head and slipped his little, nimble fingers down the back of her pants. Onyx yanked up Nightshade's blue thong so that it stretched halfway up her back. Using his gremlin magic, he then managed a sly gremlin move and hooked both her arms in the leg holes of the thong.

"ARRRHHHH! YOU LITTLE BASTARD!" Nightshade screamed and had a hell of a time walking straight. Her body was spazzing, as she turned this way and that, trying to get her thong out of her ass crack. She nearly ran into a tree because the cloak was still over her head, blinding her.

"That's for telling me what I already know, necrophiliac! Check it out. She looks like she's auditioning for a part in Michael Jackson's "Thriller". Come on, girl. Get your zombie groove on!"

Yonuh turned around and saw what was happening. He ran back to Nightshade.

He spun her around slowly, and then he growled at Onyx, "What's this shit about? I swear if we can't get home in one piece, I'll take it out of your scrawny hide!"

Onyx stayed out of striking distance and retorted, "Hey, it was better I do this to her than let my anger get the best of me. If I had, her thong would have been over and under her chin, and it would have snapped her neck like a twig! So in a way, I'm doing great at controlling my temper."

"Onyx, you need to head towards the van, right now," Raven commanded as her green eyes flared, and her fingers twitched on her wand. "I'm not going to say it again! You hurt her for saying the obvious; now that you've made your grand point, LEAVE MY SIGHT!"

Onyx had a bewildered look on his small face, and then he hung his head in shame as he slowly flew away. Immediately, though, his pride took over, and he stopped, turned, and said sternly, "I refuse to apologize for this act! She shouldn't have said what she said because, believe it or not, there are some things you just don't say to me. This could have been deadly, but—"

"FUCKING GO, ALREADY, ONYX!" Yonuh snapped, startling everyone. His eyes had a slight yellow tint to them and were pulsating.

Onyx sulked as he flew slowly away, letting out curses that would make the old navy blush.

Raven stood next to Yonuh as he ordered, "Hold Nightshade's hands and keep her steady."

Raven gave a curt nod and linked her fingers with Nightshade's. From what she could see, tears were running down the necromancer's face, and she heard her whimpering in pain.

Yonuh hesitantly reached for Nightshade's black dagger. "I'm sorry, but I'm going to need this."

"Please hurry…it hurts so bad," Nightshade said through gritted teeth.

Yonuh grabbed the black dagger and slipped behind her. He took hold of the blue thong by Nightshade's left arm and cut the band like it was butter. He then did the same to her right arm. The healer snatched the bulk of her thong off her head and let it drop harmlessly down her back.

As Raven held on to her, Nightshade collapsed to her knees.

It began to rain harder. "There, there, Nightshade," Raven cooed as she stroked the necromancer's blonde, wet hair back from her pale face. "I've got you, and you're safe with me."

Nightshade reached behind herself with a shaky hand and put it in her pants. She gently rubbed her ass crack, but when she pulled her hand out, it was covered in blood. A lot of blood. Nightshade looked at her hand and said to Raven, with quivering lips, "I...I think I'm hurt bad. Help me."

Yonuh squatted down. With a determined look on his face, he scooped Nightshade up in his powerful arms. Raven led the way to a huge, old oak tree that would keep most of the downpour off them. Nightshade held on to Yonuh, enjoying his warm, comforting energy. Feeling safe in his arms, she desperately wished to herself that he would never let go of her.

With Raven's aide, Yonuh lay the necromancer down on the soggy ground, much to her dismay. She felt cold when she lost his heat, and she shivered.

Blushing and stammering, Yonuh asked, "I...uh...need you to...umm undo your pants, Nightshade, so I can...uh...see the damage."

As Nightshade fiddled with the button on her pants, she looked over her shoulder and said with a playful smile, "Earlier, I was hoping to get you into my pants." She giggled a little. "This wasn't exactly how I envisioned it happening, though."

Embarrassed, Yonuh tried to ignore her comment. "Okay, can you stand up for me?"

"I think so," Nightshade replied as she looked at Raven. She held her hand out to her. "Would you mind...?"

"Not at all, girl, you know I'm here for you!" Raven grabbed hold of Nightshade's hands and felt that this was going to be the painful part.

Yonuh squatted behind Nightshade and took a deep breath as he slowly put his fingers around the hem of her pants. He tried to tug them down as gently as he could, but her pants were drenched and wanted to stick to her skin.

Nightshade grimaced with each tug and pull from Yonuh, which made Raven move in and embrace her. "It's going to be all right," she whispered. "I got you, and Yonuh will take good care of that sexy ass of yours."

Nightshade gave her a weak but grateful smile. "Ouch — I know he will, and I know — OUCH — that I can count on you, Raven. Oh FUCK!"

Yonuh gave her pants a good yank, and they were finally down to her calves. He gingerly put his hands on her bare ass, making her flinch at first. But she soon groaned in pain as he spread her cheeks apart. He saw that part of her thong had actually cut and dug into her skin and embedded itself in the muscles. He cringed. The healer grabbed both ends of the blue thong that hung loose and said, "I'm not going to lie. This will hurt like a mother fucker, so I'm going to yank it out quickly and begin the healing."

"I...I understand. Let's get this over — OUCH! HOLY MOTHER, HELL OF DARKNESS! GODS, AHHHHH!"

Yonuh yanked as hard as he could, and the thong came out. Blood trickled down Nightshade's thighs. He threw the bloody remnants on the ground, and then he placed his hands between her legs and on her crack. Feeling the hot, bloody liquid squish in his hands, made Yonuh start a feverous chant.

Nightshade leaned into his hands. As tears streamed down her face, her breaths came in quick spurts.

Yonuh pushed more energy into Nightshade to help calm her down and ease her pain. Raven's eyes fluttered as she felt the warm energy wash over her too, making her smile and moan. Nightshade felt the muscles moving back into place and the skin methodically mending.

She leaned in and kissed Raven softly on her forehead which caused the witch to look up. Nightshade had a happy, contented smile that spread over her pale face, and she had a look of pure bliss in her eyes. She leaned in again and kissed Raven on her soft lips and said, "Thanks! I love you, my redheaded hooker!"

"I know, you dirty little slut!" Raven said back and smiled. She could tell Nightshade was feeling better already. "I believe you will use any excuse to make out with me."

"And who wouldn't?" Nightshade replied with a ravenous look that made Raven feel like a mouse being eyed by the family cat. "How could anyone *not* want to do that with you? You're so beautiful, sweet and have one sexy body too!"

Yonuh stopped chanting and let go of Nightshade, so he could sit on the soggy ground and recover. He felt spent and wondered if this night would ever end, so he could get some much needed rest.

Nightshade reached down and tugged her pants back up. She turned and kneeled by Yonuh. She could see he was exhausted, and she felt bad for him. Seeing him this worn down and knowing she was now one of the reasons for it, she grimaced. She looked over her shoulder at Raven. "Don't get too mad because I need to do this." Before Raven could say a word, Nightshade had lifted Yonuh's head, and she gave him a long kiss.

The necromancer leaned back and said, "Thank you, Yonuh. I know you're not in the best of shape right now, but I felt this was the best way to convey how I feel about you healing me. You're a remarkable man, and I'm grateful to call you my friend."

Yonuh smiled at her as he blushed and handed back her black dagger. He sighed. "It was bad Nightshade. I'm glad I could heal you now. I just hope we can get home with no further outbursts from anyone. I've got to rest my big grizzly ass!"

Raven and Nightshade helped Yonuh to his feet, and they both curled their arms around his and started walking towards the van. Yonuh gave them both side glances and noticed they both were smiling and seemed happy. He wasn't sure if it was from his comforting energy emanating from his body, or if they were enjoying the stroll in the downpour. He gave a slight shrug of his shoulders as he decided it had to be his energy because he knew it always elicited this kind of response from others, so he went with that.

As they walked together, Nightshade tugged them to the left. "I moved the van closer when Onyx told me he planned on yanking you two out of that river back there. He never mentioned why you were going to be in the river, only that it was part of his plan."

"Well that's a relief!" Raven replied as she kissed Yonuh on his cheek. "I didn't want to walk all the way back to where we first parked because I'm worn out and so is poor Yonuh."

"How much farther is it to the van, anyway?" Yonuh asked with a half yawn.

"About a quarter of a mile, but we'll be there before you two know it," Nightshade said cheerfully.

Everyone was feeling happy, but that changed abruptly when they all heard Onyx call out to them psychically.

"Guys, I know you're all still mad at me, but I'm near the van, and I'm not alone. Long story short, it looks like we got a problem here – a big problem!"

Yonuh rolled his eyes and groaned out, "Fuck! Someone just shoot me now, so I can rest already!

Chapter Seven

Onyx felt depressed as he flew slowly toward the van. He held his chin up in defiance, and a mean smirk was on his little, dark face, but he felt anything but defiant and mean. I was right to do what I did to Nightshade, he insisted to himself as he flew along. I did it so it would soothe my inner beast and also save her life. Had I not done that, I would have killed her. I had to get even!

He enjoyed mischief and dealing it out on his friends, but he hated the idea of hurting any of them, especially Nightshade.

The sound of a feminine scream reached his acute, gremlin ears, and it made him cringe, knowing it was Nightshade wailing in agony from what *HE* had just put her through. He came to a halt and hovered in the air. As he turned around to look in the direction of where he had just come, he whispered, "I'm sorry, Nightshade. I'm truly sorry!"

Onyx gritted his teeth and tensed up his shoulders. "She may have brought this on herself, but Nightshade doesn't deserve this kind of pain, you prick!" he growled at himself.

He turned around and resumed his long, lonely flight back to the van. Onyx pulled out a Dorito and slowly nibbled on it. He was grateful that Yonuh was with her. "He'll heal her, and she'll be fine," he said barely above a whisper. Those words stabbed at his heart. He knew the healer was exhausted. "Yonuh will have to expend more of his energy because of *ME!*"

Magic has a price, always has and always will, and this is what Onyx had to pay for his use of it—the suffering of his friends who considered him family. Depression covered the little gremlin like a shroud of death.

He dropped the Dorito. Not even its wonderful and divine goodness could make him feel better, and he wasn't going to soil it with his brooding either. I'll make it up to her, Onyx thought as he gave a quick nod, whether she likes me or not. "I swear upon a field of wild growing Doritos," he whispered, "that I *WILL* make things right between us!"

The gremlin was snapped back into reality when he heard the sound of rustling grass, like someone or something was shifting in place. It seemed to have come from the direction...of where their white van was parked. Was one of the P.A.N.E.L. pricks here? Maybe the one who eluded Nightshade was lying in wait for them.

That settled it for Onyx, so he flew high up in the trees and stealthy moved along the canopy. He was happy that the rain became more of a downpour mainly because that would keep whoever was lurking nearby from looking up, let alone noticing his zipping from tree to tree. Onyx was actually hoping deep down that it would be the leader of tonight's hunting party, so he could catch him by surprise and deliver him to the others as a sort of peace offering.

The little gremlin got to an oak tree and was finally able to get a clear view of their white van. He saw a small cluster of creatures either leaning against the van or sitting on its roof. Onyx thought long and hard as he stared at the beings but, for the life of him, couldn't discern what they were.

Are they waiting for us to return, so they can steal the van, mugging style? It wasn't unheard of these days since there were no more laws or police to stop individuals from going out and taking what they wanted. Survival was the name of the game in this post apocalyptic world, and it was kill or be killed for the most part.

Onyx decided it would be best to warn the others so they didn't walk into this little trap.

He psychically called out to the others, *"Guys, I know you're all still mad at me, but I'm near the van, and I'm not alone. Long story short, it looks like we got a problem here – a big problem!"*

Onyx didn't get an immediate response, but he knew they had heard him and could tell they were moving more cautiously in his direction. He counted four creatures and did his best to sniff their energy signatures. From his position high up in the air, though, and the fact that the downpour enhanced all other smells around him, made it impossible to sniff them correctly. Lovely, he thought sarcastically. Where's Harry Potter's invisibility cloak when I need it?

"Where are you hiding, Onyx?" Raven psychically asked with her mind.

"Near the top of an old-ass oak tree watching them. There are four of them huddled around the van, and I haven't got a clue as to what they are or what they want!"

"Come on down and join us," Yonuh said with a hint of frustration in his voice that Onyx felt wasn't directed towards him.

"You sure? I could just stay up here and keep an eye out…make sure there aren't any more of them waiting to surprise us. Besides,…I don't think I'm really a welcomed sight to any of you."

"Behave and all is forgiven, you little turd!" Nightshade interjected but then added, *"I'd feel better with you down here with us anyway, so I can keep an eye on you. If you cross me or fuck with me again tonight, I will kill you without hesitation! Are we clear, Onyx?"*

"I hear you loud and clear, sugar tits! I will do my best to be on my best behavior, but no guarantees either! Baby steps and one day at a time thing, you know?"

As he felt the depressing shroud of death lift from him, Onyx happily soared through the canopy. He decided that if Nightshade was willing to welcome him back and not want to kill him, then things must be looking up for him.

Also, Yonuh wasn't doing so well at the moment, so it was best to be with the rest of his collective family and take yet another stand tonight. If another fight occurred, it would just make his inner beast happy. Suddenly, he saw his companions come into view, so he slowly came down and hovered in front of them.

Onyx had a hard time looking Nightshade in the eyes as he said, "I...umm...I hope that you can—OOF!"

Nightshade lunged and tackled him to the ground. She held him in her arms and whispered in his little, pointy ear, "It was my fault. I know that, but please don't do that to me again. I want you as my friend and not an enemy. You better understand, though, that I was being serious about killing you!"

"Point taken and if we have a private moment later...I'd like to explain myself. That is, if we live through this night. Deal?"

Nightshade smiled as she kissed him on the forehead. "Deal! Now let's find out who's hanging out on our ride!"

She let go of Onyx, and he stood up, brushing himself off. He looked up at her and said, "You're weird, you know that? But I guess that's fine considering we live in Portland now. You can add yourself to the city's old motto of '*KEEP PORTLAND WEIRD!*'"

Yonuh and Raven walked up and stood nearby. "Are you two lovebirds done making out?" Raven asked mischievously. "Maybe we should let you two sneak off and find a nice, quiet place to play."

Onyx scowled at Raven as he retorted, "Ha! Joke's on you; I'm not her type or have you forgotten that already, carrot top?"

"You say that," Yonuh said with a teasing smile as he nudged him with his leg, "but you've never actually asked Nightshade what her type really is. As always, you've just assumed things."

"I'm alive, and I'm definitely too much of a gremlin for that necromancer to handle," Onyx said as he stood next to Nightshade, grinning up at her.

"You plan on walking with me to meet our welcoming committee?" Nightshade asked with raised eyebrows.

"Yes, because if they don't realize I can fly, it could take them by surprise. We may need that if they try to hurt us or worse."

"Aww, and I thought you just wanted to take a midnight stroll in the rain with me." Nightshade made a pouting face.

Onyx kept quiet but didn't seem to mind walking with her at all. He even turned his head to hide a slight blush. They all marched together for a ways and, before long, the white van came into view, along with the creatures that seemed to be lounging against it.

One of the creatures perked up as they came out of the woods. It made a motion to the others, and the group formed a line in front of the van.

Yonuh put his hand up and waved as he called out, "Hello there! Can we help you with something?"

The tallest of the creatures moved forward, and she asked with a melodious voice, "Yes, are you the owner of this vehicle?"

"Just acquired it a month ago from some very bad individuals," he explained. "You need a ride?"

"No, I don't like the idea of being this close to it, especially when it reeks of demon magic." The female creature's eyes flared a bright white.

"None of us are demons or use that kind of magic," Onyx chimed in. "I actually tore this vehicle up to the point of being unusable. Only, the demon who commands humans to do his dirty work magically fixed it, so they could come after us."

"It's obvious that you're not demons, gremlin, but we felt the magic on it and had to investigate. We were prepared to kill the owner, if need be."

Yonuh nodded as he noticed that most of these creatures all looked similar. Only the leader and one other female looked different. The leader had a slim, athletic body and wore hunter green clothing with a hooded cloak, as did the female next to her.

The other females were the complete opposite, in that they barely had any clothing on and appeared to be nearly skyclad, with the exception of some free-flowing cloth on their arms. Leafy crowns adorned their heads, and they had green vines wrapping around their bodies in a provocative way. Yonuh figured these were wood nymphs, but he still had no clue as to what the other two creatures were exactly.

Onyx sniffed the air. "So now that you know we aren't demons, what else do you lovely wood elves and nymphs want?"

The leader pulled back her hood and said, "A show of respect for this area would be nice. We live here and would prefer you leave the dead corpses alone!"

"We didn't want to disturb them," Yonuh said as he glanced over at Onyx who seemed to want to avoid his gaze. "We had no choice in the matter."

"There's always A CHOICE!" the leader screamed suddenly, startling Raven and Nightshade. Her eyes blazed brightly as her anger grew. "Elves and nymphs are gravely ill, and we lost many faeries to those spores that you people unleashed tonight!" She glared hatefully at them, her chest heaving under her cloak. "You give me one good reason why we shouldn't kill you where you stand?"

Onyx was about to speak, but Nightshade put her hand on his head and murmured to him, "Don't run your mouth now. Let Yonuh do this, okay?"

He nodded as Yonuh walked slowly towards the lead elf with his hands spread to show he wasn't armed. It didn't keep her from yanking her bow off her back. Instantly, the bow was notched and loaded with several arrows, all aimed at the healer's chest.

"Please, I mean no harm. I know if you thought otherwise, I wouldn't be speaking right now. My name is Yonuh. The lady with red hair is Raven, and the one dressed in black is Nightshade. The gremlin's name is Onyx. If you have patience for our tale, then I'll explain to you why a shape-shifter, a witch, a necromancer and a gremlin are together out here. I can't and won't make any excuses for what happened by the river because that was completely inexcusable. I'll take full responsibility for it. So if you have to kill anyone this night, then choose me and let the others go unharmed."

Onyx flew in front of Yonuh and yelled, "FUCK THAT, YONUH! That was my plan. You had no idea I wanted to use the plague bodies to kill the P.A.N.E.L. squad! If anyone should take their arrows, it should be me!"

Raven and Nightshade hurried to Yonuh. Nightshade pleaded, "I won't have you lay your life down for me, Yonuh." She turned toward the leader and growled, "and I'll be damned if I'm letting YOU kill any of us!"

Raven stared down at the lead elf and warned, "I won't let you have him either. I'll tear your hearts out if you touch one hair on his head!"

Yonuh maneuvered past Onyx and walked up to the leader to the point where her arrow tips were mere millimeters from his chest. "So it's your choice, but what I have to say does concern you as well. What you witnessed tonight barely scratches the surface to the bigger problem we all face."

The elf eyed him intently, weighing what to do: listen to Yonuh or let her anger take over and kill them all.

The other female elf stepped up beside her and prodded, "Sicca, I would like to hear this one's tale."

"Why? We have friends who are sick and dying because of these damn fools!"

"Because you are letting your passions get the best of you, and we do need to hear them out. They may not be part of our clan, but we should treat them like they are and let our rules abide. They deserve that much. Besides, I want to know more about the ones chasing them because I've seen them on more than one occasion."

Sicca had a look of surprise on her face as she stared at the other elf. "You have seen them before, Sabic? Why didn't you mention this? Why do I have to hear this now?"

"You never asked, and they were not a concern of ours until the past few nights. These people's enemies have been capturing shifters and *weres,* but it seems there's more to this, and I want to hear it."

"If that's the case, then they shall go back with us and face our justice!" Sicca hissed at Yonuh.

Onyx walked up with his little arms in the air and asked, "How many of your friends have died so far?"

"Just the faeries so far," Sabic told him. "The spores have always been able to kill fairies in a minute's time, but the nymphs and elves that contract the plague become sick and die a slow and painful death. That's why my sister here is so angry. Why do you ask?"

"How long until they will succumb to the plague?" Onyx asked, despite knowing he was already amping up the leader.

Sicca glared at him and growled, "Three days and nights of pure hell and torment!"

"Ah," the gremlin said, "so we do have a window of opportunity for redemption then. Yonuh here may be able to help your kin *if* he can get a good night's rest."

"Onyx, what are you doing?" Raven said wearily.

"I've never tried to heal elves or nymphs. I don't know that I can!" Yonuh insisted but never took his eyes off Sicca.

"We're dead because of *my plan*," the gremlin reminded. "If Yonuh can rest up and heal the afflicted nymphs and elves, then maybe they might let us live." He put his hand on Yonuh and gave him an apologetic look. "I know you're not at your full strength, big guy. I figure after a good rest, though, you can give it your best shot because…I believe you can do it. I've seen you do some incredible feats in the short time I've known you. You're an amazing healer."

"Wait, I thought he was just a shape-shifter," Sabic said abruptly. "Which are you, a healer or a shifter?"

Yonuh said with pride, "I'm both, actually. I'm a shape-shifter and a Cherokee energy healer and energy worker. I must admit, though, I've never attempted to heal forest creatures of the plague, but I'm willing to try if it can help make amends for *our* mistake."

"Impossible! You can't be all those things!" Sicca insisted angrily. "You — oooh," she moaned as Yonuh reached out and touched her hand that held the bow. Sicca suddenly went silent as the healer's warm, comforting energy washed through her like a wave of eternal ecstasy. Everyone could see that her anger began to ebb. As Sicca's eyes rolled back in her head, she smiled like it was her first time in forever. Two of the nymphs and Sabic looked on in awe and began to inch closer to see Sicca's strange behavior.

Yonuh smiled at them and said, "I'm not doing anything to hurt her, so please don't fear for her safety. I've been told that I have this effect on all those I touch. I'm not even trying to heal her, but she is feeling that energy right now. I'm dual natured, and when my strength is better, I *will* heal your loved ones!"

The nymphs reached out and touched Yonuh on his bare back and immediately reacted to his energy.

They became giddy and giggled a lot as they rubbed their hands all over his body. Raven was ready to step in and yank them off him, but both Nightshade and Onyx stopped her.

"This is a good thing, Raven," Nightshade sternly said. "If they can feel his energy and power, it could prove to be our only way of surviving long enough for Yonuh to try and heal their plague victims."

"Maybe so," Raven growled as she stared at the nymphs and clinched her fists, "but I don't like *where* they're feeling his power at the moment!"

"He's taking one for the team, girl. So layoff and let him do what he does best," Onyx ordered.

Sabic motioned for the nymphs to move away, but they seemed to be enthralled with Yonuh and started touching themselves too. She grabbed them both and said in a stern voice, "Enough of that! Behave yourselves for a change!"

"But...he feels so damn good!" one of the nymphs pouted. "I could lay with him and never tire of that energy. Gods, I can see why that one is getting jealous," she said and pointed to Raven. "You're one lucky lady to have this one!"

Raven's anger subsided as she felt proud that this lusty creature knew Yonuh belonged to her, so she replied with a smile, "You have no idea of how right you are!"

Sabic decided to touch Yonuh just out of pure curiosity. When she did, she felt the warm, comforting energy cover her entire body like a blanket made from the very fabric of love itself. She looked at Raven and said, "A rare one, indeed. It would be a shame to kill him if he fails. I do want to know more about him and your clan."

Confused, Raven looked at Nightshade and Onyx. Was that a compliment or a threat?

Despite her cravings to stay with Yonuh and have more of him, Sabic called upon her considerable willpower and managed to let go of his arm. She now understood why the nymphs had trouble disengaging from him. Steeling herself from her own desires, she stepped away from the healer and felt her heart pang from loneliness. The nymphs were playing and petting each other. Sabic shook her head and muttered a low growl, "Nymphs!"

Yonuh took his hand away from Sicca and waited patiently to see what she would do. The elven leader breathed lightly as she rubbed her forehead. She opened her eyes and saw Yonuh standing there in front of her. The bow was now barely in her hand, and the arrows she had notched in the string were dangling from her other hand. Confused and in deep thought, Sicca waited a few moments before asking, "How did you do that--? What did you do to me? I...I don't understand, but for some reason, I'm no longer angry with you. I'm calmer now and feel at peace." Like Sabic, she called upon her willpower and steeled herself from her desire to touch Yonuh again. "What you've made me feel just now," she said and took a deep breath, steadying herself, "does not negate in any way what you did to our kin and friends tonight."

"I understand completely, Sicca," Yonuh assured her. "To answer your question, I healed the pain you were feeling for your friends and loved ones who have been hurt by the plague. I assure you if I can't heal them, I will make them as comfortable as I can."

Sicca glanced over at Sabic and wondered why she was looking at her with a clinical mind set, observing her to the point where she had to say, "What are you thinking about? I know that look, but why are you giving it to me?"

"I have a feeling this shifter will be successful," Sabic explained.

"What I've gathered from the energy he's putting out, plus what he did with you, indicates to me that he's unique and has a rare gift that could come in handy...later."

"*Ever plotting, ever deceitful! Never trust the machinations of elves, no matter how pretty they are. Never trust them period!*" Onyx said to Yonuh, using telepathy.

"What I put out," Yonuh said, "and what I can accomplish are two separate things, so don't count on a cure just yet, Sabic. Maybe if I can see them for myself, I can come up with something. No guarantees, though." His words didn't seem to faze Sabic, who still had a calculating look on her face.

"So now what?" one of the nymphs asked. "Can we leave now? I'm bored since we can't play with the shifter anymore."

"You did what was needed of you," Sicca replied as she felt her patience waning, especially with the nymphs. "Now go in peace and be merry. Let others you come across know not to tread near the river for a while. Death is there now."

"YES!" the nymph shouted. "Time to break out the spirits and make love! Merriment in the meadows!" She turned to Yonuh. "Come by later and join us. We'd love to have *all* of you!" The nymphs giggled as they danced in tandem in what looked to Nightshade as a conga line. They turned around every so often, waving their come hither gestures to Yonuh and the others as they danced off into the forest.

Onyx shuddered. "As tempting as that offer was, we have bigger fish to fry. So what was their role in all of this, anyway?"

"They witnessed what happened down by the river and barely got away from the spores that flew through the night air,"

Sicca hissed and glared at Onyx. "We were investigating your vehicle, and they informed us of what happened and who got caught in the wake of your destruction, gremlin!"

"Ah, now it makes sense," Onyx snapped back with a smirk. "For a while, I thought they were your little playthings, but I guess having fun and getting laid isn't your thing is it?"

In the blink of an eye, Sicca had Onyx pinned to the ground, with a small dagger to his throat. Her white eyes blazed with a renewed fury as she growled in a malicious tone, "As one of *your* victims, my lover is sick and in pain! Don't think I won't slit your throat, gremlin! You keep those hurtful comments to yourself, or I will take your tongue. Better still, I might tie you up and toss you into the plague corpses, so you can see just how funny your destructive actions really are!"

Suddenly, Sicca felt something cold against her neck. She whirled around and saw Nightshade's black dagger.

"You'll be dead before you can even begin to hurt him," the necromancer hissed viciously. She glanced down at the gremlin, who still lay on the ground. "Onyx, you need to do as she says and shut that big mouth of yours because you're not making this any easier for us! Does Raven need to sleep-spell you, or can you behave on your own?"

Sabic pulled out a small, wooden spear and was about to lunge at Nightshade, but her attention shifted to Raven at the last moment. The witch's wand was aimed directly at her. "Don't even think about it, bitch," Raven growled, "or I'll turn you into a human...with all their weaknesses too!"

Sabic's mouth gaped opened, and she gasped in horror. "You wouldn't dare. That's impossible!"

Raven gave her a half smirk as she replied, "Obviously, you haven't dealt with many witches in your lifetime — certainly, not the fiery kick ass witch of the Pacific Northwest!" She heard Nightshade giggle.

Yonuh felt like this standoff was happening in slow motion and wasn't sure what the best solution would be to end it, mainly because he was too tired to think. He turned his back on them and walked away, looking for a place to sit down and rest. He wandered over towards the van.

Sabic moved with her elven speed and cut him off, sticking her spear under his chin. "And just where do you think you're going?" she demanded. "None of you are allowed to leave!"

Raven was about to blast the elf with her wand, but Yonuh held up his hand, stopping her violence. "I'm exhausted and tired of the drama," he told Sabic. "So unless you can conjure up a tent, a bed, or even a chair, I'm going to lie down in our van and get out of this rain!"

"Sure, just let you slip into the only means of escape from here! Do you think I'm a fool?"

"No, but I'm heading that way whether you like it or not. Besides, I have a feeling you won't kill me...not right now, anyway."

"So bold and confident in that notion, are you? Why won't I kill you, Yonuh? Is it because I'm a female, and you think you can take me or that I'm beneath you? You seem to forget that I *can* kill you right now!"

"No, none of those thoughts ever crossed my mind. You won't kill me now because you need me to heal your friends and Sicca's lover. Also, because you want me for other reasons too."

"Ha! You think I've fallen in love with you because of your energy, or that I want to have sex with you? In your dreams, mongrel! I wouldn't soil my body with the likes of you!"

As Yonuh stared at her, his curiosity got the best of him. "Why would you think that I want sex from you? All I want to do is help you and your woodland friends heal.

I've taken an unbreakable oath to the Great Spirit to help and heal others in need, so there's no way I could possibly leave here without trying my best! I would greatly appreciate it if you could get past your own insecurities and let me do what I was put on this Earth to do. Now, if you will excuse me…"

Sabic still didn't budge from Yonuh's path, but he could tell she was thinking again, which could have been either a good thing or a bad thing. Yonuh felt like the rain was weighing him down and that his legs couldn't hold him up any longer. He took two steps back and sat down on a muddy patch of grass.

Sabic felt unsure and confused, but she decided to press Yonuh anyway. She jabbed him with her spear, just enough to let him know she meant business. "You get back there with the others now, or I'll—"

"Either let me rest or kill me, already!" Yonuh growled out, feeling furious at this creature's arrogance.

Irritable and edgy, the exhaustion made Yonuh weak, and that allowed the beast to come to the surface of the healer's consciousness. He could feel the beast's primeval surging, its readiness to pounce on the elf. With a quickness and speed that Sabic hadn't expected, Yonuh heaved his body from the wet grass and, in one terrifying move, snapped the wooden spear like a toothpick, while seizing the elf by her neck. He slammed her to the ground face first. Pinning her arms to her back, he roughly pulled them up, making her cry out in pain.

Sabic felt claws pierce into her back. She squirmed, trying to free herself, but to no avail.

Yonuh leaned forward and growled into the elf's ear. Chills flooded throughout her body as his beast spoke to her.

"Why won't you listen to us! We're tired and hungry, but you can't leave us be! Perhaps we should dine on your flesh. Maybe then you will understand! You poked the bear with your spear, and now you have us! We want rest, to help, but you can't see past your own arrogance enough to leave us be! Maybe we should take your head off!"

"Help me, someone!" Sabic screamed out in terror as Yonuh's hot breath kissed the back of her neck. Suddenly, she saw knees drop in front of her and immediately knew it was the witch. Sabic feared the worst. As she dared to look up, she saw that the witch was focused on Yonuh and not her, for some reason.

Raven reached out and caressed Yonuh's face, lifting it up so she could gaze into his eyes. She saw that Yonuh's beast was in the driver's seat. If this elf was going to survive, she had to calm the beast.

"There's my beautiful and sexy beast! Did this bitch make you mad tonight?" Raven leaned in to kiss Yonuh but noticed Sabic was about to speak. She smacked the elf and hissed, "Sorry, sister, but we're having a mate-chat, so unless you want to become bear scat, I suggest you shut your mouth! It's already gotten you into a world of hurt!"

"This thing under us has hurt us and won't listen to our pleas for rest!" Yonuh-beast growled.

"I know my love, but I think she's listening now." Raven kissed Yonuh firmly on his lips and snaked her tongue into his waiting mouth where their tongues danced.

Yonuh-beast growled in pleasure, but then he asked, *"Can I take her head off now? We will give it to you as a trophy!"*

Raven giggled as she replied, "No need for that, my sexy beast. I may take her panties instead. You probably made her wet herself."

Sicca stood by as Nightshade and Onyx held her back, explaining that Raven was the only one who could save Sabic from Yonuh's wrath.

Sicca nodded and said aloud, "The mate's call will always soothe the beast because their love trumps all. I've heard of this but never actually seen it happen. I could try to kill him, but I think I would only piss him off even more. She messed up; she deserves this."

"Wow, coldhearted much?" Onyx popped off with a surprised look on his little, dark face.

"No, that's how nature works," Sicca said. "If you're going to harass a bear, don't be surprised when it turns around and eats you. Do you really think he can do it, heal my kin…my lover?"

"I believe in him, but I want him to try *after* he gets some rest," Onyx replied. "Yonuh's a great healer and a fierce protector of others. Combine the two, and you have a recipe for success."

"Yonuh has brought me back from the brink several times, both mentally and physically, and he has made me a better person," Nightshade said with a warm smile as she looked at Yonuh. "He can touch you and your life without even trying or even knowing it, and that can't be taught. If anyone can heal your lover and friends, it's Yonuh!" Sicca nodded as her hopes grew but now wondered if she would go home without Sabic.

Raven let Yonuh nuzzle his face against her wet breasts as she said, "Hmm, how can I get my big, strong bear to leave his new chew toy alone for a while? I'm sure these could be more fun to play with than that scrawny, old twig beneath you."

"MM," Yonuh-beast moaned, *"but...but she hurt us?"*

"She doesn't understand, but I do. I can mend what she hurt and can help you rest. You have to let her go, though, so she can learn from her mistake. Come back to me, Yonuh, and let that sexy beast rest tonight. I know it deserves it."

Yonuh's eyes went from a golden yellow to a dark glowing brown, and he said, "Thank you, Raven. I didn't want to hurt her but—"

Raven kissed him gently as she guided him off Sabic, who rolled away and scrambled to her feet. Sicca walked over and made a few hand gestures in the air. A moment later, a portal opened up. She looked over at the others. "This is the quickest way to our village. Please join us, and I'll make sure you all get food and rest."

Just as everyone started through the portal, Raven grabbed Sabic by her arm. "You owe me your life tonight, elf!" she insisted in a serious tone. "Now off with those panties, and I might just call us even!"

Chapter Eight

"Seriously, Raven? You made Sabic do that?" Yonuh asked as he cuddled next to her in one of the shelters the elves had provided for them.

"Yes, I did, and she deserved the humiliation too! I guess she would take that, rather than have a witch hold it over her head that she was too stupid in the field and needed saving."

"Hmm, I can see her point," Yonuh agreed. "That's quite a blow to her pride, but I'm not sure where the humiliation would come in, other than having to give up her panties to another woman."

Raven beamed him an evil grin as she pulled out Sabic's panties. They were a dark green color, but they also had an ethereal quality to them, almost ghost-like. She handed them to Yonuh. "The humiliation came when we walked through the portal," Raven told him. "All the elves suddenly stopped walking and turned toward her, looking at her with distain and disgust. It seems they could tell something wasn't right with her. When I asked, Sabic said they knew she wasn't wearing panties because their magic connects all the elves together, in some way, through their panties. I guess it's kind of like those aristocratic people—the ones who judged others by their outward appearances. Sabic was being judged by the other elves as being lower than they were."

"They could feel Sabic's panties were gone and that's how they treated her?" Yonuh asked, his mouth gaping.

Through mischievous giggles, Raven went on to explain, "It wouldn't have been so bad, but I couldn't help myself. It was like I was channeling Onyx!

I pulled out her panties so everyone could see my new trophy, and I waved them over my head as I danced around her. I thought a few of the elves were going to have a coronary on the spot! 'So uncivilized,' was just one of several nasty comments I heard."

Yonuh burst out laughing. Even though he felt bad for the elf, Raven had promised his beast that she would have those panties as a trophy, and she had come through. Suddenly, he yawned. Before he could get one more laugh out, he closed his eyes as sleep overwhelmed him.

The shelter they were in for the night was handcrafted and made completely from earthly materials. It had walls made from dark clay, and the floor was inlayed with an array of colorful rocks and gemstones that had runes etched in each one. The décor consisted of leafy vines that had flowers blooming, along with bamboo shafts crafted and woven together to make shelving. The roof had an opening like a skylight, but no matter how much rain fell, not a single drop hit the bed or any other part of the structure inside.

The bed they lay on floated about two feet above the floor. It had neither an aesthetically pleasing look nor a comfortable look. It was just a pile of straw and ferns woven together. The pillows were nothing more than small flower petals stacked and held together in place by magical means and gave off a pleasant aroma whenever one shifted on them.

But looks can be deceiving. Yonuh felt like he was sleeping on a cloud, noting just how soft, yet, just how firm the bed was. Raven thought it was like sleeping on a bed made from pure silk, only this was softer and sleeker. The elves know how to sleep comfortably, that's for sure, Yonuh thought as he awoke the next morning.

He slipped out of bed and stretched out with a growl of pleasure while Raven looked on admiring his naked form.

Without warning, there was a quick knock on the door, and suddenly it was open, spilling in the morning sunlight. Sicca barged in. "Time to get out of bed, you two. Yonuh, I— oh my!" Her white eyes seemed to glow and pulse as she gazed at the healer.

Raven irritably sprang out of bed and stood beside Yonuh. "What do you want?" she demanded.

Sicca looked at Raven as she shook herself mentally and said, "Sorry, I caught you as you were waking and didn't realize you weren't….dressed yet."

Embarrassed, Yonuh bent over to grab his clothes off the floor. He turned his head as he started to blush. After jerking on his pants, he shoved his feet into his shoes and handed Raven's clothes to her.

"Thanks, Yonuh," Raven said as she slipped on her skirt and corset.

"I want to thank you, Sicca, for the hospitality you've shown us," he told her. "I'm sorry it has to be under these conditions, but I want you to know I appreciate it."

"You're still my prisoners," she reminded in a stern voice. "I just need you at your full strength today." She realized a shirt wasn't in the room, and she couldn't remember seeing one last night. "Hmm, I must ask, do you like running around without a shirt, or did you lose it last night?"

"It was stolen from our campsite last night," Raven explained as she sat on the floating bed next to Yonuh. She slipped her calf high boots on. "One of the P.A.N.E.L. squad snuck up and took it, probably because it had Yonuh's blood on it."

Sicca narrowed her eyes and asked, "Why would anyone want a blood-stained shirt in the first place? That person was human, right?"

Yonuh and Raven shared a glance, but it was Yonuh who spoke. "The person is human, but the one who commands him and the P.A.N.E.L. squad is a demon who goes by the name of Zordic. Have you heard of this demon?"

Sicca thought for a moment before shaking her head, so Yonuh went on, "Apparently, Zordic is the righteous right hand of Prophet Bob who preaches about the divine savior's plan where if they can exterminate *all* supernatural beings from Earth, then the world will somehow return to its former glory before the plague."

"That still doesn't explain why the human stole your bloody shirt."

"One of the humans that Nightshade interrogated, said that his master seemed to enjoy the taste of Yonuh's blood," Raven said as her eyes flared, and her hands clenched into fists. "That human had his men hunting for Yonuh, so Zordic could drink his blood and make him into his own personal…blood-slave."

"What's so special about your blood that a demon would resort to vampirism, Yonuh?"

Yonuh could only shrug as he replied, "I haven't got a clue, but my blood's the reason all those men who wear crimson clothes have been running around in your forest the past few nights. They're trapping shifters in hopes of capturing me."

Sicca put her arms behind her back as she slowly paced back and forth, thinking. She would glance at Yonuh every so often, and then she stopped. "You may not like this, Yonuh, but in order to know the why, I will need some of your blood. I won't need much—just a taste. I would like to see what's got this demon hunting high and low for you."

Raven grabbed his arm and gave him a wary look. "I don't know, Yonuh.

I'm not sure we can trust what will happen. It's bad enough to have a demon go vampiric over your blood, but who's to say she won't do the same? And we *are* her prisoners!"

Sicca rolled her eyes. "Do you think I love the idea of drinking blood? I hate the mere thought of soiling my pure blood with another's blood, like a leech! We need answers, and I'm doing my best to help provide them. Have I not treated you and your friends well since I brought you here?"

"She has a point and I, for one, want to know what's so special about my blood," he told Raven. Glancing over at the elf, he said in a firm voice, "Just understand, Sicca, if you try anything against me, I won't stop Raven from killing you. Fair enough?"

"Agreed, but I won't take much more than a few drops of your blood." Sicca pulled out her small dagger and slowly walked up to Yonuh who, in turn, extended his arm out. She hesitated at first and looked over at Raven to get her approval. The witch nodded but never took her eyes off Sicca.

The elf let out a pent up breath as she took Yonuh by his hand. Immediately, she felt that warm, comforting energy flowing throughout her body from just his touch. With a steady hand, she made a small cut on Yonuh's palm, which made him wince.

"Sorry about that, but my dagger is imbued with silver," Sicca said apologetically, which caught her by surprise. Why am I feeling bad for hurting him? She leaned in towards Yonuh. With a disgusted, crinkled up face, she stuck out her tongue and lapped up what little blood was on his palm.

Instantly, Sicca felt a euphoria flood through her entire body as if she had drunk the sweetest wine in the land, and it made her yearn for more. She felt like her body was literally on fire…burning with desire! She found her face was once again buried in Yonuh's palm, lapping up the blood that was still oozing out of the small cut.

Sicca could no longer resist what her body demanded of her, so she slipped a hand down into her leggings and started fingering her core, much to the shock of both Yonuh and Raven, who were now unable to utter a single word to protest her behavior.

The elf dropped to the floor and ran her hands over her breasts while still masturbating, seemingly oblivious that she had an audience for this performance. She opened her blazing, white eyes and had a look of pure want and hunger, ready to devour Yonuh. Her breaths became quick and shallow as her hips heaved. Finally she climaxed, letting out a scream that was both melodious and ear-piercing, forcing Yonuh and Raven to cover their ears.

After a few minutes passed, Sicca seemed to recover. She breathed heavily as she focused her eyes on Yonuh and Raven. "What? What are you two looking at?" She glanced around. "Why am I on the floor?"

Raven cleared her throat and said with a half-smile, "Umm, you might want to take a self-inventory, Sicca."

Confused as she was, Sicca did what Raven suggested. She immediately noticed her fingers were slick with…her own juices! The elf's eyes widened when she looked down and saw her green leggings were partially down her thighs, and her ethereal panties were drenched. She noted that her silk shirt had been clawed open and shredded, and her breasts were out for everyone to see. Feeling mortified, Sicca pulled up her leggings as she scrambled to her feet. She nearly fell back down from being so lightheaded.

Raven got up to help steady the elf until she got her balance back. Sicca looked at her and hesitantly asked, "Did…did I do…what I think I just did?"

The witch looked at her and said with a smile, "If you mean did you fuck yourself like there was no tomorrow and then have an ear-piercing orgasm, then the answer is yes. Yes, you did!"

Yonuh stood up and held out his cut hand. It still had a little of his blood on it, and Sicca felt inexorably drawn to it, wanting to lick his hand clean. He saw the hunger in her eyes, so he quickly pulled it away from her.

She stared at his hand and tracked it with her eyes wherever he moved it, as if she would pounce on it at any moment.

"Damn, it's like she's a junkie!" Raven stepped in front of Sicca and slapped her hard in the face, bringing her back to reality.

Stunned by the slap, Sicca looked around the room as if she didn't know where she was. She quickly regained her bearings, though, and her hand shot up to her reddening cheek. "Did you just strike me?" the elven leader snarled angrily.

"For your own good," Raven admitted. "Yonuh's blood has affected you to the point where you're looking more vampiric with each passing second."

The healer walked outside to give Sicca time to recover. There were no chairs in the room, so Raven guided the elf to the bed. They both sat down. The witch held Sicca's hand as she stroked her back and asked,"So other than the sexy orgy — party of one — what did you discover?"

Sicca thought hard as she rubbed her tender breasts, still amazed at what she had done to herself. "Yonuh's blood is literally intoxicating. I felt I had drunk the sweetest and most potent wine in all the known dimensions, and I craved for more. It was like I couldn't get it fast enough in my mouth to meet the needs of my body and those needs were — you saw those needs." She took a deep breath before she went on. "I would have to assume that Zordic is tirelessly working to capture Yonuh because the healer's blood makes him react the same way I did — the demon is hooked on the blood as if it were a powerful drug that held him captive."

"Anything else?" Raven asked.

"The blood sent my body's internal temperature to about ten times higher than it should have been, and it gave me the feeling of pure euphoria. Yonuh is a rare being, so it doesn't surprise me that his blood would be different than others. From the few times I've had physical contact with him, I found his touch to be very addictive." Sicca stared across the room in deep thought.

"His blood, though," she finally said, "is the stuff you don't want to play with. Now imagine the two together — his touch and his blood: his touch makes you feel good, warm and comforted; now add drinking his blood to that feeling. His blood makes your libido go apocalyptic. You can see now why the demon wants Yonuh. He wants a blood, sex slave who will pleasure him in different ways, but I'm sure Yonuh wouldn't enjoy it because it wouldn't go both ways."

With a sense of sadness and anger, Raven looked towards the door where she had last seen her mate. "Yonuh has had too many of those relationships in his life which has hurt him considerably. I'll be damned if I'm going to let some fucked-in-the-head demon put him through that! Too many have taken advantage of his huge, beautiful heart. And they nearly sent him over the edge not long ago."

Sicca thought for a moment. "To be like Yonuh and have that kind and caring heart in this miserable, cruel world these days might be construed as a weakness. It takes a great deal of courage to be like that, and it's what the world needs more of...if it is to truly recover and heal."

"It doesn't help to have some psychic, religious fanatic whipping humans into frenzied freaks, causing them to blame supernatural beings for the way the world is and telling them to slaughter us all. As if that will somehow magically bring the world back to the way it was before the plague!"

"Religion has always been Mankind's shield of justification for everything they've done," Sicca growled. "It has been the root of most conflicts and wars throughout their history. Does it really surprise you that they are behaving like this? In times of chaos, humans always look for a leader or an idea to latch on to for comfort. They have a nasty tendency to justify everything they do. From what I've heard from you people, the demon and this Prophet Bob have helped twist the humans, and they've molded them into killers. A question must be asked: Why is the demon working with Prophet Bob?"

Yonuh walked back into the shelter and seemed to be in deep thought. He glanced at Sicca who looked at his hands with longing, so he showed her that he had washed them. She relaxed a little. Yonuh rubbed his hand over his mouth and went back into deep thought.

"What's got those gears a grinding, my love?" Raven asked.

"Sicca, can you tell me how your best elven healing potions or medicines have fared against the plague?"

"Obviously, not well at all," she replied with a great sadness in her voice. "The potion barely takes the pain and suffering away. It becomes just a matter of time till they succumb to a painful death!" Her hands fisted tightly as she thought of losing her lover.

"I have an idea of how to help the victims while I attempt to heal them," Yonuh explained, "but...you may not like my suggestion."

Sicca and Raven both stood up and approached him. He could see a glimmer of hope in the elf's sad eyes which sealed the deal in his mind, but it all hinged on whether Sicca would go for it.

"What will you require of me that I wouldn't like?" the elf bluntly asked.

Before Yonuh could speak, Nightshade walked into the shelter, followed by Onyx.

"Well?" Sicca prodded impatiently."Would you mind telling me your plan?"

"I'll require two things from you: water and your best elven healing potion."

"That's easy enough to get, but why did you say I wouldn't like this?"

"Because I haven't said it yet; I'm going to add a drop of my blood to your potion to enhance it — at least one drop per victim."

"What?! Are you mad?" Sicca screamed out, which didn't shock Yonuh at all. "You saw what it did to me. I couldn't control myself!"

"That's because you took the blood from the source, in its purest state. I believe it will interact and enhance your potion to where the victims won't suffer or feel pain, long enough for me to heal them. How many victims are there?"

"There're twenty for the moment, but I'm not sure — "

"If Yonuh thinks there's a chance this will work," Raven interjected, "I say do it because what have you got to lose if it doesn't work? The victims may end up feeling very erotic. They might even pass away with a smile on their face. That sounds better than the alternative."

"Do you want the love of your life to suffer any more?" Nightshade asked as she put an arm around Sicca, who shook her head. "Then let Yonuh make this attempt at healing."

"I'll do this, but…it goes against everything we believe. Our magic, down to our alchemy, is connected to us all. Everyone will know something's amiss. I pray what Yonuh does will enhance it and won't destroy the potion completely."

"Then lead the way, Sicca. There isn't any time to waste," Yonuh urged as he took her hand and led her towards the door.

As Sicca walked out, she pointed to a wooden cabin straight ahead of them. "That's where the victims are, but I need to get the potion and show all of you something too."

They walked along a stony path that led to the center of the elven community. It reminded Nightshade of a town square, only it was circular. There were shops for trading and bartering set up in a circular formation, and in the center of all this was a tall, wooden platform. On it, they saw that a female elf had been stripped of all her clothing, her wrists tied above her head. She was dangling, and her back was bleeding badly from the many cuts and injuries her body had sustained.

Yonuh and the others gasped in unison as they recognized Sabic.

"Oh gods! What did she do to deserve this?" Raven blurted out.

Sicca turned and eyed her as she growled, "You happened, that's what. This is the price she paid for looking weak in the face of an enemy — also for the removal of her panties, you so happily paraded around for everyone to see."

Raven gasped in horror at what she had caused.

"Those panties were crafted with our magic," Sicca went on, "and as I said before, we all notice when something happens to our magic…it's like a warning. So when she gave them to you, she signaled to all of us that she had weakened our magical link in some way. This is the punishment for such a crime. She was already in trouble for her stupidity in attacking Yonuh. She couldn't defend herself, looking weak there too."

"I…I didn't know…I never would have asked for them if…" Raven blubbered out as tears ran down her face. "This is so barbaric and cruel! How can you stand there and not help your friend?"

"It's our custom and how we survive. Our magic protects and conceals us from the outside world. If we find a breech in our magic, the offending party must be dealt with harshly. They must be made an example for everyone to see. This public punishment is a warning to others to keep our magic safe and strong." She went silent, deep in thought.

Raven groaned as she watched Sabic's nude body gently turn in the breeze, her hands pulled over her head by a rope, her feet inches off the floor of the platform, and her eyes closed tight against the pain.

"I could save her," Onyx declared in a whisper to Nightshade. "I could cut her down."

Nightshade shook her head adamantly. "No, it might start a war. This is Sabic's punishment. It's the way of the elves."

"When I give you the potion, Yonuh," Sicca explained, "I will craft it to be manipulated by you. I'll be judged and maybe the next example if your blood does weaken our magic in the potion."

"I understand completely, Sicca," Yonuh told her. "I hope it does what I want it to do. I'll be waiting for you." He ushered Raven away from the wooden platform where Sabic dangled.

Raven wiped at her eyes. "I, for one, couldn't live like this! I'd be strung up on a weekly basis with all the experimenting I do with my magic."

"I know," Yonuh said gently, "Remember, you have more freedom than they do. This should give you a glimpse into what life is like for other beings. You should feel grateful for not being a part of this society. It's probably been this way since the beginning of time, and there's nothing we can do to change this."

Onyx hovered beside Yonuh as he stuffed a Dorito in his mouth. "Admit it, Yonuh," he stated. "You had to fight the urge to go help poor Sabic. You wanted to heal her, didn't you?"

The healer gave a curt nod and replied with a smile, "You know me too well, Onyx. But even with the urge to help her, I had to refuse. I didn't want to interfere with the laws of this community."

"So what you're about to do isn't interfering? Onyx snickered.

As they made it to the entrance of the wooden cabin where the plague victims lay dying, Sicca rounded the corner and walked up to Yonuh. "This potion is very strong," she reminded and handed him a small crystal vial that glowed and changed colors. "A little goes a long way, so only give each victim one sip of it. There's a ward on this door to keep others from entering and disturbing the victims. When I open it, go in immediately. It can't stay down for long. Your friends must stay outside. Those are the rules; are we clear?"

"Yes, and thank you for doing this, Sicca," Yonuh said and took a water canteen made from a thick animal hide. "I promise I'll do my best to help all of your friends we hurt last night."

Nightshade handed Yonuh her black dagger and said with a smirk, "Take this, I figure it'll be easier to use my dagger than gnawing on your paw for the blood."

Raven gave Yonuh a hug and kissed him passionately. She pulled away and demanded, "You be safe in there or, so help me, I'll come in there and spank that sexy ass!"

He felt a tug on his pants and glanced down. Onyx was trying to get his attention, so Yonuh squatted down in front of the gremlin.

"Don't be expecting *me* to make out with you, buddy." Onyx handed the healer a bag of Doritos. "I want you to take this for me, and I won't take 'no' for an answer, either." The gremlin got a pained look on his dark face. "I...uh...I promise on this bag of Doritos to keep the ladies safe from harm if something should happen to you while you're in there, Yonuh!"
His shoulders slumped as guilt weighed heavily on them. "This is my fault, and you shouldn't have to keep cleaning up my messes."

"Everything's going to be fine," he promised the gremlin.

Sicca sighed and shifted anxiously from one foot to another. "If Xenon is still alive….tell him I love him."

"You two will be reunited this day, I promise you," he insisted. "So be prepared to tell him yourself."

As tears ran down Sicca's face, she placed her hand on the door. A small opening appeared, and Yonuh darted quickly inside. The hole sealed up when Sicca removed her hand. "It's all up to Yonuh," she told the others. "Now we must wait…and pray."

Onyx walked over to Sicca and asked, "So is there a chance that they might be contagious?"

"We normally don't sprout the chutes like most creatures and humans do. But it *does* happen, so that's why we have them isolated from contact."

"Why not just kill them and put them out of their misery?" Nightshade asked. "Why let them linger and suffer if your people know there's no coming back from this?"

"Because there's always a chance someone will survive. If that happens, we'll use their blood to make a serum for the rest of us. We would no longer fear those dead corpses scattered throughout the world. As you can see, none have yet survived. When all the sick perish, the spell that seals this structure can be used to immolate the bodies safely, destroying all traces of the plague."

Raven looked at the wooden structure but couldn't see inside. She stroked the door, the last place she had seen Yonuh. Suddenly, something that Sicca had said just moments ago fought through the fog of her mind. Feeling overwhelming panic, she whirled around and stared at the elf.

"So your people *do* sprout the chutes sometimes," she accused. "And you didn't have the balls to warn Yonuh about it before he blindly walked through your portal? You have willingly sent him to his grave just to try and save your lover! I should fucking kill you for that!"

"That explains the whole immolation magic, right there!" Onyx growled and felt his beast becoming agitated. "They don't just get sick and die like they have the flu; they'll sprout the chutes!"

Nightshade instinctively reached for her black dagger but then realized she had given it to Yonuh, so she did the next best thing. She gave Sicca a punch to her gut, knocking the wind out of her. Nightshade got behind the elf and held her in place as Raven slowly moved toward her with her wand out.

Raven roughly jabbed her wand into Sicca's chin and got in her face as she snarled out, "Give me one good reason why I shouldn't turn you into a self-fucking toad for the rest of your life?"

"Because I'm the only one who will let him out if he succeeds," the elf cried out. "No one else here will give a damn or even lift a finger to assist you. You're stuck with me whether you like it or not!" Sicca looked away for a moment and then added, "Yonuh has just added his blood to the potion, and now the waiting truly begins, doesn't it?"

"Nightshade, can I at least take a few bites out of her?" Onyx hovered beside Raven with his sharp claws extended and showing his razor-sharp teeth, making Sicca squirm. "Hell, I'll tear her damn tongue out if you will let me. Oh please, please, please say yes!"

Raven looked at the gremlin. "I just don't get you, Onyx. Since when have you ever had to beg anyone to do anything? What gives? You've been acting strange since last night. Are you okay?"

"I'm busy deciding which part of this gamey, little elf I'm going to chew on first, so buzz off, carrot top!" Onyx hissed out.

Raven was about to turn her anger on Onyx when she noticed a large gathering of elves nearby. Sicca was right about the potion, she thought. Her people did notice and had come to investigate.

Several of the elves had drawn their swords and bows, readying to attack. As the crowd grew closer, Nightshade released Sicca and put her hands up in the air to show she wasn't armed. Raven put her wand away. This wasn't the time to threaten these would-be attackers.

Onyx didn't seem to care. He was ready to fight them all, if he had to, because he had promised Yonuh he would watch over Raven and Nightshade. He had sworn the oath on his bag of sacred Doritos, something he didn't take lightly!

The elven crowd stopped advancing, and one stepped out of the throng. He seemed to have a regal, grandfatherly air about him, despite the fact he looked to be in his twenties. He had fierce, piercing eyes, and he cast them directly at Sicca. "What have you done to our healing potion?" he demanded. "Answer me now, child! We all felt it, whatever *it* was, and we still do. Now explain this sacrilegious act against our magic!"

Nervously, Sicca stepped forward. She was on shaky ground, and she knew it. She had disrespected the sacred magic to save her lover. She could be killed for it. "There's a healer in there with the plague victims. He's attempting to save all of them. He has added his own blood to the potion to make our brothers and sisters feel less pain while he attempts to purge the plague from their bodies."

The elder elf sneered at Sicca, showing his disgust. "You willfully allowed an outsider to tamper with our magic just because you're dense enough to believe that Xenon can be saved. I should disembowel and dismember you on general principal!"

While Sicca and the elder elf argued, Raven, Nightshade, and Onyx heard Yonuh call out to them mentally, and what he said made them all gasp.

Raven dropped to her knees and pounded the ground with her fists. With a horrible, stony grimace on his little face, Onyx hovered next to Nightshade and gave her a comforting hug as tears flowed down both their faces.

None of them could forget Yonuh's message: *"Raven, I love you with all my heart and soul. I feel the same about you, Nightshade, and, of course, Onyx. Little gremlin, I guess you won't be getting these Doritos back. One of the nymphs burst and covered me with the spores. I didn't realize she was dead, but now it looks like I might be joining her…"*

Chapter Nine

Gordon entered the compound grounds through the south gate. Afraid to return to any of the vehicles, it had taken him the rest of last night and all day today to walk back. He rubbed his neck and hesitated before going any farther. He figured he would get an earful from the other men, especially for being the only survivor of the hunt, and they were sure to rag on him for being a coward. But Gordon was more worried about Master Zordic and his reaction to last night's failure. Even with the information he had gathered on the prey—their names, their photos, and the blood-stained shirt—Gordon wasn't quite convinced it would save his life.

He adjusted his backpack and decided it was high time to check in with the master because running would only make his death a lot worse. The master was very creative when it came to torture and death. Gordon walked along the winding parking lot roadways, lost in his thoughts when he ran into one of the sentries doing his rounds.

The sentry turned on him, gun drawn. "Dammit, Gordon, watch where you're going; I almost shot you!"

"Sorry Jeff, I had a bad night. It won't happen again."

As Gordon was preparing to walk away, Jeff asked, "Weren't you in charge of last night's hunt? Where are the rest of the men?"

Gordon's shoulders slumped forward, and he said in a defeated voice, "I'm all that remains of the team; the rest are dead."

Stunned, Jeff gasped. "All of them? I can't believe it! What did you run into out there, a huge pack of shifters? You took out a decent force of what…twenty of our best men?"

"I don't want to discuss this right now. I've more pressing matters to attend to with the master."

The look on Jeff's face said it all. He didn't think Gordon would live past today.

"Where's the master now?"

"He's just off stage, watching over the crowd as Prophet Bob gives his majestic sermon and future predictions."

"Good," Gordon stated, "at least this will buy me some time to get—"

"Your affairs in order?" Jeff said and chuckled. His mirth earned him a scowl from Gordon. "Can I have your stereo when you're gone?"

Gordon couldn't believe what he'd just heard. He very well could be killed by the master, and this creep was actually making fun of him. "Piss off!" His outburst only caused Jeff to laugh louder. Gordon turned to leave, but then he stopped. "Wait until it's your turn on the table, Jeff. And it *will be* someday. How funny will that be to you?"

As Gordon's words covered him like a shroud, Jeff stopped laughing. Gordon headed towards his own personal barrack, leaving Jeff gaping and speechless.

There were quite a few barracks on the premises. Some were two stories high and could hold eight people on each floor. Gordon's barrack was smaller, just a single floor and could house only two people in it. After last night's trip into the woods, Gordon had it all to himself. He hated his barrack-mate, mainly because Lee harassed him constantly. Lee often called Gordon a coward, and that moniker was legendary amongst the men. He smiled as he thanked those creatures for disposing of Lee last night.

He unlocked the door and flipped the light switch on, illuminating the room. As usual, garbage had been dumped on his bed and a bucket of yellow paint had been used to paint his bed frame.

Lee must have done this before we left yesterday—while I was with the master.

"I may be a coward, Lee," he said aloud to the room, "but I'm not the one who's rotting away in the forest."

He pushed all the garbage off his bed and into a nearby fifty-five gallon garbage can that Gordon assumed was where all this debris had come from. He chucked the open can of yellow paint into it for good measure. Gordon shoved the trash can outside and went back in, sitting down at his desk. After he fired up his computer, he shrugged off his backpack and rummaged through its contents.

Pulling out his camera, he popped out the SD card and slid it into the memory card slot on the front of his tower. While his computer was working to recognize the SD card, Gordon turned on his printer. He opened the paper tray to see if it had any paper in it and discovered that Lee had put his touch here too.

Gordon yanked out all the copy paper and found that each piece had been written on in Lee's handwriting: *Yellow chicken coward!*

Gordon screamed out in frustration. Even in death, this bastard still tormented him. He stormed over to the front door and slung all the derogatory papers in the garbage can and slammed the door shut. Stomping back to his desk, he plopped down in his chair and pulled out more copy paper from his desk drawer and put it in the printer tray.

Gordon promised himself that he would go back to the forest, find Lee's body, and take a long piss on it. Might as well make him yellow—an appropriate send off from a coward. Gordon maniacally laughed. He clicked on the file and perused the images he had taken last night. He decided to crop each of the faces, letting everyone see plainly who they were chasing after. He would warn the squads that Yonuh's friends were a deadly group. Gordon set about putting a name and general demographics to the bottom of each picture.

Suddenly, he froze. The image of the female necromancer had come up to be cropped and edited.

The ghostly image of her facial features triggered an inner fear of death, and Gordon fought the sudden urge to flee for his life. Her glowing, silver eyes stared directly into his very soul. She was beautiful, creepy, and deadly all in one package, and she had nearly murdered him last night. Gordon did his best not to stare at her image as he cropped and added text to it. But despite that, his hands shook, and his brow beaded up with sweat. Gordon figured he would rather face Master Zordic's wrath than have to look upon this Nightshade in person again.

When he finished with all the photos, he printed out a hundred of each, so all the men could get a copy. Gordon smiled at his own genius. With these images, he was sure to get approval from the others and possibly even from the master. While he sat back in his chair, with his hands behind his head, waiting for his printer to finish its job, Gordon heard a knock at his door.

"Enter, it's open!" Gordon called out, still feeling proud of his photos.

Whoever it was knocked on the door again, which threw Gordon's good mood into the toilet. He surged up with a huff and stomped towards the door. As he opened it, multiple hands grabbed hold of him and dragged him to the parking lot, where he was thrown down onto the paved driveway. Several men kicked him hard everywhere; no part of his body was safe from their combat boots. Gordon heard an angry voice shout, "We figured you'd be the only one to return without a scratch!"

Another voice chimed in as the owner of it kicked Gordon repeatedly in the spine, "Those were my friends you left out there to die, you cowardly shitbag!"

Someone kicked Gordon in the face and said with delight, "At least now you'll look the part of a hero to the master! I'm sure he's going to love hearing your whiny story!"

Gordon curled into a fetal position as the men stopped beating him. Thank goodness the beating was over, he thought. Suddenly, though, he felt some sort of thick liquid being poured all over his body. A splash on his face told him it was paint — yellow paint! Next, he saw white snow falling all around him. Strange, it isn't cold enough for snow, he thought fuzzily. As the flakes fell over and around his body, he realized they were feathers. His entire body had been painted yellow and feathered!

The kicking resumed with someone shouting out, "Cluck, cluck, motherfucker! Cluck like the yellow, cowardly chicken that you are! He needs to cluck before we can stop!"

From the metallic taste in his mouth, Gordon knew blood was coming up, so he did his best at clucking for the assholes. It was pathetic, and it came out sounding like, "luk, luk, luk, luk, luk," but the men stopped their assault on him.

One of them grabbed him by his hair and yanked him up to his knees. "Next time, we're having fried chicken for dinner. Remember that, you coward!" The man turned and growled to someone else, "Give it here!"

The man slipped an elastic cord over the back of Gordon's head and let some contraption snap hard, stinging open wounds. The contraption was a plastic cone that went over his nose and mouth. Great, Gordon thought hazily, they gave me a chicken's beak! This can't get any worse!

His attackers bound his hands and feet with ropes and slowly dragged Gordon along the paved driveway, leaving a yellow streak with feathers in their wake. Someone spit on him, and now he thought, yes this is going to get a lot worse.

Gordon groaned in pain as he felt his skin scraped raw by the pavement. He looked over his shoulder and saw a bright light come into view, but he wasn't sure where he was. As they got to the light, Gordon's body was lifted up, and his arms were held over his head.

He heard a squeaking, ratcheting noise and then Gordon found himself dangling in the air as the men hoisted him up like a sail on a boat. He felt every sore, cut, and bruised muscle in his body as gravity took hold, and his own weight made the pain unbearable.

Below him, Gordon heard people laughing and making mock chicken calls. Someone even threw little rocks at him. He looked down, the best he could, and saw Jeff standing with the rest of the men, laughing as he called out, "See, guys, it's no longer a rumor. Gordon truly is a yellow, cowardly chicken! He looks hungry. Maybe we should toss up some cracked corn, so he can eat!" Howls of laughter erupted from the rest of the men.

At that moment, the flock from Prophet Bob's service began leaving the front of the old church. Many gasped when they saw Gordon, but most of the congregants sneered and pointed at him. One lady hissed out at Gordon, "Serves you right for leaving all those brave men to die at the hand of those evil creatures!"

How did this person know? It was like she had been told of what happened by these bastards, which was unlikely or...

Gordon wriggled so he could turn his body and look around. Sure enough, there was a sign to his left that read: *Here hangs Gordon, a cowardly, yellow chicken who ran away and left twenty brave men to die at the hands of the enemy of all humans!*

Humiliation complete, Gordon thought as he heard Lee's maniacal laughter in the dark recesses of his mind. Tears rolled down Gordon's face as he felt his whole world go numb inside and out.

A commotion of shouting and painful grunts made Gordon curious enough to look down. To his shock, Master Zordic was slapping some of his tormentors and berating them.

More of Prophet Bob's flock came out. If there was one thing the master hated more than failure, it was looking incompetent, especially to the prophet's worshipers. The demon apologized to the people coming out of the old building, saying this wasn't proper and that Prophet Bob didn't condone this kind of behavior.

Jeff and another man dragged an extendable ladder towards Zordic. He pointed at an area to Gordon's right, and the men adjusted the ladder. Gordon wriggled his body so that he could somewhat face the ladder, and he heard the sound of heavy feet stomping on each rung. Suddenly, Gordon could make out Zordic's face beside him.

The demon perused Gordon's damaged body. "My dear child, why have they done this to you?"

With a crackling voice that was near the point of going out, Gordon said hoarsely through the cone, "Be-because…I'm…a coward…my…punishment…" He could feel Zordic probing his thoughts.

Suddenly, the demon gave Gordon a look of surprise. He tilted his head and said, "You realize that admitting to cowardice tends to not go well, don't you?"

Gordon nodded the best he could, and then he said, "Kill…me, Master. Information…you…want…"

"Seems like you're ready to die, but did I hear you right? You have information for me? Let me guess. You want to trade it for your life. Is that it, Gordon?" Zordic asked with a malevolent smile.

"Name…picture…shifter you hunt—"

Zordic seized him by the throat and forced Gordon to look him in the eyes. "Am I to understand that you have the name and a picture of the shifter I seek?"

Gordon nodded, and Zordic's eyes glowed with excitement.

The demon asked impatiently, "Where's the picture, my child? I so wish to look upon this creature with my own eyes."

Gordon choked out, "Bar…barracks…mine…" He passed out.

Zordic looked down at the men below him and commanded, "What are you waiting for, the next apocalypse? Get this man down from here, NOW!"

Zordic glanced around the grounds and along the streets, making sure that all the churchgoers had finally moved on. When he saw they had, Zordic took the opportunity and teleported to the ground. His use of the ladder had been for show only — to fool the prophet's congregants. Zordic could have easily flown up to him, but since this damn, incompetent squad had made a public spectacle of Gordon, Zordic had to resort to the ladder subterfuge.

The demon shook his head as he muttered, "Good help is so hard to find, even after an apocalypse." As Gordon's limp body made it to the ground, Zordic growled in a cold, steely voice, "Untie him, then gather all who took part in this, and meet me in my personal chamber room." He saw Jeff standing, staring at him. "Jeff, I already know you did this, now round the rest of the men up, or be prepared to lie down on my steel table!"

Panicking, Jeff backed away and stuttered, "Y…yes, Master! R…right away!"

Zordic walked over and picked up Gordon. Cradling the man in his arms like a baby, Zordic teleported the both of them to just outside Gordon's barrack.

The demon noticed that there was a trashcan full of garbage, along with several pages of printer paper which had more of the taunting words on them.
An empty can of yellow paint sat nearby.
The door was already open, so Zordic simply strolled in. He lay Gordon down on his bed, and then he snatched up the chair by the computer desk.

Rolling the chair over to the man's bed, the demon sat down. Zordic said solemnly, "Gordon, my child, I'm going to heal you now, so we can better talk here in private. You'll tell me everything you know, and then I'll decide if you should live or die. Is that understood, my child?"

Gordon responded with a ghostly voice, "Yyyeesss…"

Zordic ran both his hands over Gordon's body, and immediately the man felt brand new. He was still covered in yellow paint and feathers, but he wasn't going to whine about that—not after the master had just graciously mended all his wounds.

He sat up in bed and slipped the cone off his face. "Thank you, Master. I hope I can repay you with the information I have." He saw the master was waiting, so he quickly went on. "I was able to sneak up on a small campsite which had the creatures that fit the description of the ones who broke out of jail. It appears they are sticking together as a team. I printed out their pictures, and I took the liberty of adding their names and other descriptions as well."

Gordon hurried over to his desk and picked up the four pictures. He grabbed his backpack and then sat back down on the bed in front of Zordic. He flipped through the pictures until he found the one that said, *Yonuh, the shape-shifter,* on it and handed it to the demon.

With his excitement growing, Zordic studied the image. "Are you certain that this…Yonuh is the one I'm searching for?" he asked in a deadly, calm voice.

Gordon gulped loudly, but then he reached into his backpack. "I figured you would want more proof than just a photo, so I stole his shirt. Yonuh was injured, and his blood is on it for you to test. I pray it's the blood you want because the night went to shit after I nabbed this."

Zordic eyed Gordon for a long minute. He stretched out his clawed hand and said, "Do explain that last comment, my child."

Gordon gave the blood-stained shirt to Zordic. "It was like they knew we were there, somehow, and they were able to coordinate together. The necromancer took out one hunting party all by herself! The other creatures made themselves irresistible targets and drew the men out into the open. I believe the men are all dead, sir — the creatures lured them into a trap! I barely escaped with my life. The necromancer came after me, but I was able to give her the slip."

"And what makes you think they all died?" Zordic asked intently. He seemed to be resisting his urge to taste the blood.

Gordon swallowed again as he said, "Because it sounded like all of the remaining hunting parties had converged on the witch, gremlin, and your shifter. The men had them cornered by a river that was too wide to cross and too swift to jump into safely. I heard screams….so many screams. Then, dead silence on the radio. I checked again and again, but no one responded. From that point on, I knew I had to make it back here alive and give you this information."

Zordic looked down at the shirt in his hands. This man either lives or dies, he mused, depending on this blood. Lifting the shirt up to his nose, the demon sniffed it. He ran a very wet, forked tongue over the dried blood and felt his entire body reacting with wonderful euphoria. He had longed to experience this feeling again for over a month now. Quickly, he tore out the blood soaked spots. He placed one in his pocket and kept the other in his hand. Zordic saw that Gordon was on his knees, his head down, and his arms behind him.

"My child, what are you doing?" Zordic asked but felt amused by the gesture.

"I'm a coward, Master, and I deserve to die. I await my punishment."

Zordic let out a maniacal laugh as he put a clawed hand on Gordon's head. "Your cowardice has paid off, Gordon. This *is* the blood I seek! You must pass out copies of these pictures to everyone here, so they'll know who to grab and who his friends are."

Gordon let out a pent up breath. "I have all those ready, my master. I was coming to tell you all this before I was—"

"Go clean up, my child. You have much work to do. I'll deal with those who have hurt the one person who has made me so happy!" Zordic stood up and lifted Gordon to his feet. "Be well, Gordon, but no more fuck ups!"

As Zordic teleported from the barrack straight into his own personal chamber, where Gordon's attackers awaited him, the cowardly, yellow chicken decided to follow the demon to see what fate awaited them.

When Zordic appeared in the middle of the room, the men sprang to attention. They look quite nervous, the demon thought. Good! "What all of you did tonight was unwise. You could have very easily upset that which the prophet and I have worked so hard to create. You punished one of your own without my permission, and then you deliberately paraded him in front of the congregants. For this, I should steel-table you all…but I won't. You have a higher purpose this night, one that shall make up for the embarrassment you've put us through."

The men were visibly shaking but remained where they stood. Zordic let a toothy smile cover his visage as he said to them with a beckoning hand, "Come forth, all of you! You are needed for a summoning, so please do stand around that black circle on the floor there and, for your own good, don't disturb the circle or things could get….messy."

As the men surrounded the black circle, Zordic came up behind each man and cut him with his claws. When one man nearly panicked, the demon cried out, "Stand your ground and don't move! Your blood is needed for this summoning to work properly!" One by one, Zordic slashed each man's arm and felt a bit of satisfaction as he hurt them. Blood pooled by each man, and the black circle seemed to draw all the red, sticky fluid to it. The men exchanged wary looks with each other but not a word was spoken.

Zordic smiled as he clapped his hands together. "Good! Very good, my children. Now I shall begin the summoning. Don't be alarmed at what shows up in the middle of the black circle, for it's here to help us!"

Loudly and fiercely, Zordic began to chant in a mix of Latin and his demonic tongue. Before long, the men noticed a black form starting to appear. The creature was black, but it seemed way darker than that, and it didn't take on any kind of human shape.

Despite being frightened by the creature, the men all stayed in place as the master had instructed them. One of the men, though, broke the silence. "What is that thing, Master? It looks a lot like a tattered piece of cloth."

"That, my child, is known as a wraith, and it's here to assist me in finding the shifter that had no name or image either until tonight. Gordon brought me both from last night's hunt. Oh, you all seem surprised. The coward did what many of you couldn't do!"

"Sir, are you…uh…sure he has found the right one after all this time?" Jeff asked with a shaky voice.

"He brought back its blood, and I confirmed it to be the one I want! Now do you wish to question my judgment anymore, Jeff?"

"N…no, Master," Jeff replied as he hung his head to avoid Zordic's piercing gaze.

The demon smiled as he picked up a small crystal and held it in his palm. He cut his hand and dripped his blood on the crystal. Holding out his other clawed hand, Zordic chanted. The wraith reacted violently by thrashing about in the black circle, but it was trapped there. When Zordic stopped his chant, he put his clawed hand over the crystal, and a bright red glow flashed. The demon hovered in the air so he could direct the crystal at the wraith. "You know why you are here, wraith. I've just bound you to this crystal for added insurance."

"*Yyyeeessss, Zordicccc, I remember,*" the wraith hissed out. The men cringed with fear as they heard the horrid thing's voice. It continued, "*I'm to be your damn bloodhound, aren't I?*"

"More like a bounty hunter," the demon corrected. "If you fail me, I can and will send you back not to your realm, but to oblivion. You're bound to me until I release you from our deal!"

The wraith sneered, "*I haven't accepted your terms yet, demon! I want more for my services. Being bound to you won't make me do anything at this point, but you know that already, don't you?*"

Zordic produced a couple of his spheres that contained the prized life forces he had been collecting. "These spheres are filled to the brim and should feed you quite nicely." Zordic made a flick of his fingers, and the two spheres were in the black circle with the wraith. It absorbed both the spheres and seemed pleased with the payment.

Zordic waved his hands out at his men and said, "These are the men who are willing to help you in your search for the shape-shifter known as Yonuh. Their blood is bound to the circle which makes them yours to command as you see fit."

All the men dropped dead on the floor!

As his life force drained from him, each man's ghost became trapped in the black circle with the wraith. The spectral being touched each ghost, and it was converted violently into a shadow person and under the wraith's control.

When the wraith was finished, it said in a cold, unearthly voice, *"Payment accepted, now release me!"*

Zordic flew down by the black circle and broke it with his foot. Immediately, the wraith shot up into the air. The demon pulled a piece of the blood-stained shirt from his pocket and held it out to the wraith. "This is the blood of the one I wish for you to find. He's to be captured and brought to me — alive, of course! His name is Yonuh, and he's a shape-shifter who has surrounded himself with three others: a witch, a necromancer, and a gremlin. All of whom, you may kill."

The wraith touched the blood-soaked cloth but didn't take it. *"With this blood, I have tasted; this Yonuh will have nowhere to hide from me!"*

A cold sweat broke out all over Gordon's body as he spied through a grimy window in the back of the room. What he witnessed shook him to his core. In that moment, despite his cowardice nature, he knew that he had to act.

Chapter Ten

Yonuh walked along a narrow aisle that separated the beds, wondering how to begin or where he should start. There were ten cots on each side of him, and a lot of moans and groans came from all the beds, except one. Apart from the beds, the cabin was bare—no decorations to brighten up the room, no furniture to sit down on, or do any kind of work from. Even the floor was made of packed down dirt, and there were no windows to let in the sunshine. The cabin was literally a tomb; there was no recovery after exposure to the plague.

Yonuh felt bad for these creatures and desperately wanted to make things right. They were innocent victims of a battle they weren't apart of in the first place. The healer sat on the floor and set the elven potion down in front of him.

He took a drink from the water canteen and moaned with pleasure. The liquid was so pure and refreshing that he wondered if it was enchanted somehow. Yonuh replaced the cap on the canteen and decided he would first prep the potion. He took the cork stopper out of the vial, and a wispy vapor escaped out. Yonuh pulled out Nightshade's black dagger and made a small slice at the top of his left index finger.

Blood dripped into the vial as he squeezed his finger. "One drop per victim," he reminded himself. As the last drop entered the vial, he pulled his hand back and made a fist. He chanted. Yonuh's hand glowed white for a moment and then went dark. He opened his fist and saw the cut had healed completely.

Slipping the black dagger back into its sheath on his belt loop, he stuffed the cork stopper back in the vial.

He shook the vial and noticed the potion seemed to accept his blood. It shined brighter than before, like it was alive. He concentrated on the potion and chanted, directing the energy in his blood to work in tandem with the potion.

After a few minutes of chanting, Yonuh took a deep breath and exhaled, so he could center his own energy. He stood up; it was time to right this wrong.

Yonuh walked over to the first two beds which had female elves in them. Wincing and grimacing, their pale faces bespoke of their pain. Yonuh pulled the cork stopper from the vial and gently poured a sip of the potion into their opened mouths. The female elves reacted immediately as they both let out a sigh of relief and seemed to be at peace for the moment. He felt encouraged by this reaction, so he wasted no time in going in between the beds, from one side of the room to the other.

The reaction from everyone was the same: relief!

As Yonuh got to the last two beds, he saw one was a male elf who was thrashing his head back and forth on his straw pillow. He looked as if he wanted to unleash the contents of his stomach. The elf opened his eyes and saw Yonuh. "Who…are you? How did…you enter?"

"I'm Yonuh, and I'm here to help all of you. I—"

"You damn fool! We're…plague ridden. You could…get…infected and spread it…to others!"

"An elf named Sicca let me in here. I can either cure you all or, at least, slow everyone's suffering. It's the least I can do; it's my fault you're all sick."

"Sicca…she lives? Is she…okay? The male elf narrowed his eyes at Yonuh. He sat up, looking as though he wanted to double over from cramps. "Did you…say this is…your fault? I should…kill you for putting…us all through this hell!"

"I don't blame you for wanting that, and you may have that chance later. For now, though, I need you to drink some of this potion."

"Our…potions don't…help!"

"You're Xenon, Sicca's lover, aren't you?"

The elf nodded. "But potions…don't help," he insisted. The exertion of even speaking was too much for him, and he lay back on the cot.

"I've given it to the others, and they seem content and happy for the moment." He waved his hand toward the other elves. "You and the person under the covers, there, are the last to get this special potion. Will you drink it now, Xenon?"

The elf listened for a moment and then rose up on one elbow, looking around. When he saw everyone was quiet, and some even snoring peacefully, he looked back to Yonuh in surprise. "Yes, I'll drink it, but…how did you know my name?"

The healer sat down and helped Xenon take a sip of the potion. When the elf was finished, Yonuh guided him down onto his back. Xenon's eyes rolled back in his head as he sighed in relief. "This is and yet isn't our potion. How is this possible?"

Yonuh patted the elf on his shoulder and said in a soothing voice, "Just relax and don't worry about that. Rest now, for I'm about to begin healing all of you."

Xenon didn't need any more coaxing. He stretched out and rolled on to his side, snoring loudly.

Yonuh turned to check out the last victim who was completely covered with a blanket, as if cold. Pulling the blanket away to see better, he heard a pop.

Plague spores!

Panicking, Yonuh desperately hit at the spores, trying to wipe them off his body. Terrorized by what had just happened, he whirled around and around, slapping at his clothes. But the spores didn't budge!

Suddenly, he felt the spores begin to penetrate his skin, using him as an incubator.

As fever flushed his body, he stopped hitting and whirling. Realization hit him; all he could do now was die!

Yonuh groaned in pain as he fell down on his side, thrashing uncontrollably. When the movement eased up a little, he looked in his hand and saw the potion was spilling everywhere. "What the hell," he grimaced, and drank a couple of sips of it.

Yonuh was sweating profusely, but the potion seemed to help calm the spasms. His skin felt like it was on fire. He concentrated hard and created a temporary healing bubble around his body. When the worst of the pain and burning subsided, Yonuh resigned himself to tell the others what had happened. If he didn't do it now, he might never get another chance.

Yonuh mentally called out and said calmly, *"Raven, I love you with all my heart and soul. I feel the same about you, Nightshade and, of course, Onyx. Little gremlin, I guess you won't be getting these Doritos back. One of the nymphs burst and covered me with the spores. I didn't realize she was dead, but now it looks like I might be joining her…"*

Yonuh didn't receive any response back, but he could feel psychically that his words did get heard and they all reacted. He felt sorrow mostly and...betrayal? This confused him, but he decided now wasn't the time to be reading into their emotions. The time to purge the plague was at hand, and now he was under the gun to do this as quickly as possible.

Yonuh crawled to the middle of the room and slowly sat up, feeling his stomach juices churning. He went into a deep, meditative state and began scouring his body, examining the spores to see what he could learn.

He quickly learned they gravitated to any part of the body that could carry them, like veins as they moved to get into his heart and lungs. Interesting, he thought, and put up a small energy barrier near his heart chambers to slow them down while he worked.

It looked like a bad traffic jam of spores as they clustered against the energy barrier. Then another thought occurred to him. If the spores loved the heat so much, then maybe he could trick them into leaving the body — make them think there was a new route to spread about on. Outside the body, without heat, they could exist for only a very short time. Once they infested a body, though, they could sustain its core temperature by feeding on the brain, especially the hypothalamus. There, the spores could thrive.

Yonuh studied the dead nymph and saw his theory had credence because her brain was infused with the spores. Now that the body had burst its load, the spores in the brain were dying from a lack of heat. They had no way to contain what heat was left in the nymph.

Yonuh placed a strong energy barrier around his brain and grounded it to his crown chakra so he didn't have to concentrate on it. He heard a voice to his left and saw Xenon looking directly at him.

"Did you say something, Xenon?" Yonuh asked.

"Yes," the elf said with pity in his eyes. "I'm sorry you're now a victim of this plague. No one should ever experience this kind of pain and suffering. I lament that I won't see my precious Sicca again and..."

"Don't give up on me now, Xenon. All hope is not lost, not as long as I'm breathing!"

"Face it, Yonuh. You're a dead man who doesn't know he's dead."

"Then this dead man is going to work until he's finally called back to the sky vault. One of the elders I knew long ago had a saying: *In a world of darkness, where evil lays waste, a beacon of light arises!*"

"What does that mean?" Xenon asked curiously.

"When life is at its worst and everything is against you, no matter what the odds, there is always hope! Hope that things will get better.

No darkness or hate can bring you down because hope has made you a beacon of light to burn away the darkness. Now let me be a beacon for you and your friends here, Xenon!"

The elf gave Yonuh a soft smile as he lay his head down on his pillow. Yonuh thought about what he had just said. It was time to become a beacon of light and draw out all the spores to him, like the proverbially moths to a flame.

He turned his body so he faced the way he entered the structure. Holding his hands high in the air, he began chanting loud and violently, demanding that the energy he created become as pissed as he was right then. Suddenly, an energy pocket formed over his head. It pulsed and throbbed with a frightening power. As he rotated his arms in the air, the energy pocket grew larger. Once Yonuh felt it was large enough, he split it into two energy pockets and maneuvered them over the beds.

Concentrating on the row of beds to his right, he gently let the energy pocket hover inside each victim. He moved his left hand and lowered the other half of the energy pocket over the other victims. Xenon and several others squirmed, but they didn't say or do anything else.

Now with the energy pockets in position, Yonuh focused on making them as hot as he could. He thought of the sun on a sweltering day and then decided that wasn't hot enough, so he threw his own core temperature into the mix. Believing the energy pockets were nearly two hundred degrees, he held them in place as he chanted harder, adding swirls of energy inside them to entice the spores.

He kept his eyes shut as he chanted, preferring to use his third eye to look at his surroundings. He was pleased to see that the spores were reacting as he hoped they would. Since the energy pockets were touching the insides of the victims' bodies, it didn't hurt them as much when the spores jumped into the swirling mass above them.

Yonuh's body was reacting as well. The spores inside him were demanding to go into the energy pockets. Only, none of the swirling mass touched him, and the spores caused him considerable pain as they jumped.

Yonuh wanted to make sure he got all the spores out of the bodies, so he made the energy pockets even hotter. More spores came out in spurts, so Yonuh felt it would be best to now dip the energy pockets into the victims and gather all the spores like he was out fishing in a river with a net.

He let the swirling pockets lay on the victims who responded to the heat by fanning themselves. They didn't seem to be burned by the energy at all. After one last scan of everyone's body, Yonuh lifted the energy pockets high in the air, and then he combined the two together. He twisted and turned his arms until the two pockets formed into one giant sphere. He then made a strong barrier on the outside of it to keep the spores from escaping.

Now that he had captured the spores, Yonuh immediately sucked all the heat out of the sphere and dropped its temperature down to practically freezing inside. The spores reacted violently, trying to break free from the sphere. When Yonuh saw the spores merely bouncing off the energy barrier, he smiled. Each of them finally shriveled up and died. No host, no life, he thought.

To be certain the spores were actually dead, Yonuh heated up the sphere to two hundred degrees again. After a few minutes and no signs of movement, he concluded that the spores were indeed dead. Shrinking the sphere, he moved it off to one corner of the room and out of the way. He struggled to stand up, feeling the spores moving around inside him, causing a lot of cramping.

Yonuh lowered his arms but left his hands splayed and open. He called upon the natural healing energies from not only the Earth but from the moon as well.

Filling the whole room with swirling, healing energy, he started feeding it to all the victims. After a few minutes, elves and nymphs began moving around, feeling a lot better.

Several nymphs sat up, caressing their bodies. "He…he saved us; I can't believe it," one nymph exclaimed. "I feel like running and dancing in the meadows!"

"Amazing…extraordinary! I'm afraid those words don't even begin to describe what you've accomplished," a female elf stated.

"Nesara, please, let Yonuh finish what he's started," Xenon reprimanded.

Nesara laughed as she replied, "How can we repay this man?"

"Nothing could even begin to repay this kind of debt," Xenon declared. "Once infected, no one has ever survived the plague. Now we have an outsider here in our midst that has cured us all…but at a great cost to himself."

Several more elves stirred back into consciousness and sat up feeling well and bewildered. All eyes were on Yonuh as he stood in place, still chanting until he finally collapsed and dropped hard on the floor. Several elves rushed over to aid him, but Yonuh commanded, "Stay back. I'm still infected."

Xenon hurried and picked up the elven potion and poured it into Yonuh's mouth."

The healer felt the cramps subsiding and nodded.

"Now the healer is in need of healing," Xenon said and smiled.

"Water…please?" Yonuh asked as he felt the spores fighting to break through his energy barriers.

Nesara picked up the water canteen and knelt down beside Yonuh. She took the cap off and held it up so he could drink. When he finished, he gently pushed the canteen away and said, "I'm ready to finish this, but I ask that you leave me alone…just in case I should fail."

As the nymphs rushed passed him, one yelled out, "You don't have to ask us twice to leave!" Most of the elves moved towards the area where he had come in, except for Nesara and Xenon who were hovering over him protectively.

Yonuh looked at them both and said with a cringe of pain, "You both should go as well."

"I'm staying here with you whether you like it or not," Xenon proclaimed with a grin.

"Sicca has my friends and intends to kill them if I fail in here," Yonuh explained. "I need you to go and tell her you love her and that I made good on my promise to her."

"And what did you promise Sicca?"

"You will have to ask her yourself because I'm not saying."

Xenon glanced over at Nesara. "Would you be willing to stay and help?"

She nodded. "Go be with my sister and be well!"

Xenon stood up and put his hand on Yonuh, feeling his warm, comforting energy. When he took his hand away, the sensations stopped. He wanted to touch the healer again but didn't. "Be well and heal fast, my friend!" He walked towards the others. When he put his hand on the wall, nothing happened. Confused, Xenon looked around. "Something's wrong."

"It can only be opened from the outside," Yonuh explained. "Sicca said it was for containment purposes. Give me a moment, and I'll see what I can do." The healer mentally called out to Raven. *"Raven my love, no time to explain. Have Sicca open the door. Tell her he's well and waiting for her, please."*

"Okay and....it's good to hear from you, Yonuh!" Raven replied which made his heart swell with love. A few minutes passed, and then the doorway opened. Two nymphs wasted no time in leaving. All the elves walked out in a line with Xenon bringing up the rear.

Sicca's eyes flared brightly when she saw Xenon. As she closed the doorway back, Yonuh could see Raven, Nightshade and Onyx looking in at him. He grimaced as he held his abdomen and waved at them before the doorway closed up once again.

Yonuh sighed heavily and dropped into a meditative state. He put his arms out with his palms open like he was going to catch something and then started making circular motions, building up energy and letting it swirl in his hands.

Nesara watched in awe as he created energy from nothing. He wasn't pulling it from the Earth or any other source. Was there nothing this man couldn't do? She thought.

The energy globes Yonuh created were the size of basketballs and radiated out the purest white light that Nesara had ever seen. She watched in awe as he pushed the energy globes together, creating only one which he held in his hand. Using his other hand, he created an energy vortex inside the globe, similar to what he had done earlier. Once he felt the energy globe was ready, Yonuh slid it part of the way into his body.

He began chanting hard and fast, concentrating on making the energy globe heat up to four hundred degrees. He wanted to make sure it would be an enticing treat for the simpleminded spores. Yonuh's face crinkled in pain while he chanted, but all the spores began pouring out of his body. He felt a rush of relief as the traffic jam of spores finally moved out of his body and into the energy globe.

With better control and concentration, Yonuh let the energy globe stretch and pass slowly through his body to corral any stragglers. As the energy globe passed through his feet, he put out his hand and guided the globe back, weaving an extra protective layer around it. Yonuh grasped it with both his hands and changed the temperature from a sweltering four hundred degrees to a freezing twenty degrees, shutting down the energy vortex as well.

The spores reacted like the other ones had, violently searching for a way out of the globe. They merely bounced off the energy barrier, and one by one, each of the spores fell to the bottom of the globe and didn't move. Yonuh used his third eye and saw there were no energy signatures emanating from any of the spores. Like before, Yonuh heated up the energy globe to two hundred degrees to test them, but the spores didn't react. They were all dead.

Chapter Eleven

After being thanked repeatedly by the elves and nymphs, the healer was allowed to pass through the portal where Raven, Nightshade, and Onyx were waiting.

"Good buddy," Onyx called out excitedly as Yonuh approached them, "you should pimp out your blood more often. You've got to see all the stuff the elves, nymphs and even the faeries gave us as gifts of gratitude."

"Onyx!" Raven scolded.

"Yeah, yeah, I know. But you can't deny it got us a lot of goodies that we can barter with. This kind of stuff will trade well in the supernatural shops."

Nightshade walked up to Yonuh and gave him a hug and a kiss. "It's good to see you're well."

"Thanks," he told her and handed her the black dagger.

Raven took Yonuh by his hand and led him toward the side door of the van and ushered him in. "You need to get off your feet. I can tell you're beyond exhausted. Nightshade's going to drive us home, so get that sexy ass of yours in here so we can cuddle."

She was right, so Yonuh slid down the bench seat. As tired as he was, he wasn't going to argue with her. Raven slid the door closed and walked around the van to speak to Nightshade.

"You need what?!" the necromancer exclaimed.

"I need you to…cut me," Raven repeated.

Nightshade backed up slightly and eyed the witch. "Well now, that's a new twist. My hooker's branching out into the world of sex pain? Myself, I'm not into that sort of thing; I've had enough pain in my life already."

"Forget the sex for now, okay? I have to use my blood to activate this charm, and well...I don't like the idea of drawing my own blood, let alone cutting myself."

Nightshade made an "O" with her lips, and she pulled out her black dagger. "Where do you want it? I will stick you anywhere you like, Raven, especially in my bed!"

Raven rolled her eyes. "You've been around Onyx too long, and he's rubbing off on you, girl! This charm is supposed to help protect against demons. For it to work, though, it needs to be tied to the user." Raven took the charm from around her neck and held it up for the necromancer to see.

Nightshade lowered her dagger and looked at Raven for a long moment. "Where did you get this charm?"

"I got it the day I went on the shopping spree at the mall...the day Onyx got shot."

"Why did you buy this in the first place? At the time, we didn't know we were up against a demon."

"It...called to me," Raven swore. "Well, more like it screamed out for me to take it home. Emma, the shopkeeper, explained to me that it was to protect against demons. I figured since it reacted to me, I should take it and get it prepped for demon activity."

Nightshade thought for a moment. "I don't think I want it bound to you."

"Beg pardon?" Raven blurted out and felt like she had been slapped in the face.

"It may be for protection; it may have strongly called to you, but—"

"But what?" Raven demanded irritably.

"Who do we know that's in the greatest danger from a demon attack?" Nightshade looked past Raven. The witch turned and followed her gaze.

Yonuh!

She looked back at Nightshade. "You think we should bind it to him?"

"Yes, I do. Just because an item wants you to find it, doesn't necessarily mean that it was meant for you. I believe it's meant to be passed on to Yonuh. The charm knew danger was arising. It felt you were the one to put it where it was needed most. I, for one, would feel better knowing it could give Yonuh an edge if Zordic showed up."

Raven stared at the charm she held. What Nightshade said was true. Magic had its own form of psychic consciousness, and it tended to react for reasons most people didn't comprehend. Any item — talismans, amulets, charms or jewelry — that got imbued with magical properties tended to retain a memory of those properties, as if they had been programmed. The magic would seek out those who could best use it. It was like magic could go on its own quest and could do good or evil, depending on its programming.

"I'll ask him about it and see if he wants to use it or not," Raven said as she slipped the charm's cord back around her neck. "I'll ask about adding magical protections to our home too."

Before Raven could leave, Nightshade gave her a hug. "I want you to be safe too, but I believe Yonuh needs more protection. We know how to handle demons on our own, which is why Zordic wants us dead. He feels threatened by us. I love you and Yonuh both, and I'll gladly trade my life to save either of you...and that goes for Onyx too."

Raven returned Nightshade's hug. "I know you would, but I think it would be better just to kick the bad guy's ass. Now, tell me, what's going on between you and Onyx? Why the hell is he obeying you, let alone asking you for permission to do things?"

Nightshade let go of Raven and walked around her. "Let's just say the night we spent together was…enlightening for both of us," she said with a sly grin.

Onyx poked his head over the van and shouted, "You ladies done fondling each other yet? I want to get back home and decorate my room with all these treasures!"

Nightshade stopped by the driver's door, crossed her arms over her chest, and stared down the gremlin. To Raven's astonishment, Onyx began to squirm under the necromancer's gaze. He quickly scampered into the van. Raven went around and climbed into the back with Yonuh, who was trying to nod off but couldn't. Onyx was a non-stop chatterbox as he examined the myriad of gifts.

Nightshade got into the driver's seat and started up the van. Looking in the rearview mirror, she commanded, "Onyx, leave that stuff alone and get up here with me!"

Onyx didn't hesitate. He flew up front and sat down quietly, holding what looked like a small chisel hammer.

Raven's mouth gaped open. "How the hell did you make him do that? Please spill the secret!"

Nightshade turned her head to look at Raven and said with a mischievous grin, "I have my wiles, and that's all I'm going to say about it!"

"Okay then, Onyx, what did she do to you? Did she cast a spell over you? You're obeying like a trained dog. What gives?"

Onyx looked back at Raven and calmly said, "I think you should relax with your bear and enjoy the ride home."

Worry and suspicion filled Raven's mind. "I think the elves must have left a pod in your hut because that's NOT the Onyx who went in there last night! Who are you and what have you done with my Onyx?"

The gremlin smiled as he pointed at Raven and shrieked loudly, which made her shake her head as she pinched the bridge of her nose. "Okay, that's definitely you, Onyx. You got that movie reference, but seriously…what did she do to you?"

"Nothing, we just had an…enlightening chat. That's all I'm saying."

Raven rolled her eyes and decided she would cuddle next to Yonuh. He gave her a weary smile as he put an arm around her. "You're tired," Raven told him. "Lay your head on my lap and stretch out. Rest until we get home, my love."

Yonuh didn't argue and did as he was told. Raven lovingly looked down at him as she ran her fingers through his long, black hair. "I'm going to give you something when we get home," she said softly and thought of the charm. "It will protect you. I—"

The healer snored lightly.

Onyx crept up to Raven and hovered in the air. In his little hands, the gremlin had a small throw blanket which he spread over Yonuh's sleeping body.

Raven smiled. "Thanks, that was very thoughtful of you, Onyx."

Onyx replied in a soft whisper, "He needs it more right now. It's one of the many gifts given to him from the elves. It's supposed to help travelers get a restful sleep when they're far from home. I still feel bad that he ended up getting exposed to the plague. We can blame Sicca all we want but, in the end, it was all my fault."

Raven put a hand on his little shoulder. "That's *your* demon, and you'll have to wrestle with it for now. Just understand, though, he would never see it as your fault. It was probably meant to happen because now we know he can destroy the plague. The elves can actually make a cure now, and they can learn a lot from those dead spores." She gazed into Onyx's tired eyes. "Please stop beating up yourself over this. I don't blame you, and I'm sure Nightshade doesn't either."

"On the contrary," Nightshade chimed in as she swerved around debris on the road. "I do blame him for what happened. Only, I've got a different twist to it."

"Well, please explain this so the whole class can understand." The sarcasm in the witch's voice was blatantly evident.

"It's his fault because he didn't tell us his full plan. He didn't trust that you and Yonuh would go for it. Since there was plenty of time to set his plan into action, Onyx could have searched the woods and made sure that any supernatural creatures were made aware of the dangers of his plan. They could have gotten out of the area before he sprang his trap on the P.A.N.E.L. squad."

"I see your point, but—"

"No you don't, actually. Onyx needs to trust us more. He needs to consider the consequences of his actions—ask himself: 'is this going to hurt anyone?' It's a hard lesson, but he has to learn from this. He's got to get better control of his mischief streak, or one day it'll get us all killed. Isn't that correct, Onyx?"

Onyx grimaced and closed his eyes as a single tear ran down his face. "Yes, you're correct, Nightshade, and I'll work harder to…trust all of you." He turned around and slowly flew back to his seat, where he fiddled with his small chisel hammer.

"Nightshade, is this how you're keeping him on a short leash? This is a bit much, even for you. It seems very cruel."

"Life's cruel, but he's the one imposing this torture on his little mind, not me. This isn't how I'm keeping him on a short leash, as you put it. That's an entirely different subject that you're not ready to hear about."

"More like you don't want me to know from the sounds of it. You act like I can't handle what you have to say. But guess what? I'm a big girl, and I can handle whatever it was that you did to Onyx."

Nightshade snorted a laugh. "Don't be so dramatic, Raven. It's not like I've brainwashed him. We just had an—"

"Enlightening chat—I know, I know! What the hell does that mean? Oh, never mind, you're both giving me a migraine!" She let out a frustrated huff and decided to focus on Yonuh. Going back to playing with his hair, she relaxed. Yonuh suddenly shifted and wrapped his big, strong arms around her waist.

It made her happy until she saw Yonuh grimace and grunt slightly, like he was in pain. She thought it was possible that he was having more of those visions of torture, so she gently stroked his forehead. Her hand felt wet from the sweat on Yonuh's brow, and she worried that he could be getting sick.

He jerked several times like he was having spasms. "Yonuh, are you okay? Wake up, my dear." Raven shook him several times, but he didn't respond. "Wake up!" she ordered loudly.

"What's the matter?" Nightshade asked as she looked at her through the rearview mirror.

"I'm not sure," Raven said worriedly. "He's sweating and grunting like he's in pain, and he's having muscle spasms. I can't tell if he's sick or having another vision of torture!"

Nightshade pulled off to the side of the road and parked the van. Onyx flew to the back and studied the healer for a few moments. "He might be so exhausted that his muscles are finally relaxing," he said hopefully.

Raven looked at him and nodded her head, but she still felt like something wasn't right.

The side door opened and Nightshade crawled inside the van and sat on her knees beside Onyx. Putting her hand on Yonuh's chest, Nightshade instantly felt something hot and wet which she assumed to be sweat. She pulled back her hand to wipe it off and glanced down at it as she did.

Blood!

"PULL BACK THE BLANKET, NOW!" Nightshade exclaimed frantically. As Raven yanked it back, everyone gasped. Yonuh's chest and abdomen were covered in fresh cuts.

Onyx shook Yonuh roughly, but he still didn't stir awake. As more cuts appeared on Yonuh's body, Onyx cried out, "Shit! This is like watching a Freddy Kruger movie! Wake up, buddy!"

"He looks like he's been put to sleep with a spell," Raven anxiously pronounced. "Who would do that?"

"Zordic!" Nightshade growled.

Onyx stared at his best friend and shivered as new cuts appeared on the healer. "Here's a better question: how did Zordic sleep-spell him from afar?"

"The only way he could do this is if Zordic has his name and some of Yonuh's DNA, like the missing bloody shirt." Nightshade said with a hint of irritation.

"What can we do for him? We can't just leave him here to be carved up in his sleep!" Onyx said frantically.

"Raven I have a counter spell in mind that may work I will need your help doing it. Onyx, do your best to cover his wounds so he doesn't bleed out or goes into shock from the blood loss."

Chapter Twelve

Yonuh found he was in a peaceful meadow where there were wild flowers of all colors growing. A gentle breeze wafted across the land, making the flowers dance, and his long, dark hair sway in all different directions. A forest of large oaks and pines surrounded the meadow, and the smell of fresh water from a crystal clear creek assailed his nostrils.

Yonuh pulled out a wooden flute, crafted from cedar. It was adorned with a white, a yellow, a red, and a black feather that represented the four cardinal directions for his people. He played the flute and danced around the meadow without a care in the world. Birds chirped in the distance, and Yonuh heard the sound of frogs croaking nearby. The sun was high and bright in the sky, but the day wasn't hot or cold. It was a perfect day in Yonuh's mind, or it would have been with Raven by his side.

Suddenly, the flute changed drastically. The wood became brittle and cracked, and then it crumbled to dust in his hands. He looked up and noticed that every single flower in the meadow was withering and turning black. As everything aged rapidly, he felt like he was watching a time lapse recording. The creek water stopped flowing and became a dark, slimy muck that had a consistency of tar, and all the fish and frogs were stuck and slowly dying.

A blast of icy cold air hit his back, and he turned around. Yonuh cringed as he watched dark, ominous clouds rolling in fast, and a bad feeling from the pit of his stomach warned of things gone terribly wrong. The arctic storm blew through the meadow, taking with it all the now-dead flowers. Trees bent and broke under its gale-force winds. Yonuh hugged himself, trying to stay warm as the temperature plummeted, and now he could see his own breath.

Lightning bolts crackled through the clouds, and thunder boomed loudly and painfully in his ears. He instinctively lay down on the ground to make himself less of a target for the lightning. On his back, he felt vibrations coming from beneath him, and his first thought was earthquake. He quickly dismissed that cause when he saw the ground morphing all around him. The meadow changed into a dirty concrete floor, and Yonuh understood.

"Invading my dreams now, are you, Zordic?"

He had a sickening feeling the drama would be over soon, and the demon would finally come out of hiding. Without warning, he felt something cold and hard rise up under him, lifting his entire body up in the air about three feet. As he struggled to see what was happening, his arms and legs were suddenly pinned to whatever was under him. To his horror, he saw that he was bound by straps—straps all too familiar from his dreams.

Strapped down on Zordic's steel torture table, Yonuh couldn't move!

He heard a commotion coming from somewhere past his feet and saw a shadowy figure move into his line of vision. The healer recognized Zordic from his dreams.

The demon looked down at Yonuh and flashed a toothy grin. "Yonuh, my wayward son, how nice it is to finally see you in the flesh…so to speak!"

Playing ignorant of who Zordic really was, the healer decided to stroke the demon's giant ego. "You seem to know my name, stranger. What's the name of the one who successfully invaded my peaceful slumber?"

The demon arched his brows and seemed pleased. "My dear child, I'm Zordic. I've been waiting a long time to meet you. I've sent many of my own children to fetch you, but sadly only one has managed to return to my flock."

"I must say, they weren't the best at relaying your invitations to me. They seemed more prone to use brute force and guns. I can't imagine a being of your importance condoning such actions. They were human, though, and we both know how they can be a pain to work with."

"Yes indeed, Yonuh. Do you really believe they wished to do you harm instead of coming and telling you I wanted to see you?"

"Well, Zordic, only one of them returned to your flock, so I can only assume they defied your orders. I hate that this has caused us both considerable trouble. If I didn't know better, I would've assumed you wanted me dead instead of having a civil chat."

Zordic eyed Yonuh intently, wondering if he was being honest or trying to patronize him.

"Zordic, are these really necessary?" Shaking his wrists and legs so the shackles rattled, Yonuh continued on. "I know you want me as a captive audience, but I'm not planning on leaving here because you have me curious now."

"I'm afraid your shackles *are* necessary," the demon said with mock sympathy in his voice. "I'm not sure of your intentions towards me. So tell me, what's got you so curious?"

"My apologies, Zordic. I'm curious about what your true intentions are for *me* since those fools only wanted to kill me and, obviously, that wasn't your wish at all."

The demon thought long and hard on what he should say as he walked around the steel table. "My child, I've wanted you since the day you broke free from my jail. I want what you have inside that plump body of yours. I want to drink your blood, Yonuh."

The healer concealed a laugh as he feigned surprise and shock. "You're a….vampire?"

"No, Yonuh, I'm not one of those nasty leeches! I got a taste of your sweet blood and well…"
Zordic jabbed Yonuh in his side with one of his black claws, drawing blood. He lifted his finger to his mouth and licked it greedily. "I can't resist what you have to offer me, my child!"

"Oh, that's a relief to hear. For a moment there, I thought I was going to have to kill you like the last vampire I ran into, not too long ago. Nasty creature! It went by the name of Drexel."

Zordic froze. Two things sprang into his ever-calculating mind: how did Drexel make it back to this plane, and how did Yonuh kill him? Zordic eyed the healer with suspicion.

"He did mention your name to me," Yonuh went on. "He was quite angry that you were willing to help necromancers cast him into the void."

"What else did he say?"

"He wanted payback," Yonuh explained. "He wanted to know where you were. He used a lot of colorful words to describe you. If he could make you last that long, he wanted to drain your energy for weeks…months, even."

"Hmm, and you say that you and your friends killed him? Are you certain Drexel is dead?"

"Dead and decomposing!" Yonuh noticed that the demon physically relaxed, so he concentrated on his own shackles.

He knew the restraints nullified magic and his shifting abilities, so Yonuh decided to manipulate the energy that was imbued in the shackles and bend it to his will. It was energy, after all, and Yonuh could work it easily enough.

"I can see you're not lying," Zordic said and smiled. "And thanks for taking care of that old pain-in-the-ass for me, but now I must enjoy what you have to offer me. No hard feelings, Yonuh. I must admit that my men were not out to kill you, but the company you keep was on my hit list."

"Why would a...demon be so adverse to the company I keep? Have they wronged you?"

Zordic slashed his claws across Yonuh's chest several times, making him grunt in pain. The demon leaned in and began licking the blood that poured from his wounds. "I won't have you cowering behind those creatures. I'll kill them all if I have to, Yonuh, just to possess you. You will be mine!"

"But there's nothing special about me, and I would rather you didn't hurt my friends!" Yonuh grunted more as Zordic cut him along his abdomen.

"Oh, but you are far more special than you let on, my child! If you'll come willingly to me and become my blood slave, I swear I'll spare your friends," Zordic said through heavily lidded eyes as Yonuh's blood coursed throughout his body, making his male member hard.

"Take the word of a demon, huh?" Yonuh said and chuckled. "I go to you, and you spare my friends? I doubt it since I know you'll send your cronies after them no matter what I do. Don't take this the wrong way, but I don't make it a habit of trusting demons."

Intoxicated and euphoric from the drinking, Zordic's body was as obsessed to Yonuh's blood as a heroin addict was to opioids. And now his body urged him to drink and fuck Yonuh like there was no tomorrow. Unbuttoning his pants, Zordic struggled to pull them down to his knees.

Yonuh used the demon's distraction to release himself from his shackles and gave Zordic a hard knee to his balls. The demon groaned in pain as Yonuh slid from under him and got on top of Zordic's back. He slammed the shackles around Zordic's ankles while he was too busy holding his pain-riddled member.

"Seeing that you're enjoying yourself right now, I'll leave you a little alone time." Yonuh smiled as he gave Zordic several smacks on his bare ass, channeling his inner Onyx.

"Impossible! No one has ever escaped my table!" Zordic snarled over his shoulder, his black eyes blazing with fury.

"This is a dream, remember? So chances are that your perfect streak is still alive and well! Don't cut yourself on your table, Zordic. That would be painful, and you might end up cutting your dick off before you come!"

Zordic looked down and saw he was involuntarily thrusting and rutting on the steel table so hard that he had pierced a hole in it and was bleeding everywhere. He had an "Oh shit!" expression on his face and then pleaded to the healer, "Yonuh, my child, please! Untie my feet and I will ensure—OUCH! ARRGHH! I will stop trying to kill your friends!"

Yonuh looked at him curiously. "Like I said before, this is just a dream. Remember, you're the one who invaded my dream state so just wake yourself up and leave."

Yonuh heard voices from far away. Someone was calling to him, and they seemed to get closer with each passing moment. Suddenly, he awoke to find Raven and Nightshade chanting over him. Onyx's little hands dabbed towels on his abdomen to stop the bleeding.

None of them had noticed he had woken, so he put his hands on both Raven and Nightshade. They looked down at him. "Yonuh, are you okay?" Nightshade asked, worry still in her voice.

"Speak to me, sweetheart!" Raven exclaimed with a sigh of relief that he was back.

"Look who's back from the dead!" Onyx called out, looking just as relieved as the women. "What happened? You looked like you were having a bad dream on steroids!"

"I'm doing okay," Yonuh answered with a grin. "Zordic's going to be having a bad day though."

"So I was right," Nightshade said. "It was that damn demon doing this to you. Raven has a charm with her that could possibly protect you from a demon attack, but it needs a little of your blood to tie it to you. Would you like to try it?"

"Yeah, if it's okay with her—"

Something very cold touched his abdomen, and he gasped. Raven slipped a cord over his neck, and he figured it held the charm. He noticed the amulet got warmer as it continued to touch his bare skin.

"Thanks, Raven, I'm sure this will help keep him out of my head…I hope."

"This is all lovely and heart-warming, Yonuh, but could you start healing your ass because I'm getting tired of playing your wet nurse."

Yonuh closed his eyes and let out a faint chant, sending healing energy to all the areas of his body that hurt. He felt his skin pulling and mending together, and soon all the pain was gone.

Suddenly, Yonuh burst out laughing uncontrollably, leaving everyone baffled. Tears streamed down his face. As he calmed down, Onyx grinned and asked, "All right, Teddy Ruxpin, what's so funny? Do share with the rest of the class."

"The name Onyx loves to call Zordic is so appropriate right now—sore dick!" The healer wiped his eyes. "I was thinking about poor Zordic and the way I left him in my dream state. He was face down on his steel table with his pants around his knees, fucking a hole in the table, literally slicing his dick up with each stroke! He's going to have a sore dick, that's for sure!"

Chapter Thirteen

Raven felt as if her arms were burning and would fall off at any minute. She and Nightshade had gotten permission from Yonuh to place their magical protections and different wards on the old Costco building. The healer had tried to remind them that Costco was as much their home as it was his, but the women still wanted his permission.

Raven didn't like the idea of doing something to another person's house, especially casting magic, without getting their permission first. It seemed like the polite thing to do, and since Yonuh gave her permission, her protections and wards would hold better. After an hour of sprinkling holy water and placing multiple incense sticks around in the huge building, Raven began to regret taking on the enormous task.

Onyx had crafted an incense holder that would snuggly hold ten sticks at one time. In a weird way, it reminded Raven of a menorah used at Hanukkah. The gremlin had used an old wooden handle from a plunger, fastened and balanced a PVC pipe to the end and added tiny holes for the incense sticks. It made it much easier and quicker for Raven to get the smoke to cover the vast amount of space in the massive warehouse.

After Nightshade made a few slashing X motions over each wall and other places like water drains and vents that a demon's evil could easily get through, she declared she was done. Raven was annoyed at how little work the necromancer had actually done. Even though Nightshade was in the center of the old warehouse meditating and chanting her protection spells and wards to activate them, Raven felt her way was the better way because once she finished, she was done.

Onyx got the heavy-duty scissor ladder lift working so Raven could put her wards and protections on the ceiling. Raven figured he was enjoying the fact that he could contribute to the work. Plus, he got the added bonus of a new toy to play with.

Raven still couldn't help but wonder why he was being so nice and cooperative. She had asked him about it while he drove the scissor ladder lift for her, but all he did was give her the same old line Nightshade had been giving. The whole "enlightening chat" was beginning to chaff her ass. Although, she did wonder if Onyx was actually under Nightshade's spell.

If he was, Raven thought, it would serve him right for all the crap he had put both her and Nightshade through this past month. On the other hand, she mused, if he was and the spell finally broke, Onyx would be severely pissed, and the necromancer wouldn't have anywhere to hide. He would probably torment her to death. Magic always has a price, and lately it tended to be a deadly debt collector.

"Coming up on the last part of the ceiling," Onyx called out as he looked over his shoulder. "Do you want to do the roof as well?"

"No, it would be pointless," Raven answered. "Any incense smoke would be hit or miss outside." She glanced at the gremlin wondering again just what Nightshade had done to him. She decided she wouldn't press the issue. "Thanks for doing this, Onyx. You've been a great help today."

Raven caught a hint of a blush on Onyx's dark skin as he turned and looked ahead. She thought it was cute how he tried to act all big and tough, but the simplest compliments or praises always made his face redden.

"Ah, I didn't have anything better to do." He patted the scissor ladder. "Now that I have this little beauty up and running, I can work on the solar panels and get them operating more efficiently."

With one final swipe with her homemade incense holder, Raven was finally done. "Fuck yeah! All done and now it's time to unwind, little buddy!" She collapsed on the lift and just sat there rubbing her sore arms.

Onyx flipped the switch, and the scissor lift slowly descended. He turned around and looked at Raven. "How do you plan on unwinding?" he asked with a snicker. "I'm sure Yonuh could assist you with that and so much more!"

"That would be nice, but I'm more in the mood to treat myself with something special. Although, I'm not sure with what."

"You could go down to the river and go swimming or sunbathe. I think I saw a small hole in the clouds that might let you get, maybe, five minutes of sun."

"I just worked my ass off putting my protections and wards on a fucking, huge-ass warehouse! Do you really think I want to swim?" She rubbed her sore arms.

Onyx shrugged. "Like I would know what a cranky, old witch would want to do? I, for one, would like a peaceful day where we aren't fighting with each other or some other jackass who wants to kill us all. Is that really too much to ask for?"

Raven couldn't argue with that; she was in total agreement with him. It would be nice to have some much needed downtime and recharge the old batteries. She thought about climbing up the wall ladder that led to the roof and simply stretch out up there amongst Yonuh's garden of fruits and vegetables. She remembered that the garden was in a greenhouse, and she groaned, "Too hot!" She considered what else was on the roof, and she moaned, "Solar panels are up there — too hot." She wouldn't be able to meditate or relax.

Once they reached the floor and came to a stop, Raven stepped off the scissor ladder. Onyx hovered by her. "So what's your grand plan of relaxation, carrot top, or are those little gears in your head stuck?"

"Does turning you into a toad with a fly for a dick work for you? I could watch you snap your tongue out, trying to eat that little fly, all day long if I had to."

Onyx gave her a mean scowl as he covered his member with his hands. "Ha! Very funny but that still falls under fighting which isn't part of the whole relax-my-ass plan, you know!"

"True, but if you bug me today, my threat still stands. I'm fresh out of patience!"

"Just remember, if you did that to me, I know where you sleep. One morning you'll wake up baldheaded, and all those lovely locks of red hair will be super glued to that heart-shaped ass of yours!"

Raven rubbed her face in frustration. "I guess there's no such thing as a day of peace around here, is there? We can't go a whole two minutes without threatening each other, can we?"

"It's all done out of love, Raven," Onyx declared. "Haven't you figured that out yet?"

"Excuse me?" Raven said with a confused look on her face.

"We love each other so much that we can only express it through fighting and arguing. You're like a big, bratty sister that I never had," Onyx insisted with not only a smirk, but pride too.

Raven raised her eyebrow speculatively so Onyx added, "Have I actually done anything to you, other than threats?"

"I seem to recall you knocking me on my ass when we first got here, causing me to expose myself in front of Yonuh. I also remember the ass slaps."

"Ah, come off it, will you? That's the key right there, isn't it? We first met. We were testing each other; all of us were doing it.
Well, maybe not all of us. I'm sure Yonuh was being his normal clueless self in the beginning because that's who he is. But since then, you and me bicker and bitch at each other, but has either of us done anything to the other? No! We have a friendly banter back and forth with deadly intent, but who doesn't do that?"

"Sometimes I worry that one day we may go farther, and it won't be banter anymore. I don't want to see that happen….because, deep down, I do care about you. I don't want to see you get hurt, especially by me."

Onyx floated down and landed on the floor. He looked up at Raven and asked, "What makes you think you could ever hurt me?"

The witch dropped down to her knees, so she could look him in the eyes. "Because I have a bad temper, at times that has gotten me into trouble in the past. I do my best to keep it in check, but there're times when you push my buttons, and it takes all I've got to keep from either killing you or sending a magical surge through your body that would do permanent damage."

Onyx cocked his head to the side. "I see, and I take it you've done this before and now fear for my safety?"

Raven looked away in shame as she slowly nodded.

Onyx tightly hugged her, surprising her, and whispered in her ear, "You shouldn't beat yourself up over what happened in the past because that's where it is—in the past! You control what happens in the here and now. I'm not afraid of your anger because I know you care about me. That's why I push your buttons, to give your anger the outlet that it needs. That's also why I back off when your bitch-kitty is in *pissed mode*. I might be crazy, but I'm not a dumbass."

Raven laughed as she hugged Onyx back. "You're not a dumbass, just an ass! But you're my friend, and I never want to lose you. I was scared you would die that day you got shot, but now I know I couldn't bear to see you die."

Onyx didn't let go, so Raven continued to hold him. It seemed odd to her that he was acting this way, but she wasn't going to complain.

The gremlin finally disengaged and backed away from her. She grabbed him and pulled him back to her again. Kissing the gremlin lightly on the forehead, she said, "Sorry, but I couldn't let that go without a proper *thank you*."

Onyx lightly rubbed his forehead as he turned his back to her, which made her giggle. She knew he was blushing and too embarrassed to let her see. "Well duh! It's hard to resist my charms, but I'm not one of your romance novels' leading men." He turned back to her. "I do, however, possess a few skills that only those fictional hunks wish they had."

Raven looked at Onyx for a moment as if he had just slapped her. Suddenly, she beamed a big smile and said, "That's it, Onyx! Now I know what I can go do for a peaceful day. You're a genius!"

"Of course I am. Now what the hell are you babbling on about?"

"Books, of course—not those sappy romance books, either. I want to go shopping for them, and what better place is there than *Powell's City of Books* downtown?"

"Hmm, it might be a good idea to not only grab some of Yonuh's meats but also some of the gifts the elves gave us. As unique and beautiful as elven craftsmanship is, you won't have any trouble getting what you want."

"Good idea. I'd hate to go all the way out there and they say no to my offer. I think I'd be breaking some heads if I couldn't take home all the books I wanted because they don't eat meat," Raven said as she turned and walked towards her room.

"If it's all the same to you, I'd like to come along."

Raven froze as thoughts of the last time they went shopping flooded her mind. That was when Onyx had gotten shot.

She wasn't sure if she could handle more guilt if something happened to him under her watch. She had an uneasy feeling in the pit of her stomach, like this wouldn't turn out so well.

Turning around slowly, she saw Onyx hovering in the air just out of her reach with his arms folded across his chest.

She was about to protest, but the gremlin spoke up first. "I know you have some reservations about taking another road trip with me, but you need to get over it. We weren't very smart last time, and we underestimated the P.A.N.E.L. squad. If we stick together, we'll be fine. It's safer to go together. Remember, Nightshade went off alone and look what happened to her. You need backup, and I'm the one for the job!"

"I guess there's no talking you out of this, is there?"

He shook his head. "You could give me all the Doritos in the world as a bribe, and I would flat out refuse to take them! That's how serious I am right now. I'm going to grab a few of the elven gifts and meet your heart-shaped ass in the van, so you get a move on, girl!"

Stunned, Raven watched as Onyx darted off. She hadn't expected this kind of response from him. She mentally shook herself and walked towards the reach-in freezers. Since Onyx was grabbing the elven trinkets, Raven figured she better grab a few handfuls of assorted meats. She snatched up an old box that was nearby and then began gathering the meats. She felt that if she brought a variety, it would increase her chances of walking out of the bookstore with several piles of books, maybe more if she was lucky.

Times were tough and good quality meats were a premium item to barter with, especially since most of the generation that survived the plague didn't have a clue where meats came from.

Raven closed the reach-in freezer door and carried the box full of meats on the side of her hip.
As she made her way through the warehouse, she came across Nightshade who was still sitting and chanting. Calling out to the necromancer, she explained, "Onyx and I are heading to Powell's bookstore. If anything happens, just give us a mental call."

Nightshade gave Raven the thumbs up but never stopped chanting or even looked up. Raven sat the box on the long countertop and wandered over to Yonuh's room to check on him. She peered into his dark bedroom and saw he was sleeping peacefully. She smiled and resisted the urge to crawl into bed with him. Silently, she closed his door. She turned around and saw Onyx by the red garage door, patiently waiting and mocking her by giving her the naughty hand gesture.

"Oh, knock it off!" Raven growled as she picked up the meat box. "I wanted to make sure he was okay before we left, that's all."

"Yeah, I can smell it all the way over here, you horny witch!" Onyx snickered.

Raven ignored him as she walked past him and into the garage. The gremlin held the red door open for her. Onyx left the side door open so it was easy for her to put the meat box in the van.

On the seat, she noticed a small linen bag and a red satchel with Onyx's name on it. Closing the door, she said, "Thanks for holding the door open. That was very nice of you to do that."

Onyx shrugged his little shoulders as he got into the passenger side. "Sometimes you got to help the helpless and guess what? You're over-qualified in that department!"

"You know you could always fly out there yourself; I don't have to drive your boney, lizard ass around!"

"True, but I like the a/c in the van and having a chauffeur is kind of nice too!" As Onyx pressed the remote button to open the garage bay door, he pointed ahead and said, "Forward, Ms. Jeeves!"

Raven rolled her eyes as she started the van and pulled out of the garage, wondering if Onyx was going to survive the trip because the urge to strangle him was growing exponentially.

Chapter Fourteen

Nightshade fell into silence as she took the time to catch her breath. Pulling out a piece of chocolate, she nibbled on it to help give her an energy boost. She downed a bottle of water, quenching her parched mouth and looked around at the warehouse. Her protections and wards were strong and holding up nicely. She could see that Raven's work complimented her spellwork nicely.

Nightshade stood up, still feeling lightheaded from her magic work. She walked over to the nearest wall while opening up another bottle of water. As she gulped down half the bottle's contents, she got to the wall and placed her hand on it. She felt the wall vibrating with an energy that should keep out most supernatural beings. Humans, on the other hand, would either feel uncomfortable or nothing at all. Nightshade wished that she would have thought about it and included a ward that would instill terror into humans. At the moment, though, she was spent and wanted to lie down.

Halfway to her bedroom, Nightshade stopped at Yonuh's door. She bit her bottom lip as she reached for the knob and gently opened his door. Nightshade looked over both her shoulders like she was a thief on the prowl before slipping silently into the healer's room. It was dark inside, but she could see well with her excellent night vision. She stopped for a moment, admiring Yonuh's body. He was barely covered by his sheet, and it gave her a wonderful view of his ass and a glimpse of his manhood as well when he sleepily rolled over.

Nightshade let out a moan of satisfaction as her silver eyes glowed. She decided it was her time to play with Yonuh, now that they were all alone. I want to lick every inch of his big sexy body, the necromancer thought as she wet her lips with her tongue.

Raven might very well get pissed, but Nightshade didn't care at this point. Hell, Raven would be a hypocrite if she got mad, she thought, because the witch had no problem having sex with her. That sealed it in Nightshade's mind as she sat down on the edge of Yonuh's bed.

She quietly pulled off her boots and climbed in bed as stealthily as she could, curling up behind Yonuh. Mere inches away from his bare skin, Nightshade could feel his body heat, and it made her want to get closer to him. She held her breath and tentatively reached her hand out to touch him, but she paused. She was now wondering if she was making a terrible mistake in coming in here, assuming Yonuh would allow her to touch him. As she started to pull her hand away, Yonuh grunted and grabbed hold of her hand, pulling her to him.

As her body pressed against his, Nightshade felt his warm, comforting energy fill every inch of her body. And he was still asleep! She smiled as she thought this was a lovely thing to have happen to her because he seemed to want to cuddle with her even in his sleep.

She had never experienced this sort of thing in all her life. Certainly none of the women she had been with ever made her feel like this. His one simple gesture made her heart swell with love. Suddenly, a thought occurred to her that Yonuh might think she was Raven climbing into his bed. Jealousy poured into her mind towards Raven, but she also felt envious of the woman. She wondered if this was how Yonuh greeted Raven, by pulling her into his bed.

Nightshade nuzzled her pale face into the healer's neck and softly kissed him, licking him too. She felt she might as well let him know who he had in his bed. Yonuh groaned, making Nightshade's stomach fill with butterflies. She let go of him, and he rolled over, facing her.

"Yonuh, it's me Nightshade. I didn't want you to think I was someone else."

"Belladonna? What brings you in here?" he asked in a panicked voice. "Is there a problem or — "

Nightshade put a finger on his lips to silence him. "Everything's all right. We finished putting the protections and wards up, and now we're taking time to enjoy ourselves. Raven and Onyx left to go to that big bookstore downtown. I guess she wants a few books to read other than craft books."

"And how did you plan on relaxing, Belladonna?" Yonuh asked with a smile.

"I'm worn out from all the magic work. I was heading to my room but, for some reason, when I got to your door, I found I couldn't go any farther. If you don't want me in here, I'll go. I know I wasn't supposed to do this, but..." Nightshade paused as she gazed over Yonuh's body, "I couldn't resist."

Yonuh blushed. "You can stay in here with me. I never mind the company of a beautiful lady. May I ask, was your plan to rest in here with me, or did you have other plans in mind?"

It was Nightshade's turn to blush, and she was thankful that it was still dark in Yonuh's room. She replied, but it came out more like babbling, "A bit of both, actually. I haven't had any good alone time with you. I've been wanting some—alone time, I mean. Ever since you saved and healed me from what Drexel...did to me." She shuddered, remembering. "I want to show you how much I appreciate all that you've done for me—all of us, actually, but mostly for me."

"You don't have to do this if you don't want to, Belladonna. I've not done all those things for you just to get you into bed with me. I've done it all because I care about all you. I care a lot about you, Belladonna, so I want you to be certain this is what *you* want."

Nightshade thought about it for a while but got snapped out of her musings as Yonuh turned on his lamp by his bed. Damn, he looked so much better in the soft light, and she got a good view of his ass before he rolled over onto his side to look at her with his gorgeous, dark brown eyes.

She finally spoke. "I do want this—I mean, I want you, Yonuh!" She felt her cheeks heat up, and he smiled as he noticed them reddening. "I've never had a man in my life. Drexel showed me the cruelty and violent nature of sex, but you took the time to heal and care for me when you really didn't have to. I believe that you're the one man who could show me the tender and wonderful side of lovemaking that Raven gets to experience—lucky witch! I want you, Yonuh, to officially be the first man to make love to me. You have done more for me than you could possibly know, and I want to experience you on so many levels. I...I...love you, Yonuh."

"I love you too, Belladonna. I would be honored to be your first, but I hope I can live up to the expectations you have of me," Yonuh told her as he sat up on his knees and pulled Nightshade up to him. He softly kissed her lips. She groaned as his energy filled her body, and her core immediately responded.

As they kissed, Yonuh ran his hands down Nightshade's body until he found the hem of her shirt. He gently tugged it up.

The necromancer stretched her arms up in the air and allowed Yonuh to pull her shirt off, as well as her cloak, which he dropped behind her. She leaned back to show off her round, plump breasts to him and swayed her body.

Yonuh's eyes glowed as he bent forward and kissed her neck. He slowly worked his way down to her chest. Putting one arm around Nightshade's back, he cupped his other hand on the back of her neck. He put his wet lips around her nipple, sucking and nibbling on it.

Nightshade's eyes flared with passion as they rolled back in her head. She dug her nails into Yonuh's back as he went back and forth from each of her breasts, making her nipples swollen and sensitive. He slowly lowered Nightshade onto her back, and then he kissed his way down past her breasts to her soft abdomen, sucking skin gently with his lips. She ran her fingers through his long, thick hair as he worked the button free on her black pants. Looking down, she saw his eyes flicker with a gold tint as he gazed back at her, making her squirm as if he was going to devour her.

He slowly pulled her black pants off and let them drop to the floor. He slipped his finger around her white panties—the ones with little rainbow patterns. Nightshade blushed. "I've lost several nice thongs since I've been here, so a girl can't be too choosy these days. I…I wasn't expecting this today."

Yonuh smiled as he bit into her panties and pulled them down, using his fingers to guide them. She felt her whole body heat up with some sort of primal energy from Yonuh. He let her panties drop by her pants. Draping Nightshade's legs onto his shoulders, he slowly licked her wet core and suckled on her clit.

Nightshade was used to receiving oral pleasures from women, but the enjoyment she received now from Yonuh was way different and more intense. The energy he gave off increased with each swipe of his tongue. Her body sizzled with desire and need as she unconsciously rocked her hips in sync with his rhythmic swipes.

He opened her wet core and then slid a couple of his energy-charged fingers inside her. As he fingered her, he took her clit between his lips and suckled it, running his tongue over it repeatedly. Nightshade came with an intensity she had never known before. As she screamed out in ecstasy, her eyes blazed brightly with passion overload.

"Mm, I think you're about ready to receive me. Do you want me inside you, my sweet Belladonna?"

Nightshade gasped, "Y...yes, please! Take me now. I can't...wait. I need you!"

Yonuh grinned as he spread Nightshade's legs wide open and rose up onto his knees. He positioned his member at the opening of her dripping core. Slowly, he rubbed the tip up and down her folds, making her squirm as his tingling energy made her even more sensitive.

Nightshade whimpered as she begged, "Yonuh...please! Please! Oh, mm, FUCK!"

Yonuh gently pushed his way up Nightshade's tight sheath so she would enjoy the feel of him and let her core have time to adjust. He slowly pulled out and slid back inside her again and again until he felt her core completely open up to him, and then he thrust harder and faster.

Nightshade felt lightheaded as she had trouble catching her breath. She wrapped her legs around his waist, urging him on to fuck her harder and faster. He grabbed her hands and, with a wicked grin, he began yanking her forward in rhythm with his thrusts. Another wave of ecstasy pulsated throughout her body, making her thrash her head from side to side. She screamed in ecstasy long and loud as she came even harder than before.

He pinned her legs together while he was still inside her, which made her core feel tighter. Yonuh pounded her harder and faster. He got even bigger inside her, and he seemed to be pulsing too.

She looked at him through heavy lidded eyes and saw he was sweating fiercely. His eyes were glowing gold with hints of brown.

"I...I'm coming, Belladonna!" Yonuh exclaimed as he panted.

"Mm, give it to me, Yonuh! I want to feel it. Come for me, you big, beautiful man!"

He didn't need much coaxing as the pressure and energy built up rapidly in his member. He let out a guttural roar of primal ecstasy as his semen burst forth in long, pulsating streams that overfilled Nightshade's core.

Yonuh rolled over and onto his back, dragging Nightshade on top of him to rest on his body. They both were out of breath, panting hard and smiling at each other.

"I never thought...sex would feel so...intense...damn!" Nightshade said in between breaths.

"If it's done with the right person, it will feel like a high that you never want to come down from, Belladonna. I hope that you enjoyed it, and that I satisfied all of your needs."

Nightshade laughed. "I'm not sure I even know what all my needs are supposed to be, but you definitely satisfied me, Yonuh! The energy you naturally put out seemed to be in overdrive. My body responded to it in ways I never thought possible. Thank you!"

Yonuh blushed as he smiled. "You're welcome, Belladonna. If there's a next time, I promise to do better."

Nightshade looked at him with a confused look on her face. "Excuse me? Did you say you will do better?" She grinned. "I hate to tell you this, Yonuh, but I'm not sure you can do better. How do you beat perfect?"

Yonuh pulled Nightshade to him and kissed her gently on her lips. "Oh, but I can! I can go longer than that too and use more of my energy to overwhelm your senses. When I do that, you won't be able to talk, let alone be conscious. Hmm, maybe I should demonstrate my *'beat-perfection'* technique...now."

Nightshade felt Yonuh guide her hand down towards his member which was once again erect. She stammered with surprise, "I...uh...thought when a guy...uh...blew his load, he was done!"

Yonuh's eyes had a golden glow about them, and he looked at her as if she was his prey. "I'm not most men, Belladonna, and I'll show you why!"

Nightshade's eyes widened as both a feeling of dread and excitement overwhelmed her at the same time. Yonuh put her on her hands and knees and started making love to her again.

Chapter Fifteen

Onyx sat in his seat, pouting with his arms across his chest. He scowled at Raven, but she ignored him and wouldn't even glance at him. He let out an overly-exaggerated breath. "Why can't we stop there? It's on the way to Powell's, so what's the big deal?"

Raven drove on, still ignoring him, which only irritated him more.

"It figures you would be so cruel to a poor, little, malnourished gremlin. Damn witches are all the same—no matter where you go!" The gremlin put his little hand over his heart and began singing, "*Nobody knows the trouble I've seen! Nobody knows my sorrow! Nobody knows but…Gizmo!*"

In spite of herself, Raven cracked a smile. "You're laying it on pretty thick, don't you think?"

"No, I'm not. I'm preaching the truth. When I get through, everyone will know just how mean your kind is, especially to my people! You're oppressing me and my rights!"

"Look, just because I won't stop at **Voodoo Doughnuts** doesn't make me oppressive; it makes me the driver who has the final say as to where we go."

"I sense a plot to emaciate me! The dark side of witchcraft surrounds you like a fart on toast!"

"You shove too many Doritos down your gullet. I'm pretty sure you're *not* emaciated. Besides, you can always fly over there and get the doughnuts yourself. Unless, of course, they have a sign that says you have to be this tall to enter?" She hit her knee with her hand, pretending to measure off his height.

"But we can't be going off by ourselves," he growled. "It's too dangerous. You should come with me to get doughnuts. Remember, safety first." He grinned as he wagged his finger at the witch.

"Nice try, gremlin, but I don't want a doughnut. I want to go to Powell's and lose myself in all those wonderful books and…" Thinking of books, her thoughts drifted her away.

"Voodoo Doughnuts are way better than those dusty, old books at Powell's any day of the week," Onyx said in a pouty voice as he looked out the window. "I'd buy the others doughnuts too!"

"Sheesh!" she exclaimed. "It's like riding with a whiny five-year-old!" Onyx stuck his tongue out at her, and she rolled her eyes. "I guess we can swing by Voodoo *after* we hit Powell's, you little brat!"

Onyx hopped up and started dancing in his seat, shaking his ass and doing his best Saturday Night Fever impression, which Raven thought wasn't half bad.

"How long is it going to take to get you a couple of books?" Onyx asked excitedly.

"A couple? If I have my way, I'm going to grab at least two, maybe three, bag loads of books!"

"What?! Damn, are you planning on bringing the whole bookstore home with you?"

"I wish," she mused and then glanced at him. "Don't give me that look. Your doughnuts will still be there waiting for you when I get done shopping for books. I lost my house to a fire, and my library went up in flames. I plan on rebuilding my library, three or four bags at a time."

"I guess it's a good thing we have a van," Onyx chortled. "It sounds like we'll need a lot of room for your shopping needs." He had a sudden thought. "Do you think they have any do-it-yourself manuals for electronics or mechanical stuff?"

She stared sideways at the gremlin, her mouth gaping open. "Wait a minute, Onyx. I thought you already knew all that kind of stuff. Why would you need manuals?"

"It's a little known fact that gremlins tend to steal those kinds of manuals and pass them on to the next generation. Sure, we're gifted and talented in those areas already, but the manuals give us more of a concrete understanding which makes us quicker at our mischief. Same thing can be said for a natural witch. Magic comes easily to them, but give them the proper spell books or a tome full of knowledge handed down by other witches, and they can excel faster in their craft. Make sense?"

Oddly enough, it did make sense to her. "Sorry, I just never thought about it that way...about your kind, that is. I figured it was part of gremlins' magical talents to know about technology."

"Some do, but I was never one of those. I spent my time snatching manuals as often as I could because I wanted to be well versed. There're things I still want to know, like the solar panels and how I can make them work more efficiently. I've worked on them some, but a better knowledge of their wiring would make things click into place faster for me."

Raven nodded her head as they drove over the Burnside Bridge. The few vehicles abandoned on the bridge had been moved over near the guard rails, making it easier for people to cross over the Willamette River.

Most of the people who lived in the area used smaller modes of transportation, like bicycles or motorcycles. There were more bartering sections set up on every other corner, but the biggest one in the area was by the waterfront where the Saturday Market was before the plague hit. It still thrived seven days a week and was referred to as the Waterfront Market.

Raven figured that the variety of meats she was bringing would trade well since most around here were used to getting fish and other aquatic animals for their protein. She remembered Yonuh saying he was on his way to the waterfront before he got tranquilized and captured by the P.A.N.E.L. squad goons, so it seemed reasonable to assume he would have probably brought some of his meats to trade.

After driving a few more blocks, Raven spotted the bookstore. It literally took up a city block. At 68,000 square feet, the store had four floors of books and housed one hundred and twenty-two major subjects and had thirty-five hundred subsections of books in nine color coordinated rooms. It was book-worm-nirvana with over a million books on hand, along with a room dedicated to rare books, like signed first editions and other out of print classics.

Raven parked the van. She grabbed her meat box and slung a small, linen bag that contained the elven items over her shoulder and walked briskly across the street.

Onyx closed the van's door and slipped his red satchel over his shoulder. He shot across the street, catching up to Raven. "I'm glad I have a psychic link to you. It would be a bitch trying to find you in there," he said, eyeing the huge building. "If it's all the same to you, I'm going to hit their technical bookstore over there." He pointed across the street.

"Oh really? What happened to the whole 'stick-together-for-safety' crap that you've been spewing all the way here?"

Onyx grinned. "I know, but I'll only be across the street so quit being an ass." He smacked Raven hard on her ass as he flew off and call out, "Go play, carrot top!"

"Hey! You little--grrr! If he's not careful, the van is going to have a new hood ornament!"

"I heard that!" Onyx cried out before he went into the technical bookstore.

Raven walked up to the store entrance. She put her hand out to open the door but stopped. An odd feeling settled over her, like she was being watched. She turned around, searching everywhere, but only saw several crows fighting over the remnants of what were the contents of someone's stomach. Raven crinkled her nose as a slight breeze wafted the putrid odor up to her nostrils. Not wanting to lose her own lunch, she turned around and hurried through the door.

Once inside, her nostrils were assailed again. The distinct odor of old pages filled her senses and brought an uncontrollable bright smile to her face. "Books!" Raven was giddy and delighted as she walked, with a strut, down the long ramp into the Orange room.

This was not only pure bliss, but the prefect sanctuary for her. She had often wished that she could have taken over this building like Yonuh had with the old Costco. She sighed. This place was protected by many people and not just book lovers, like her.

It had been decided that if there were any survivors of the apocalypse that mankind's literature should be preserved for future generations to read and cherish. It would be a crime to lose all these books and have people fall farther into ignorance.

In the beginning of the end, Powell's bookstore had been harassed by looters, looking to destroy whatever they could. But with the aid of several witches and a small, white dragon, the looting attempts stopped as word spread. Humans and supernatural beings worked together because neither group wanted to see this reservoir of knowledge lost.

The witches helped with bartering trades that dealt with specialty items that weren't man-made. The humans kept the bookstore tidy and the shelves full.

Most were happy to work there because all the staff actually lived there. The basement had been converted to bedrooms, and a couple of shower stalls had been installed. The room on the top floor known as the Gray room housed all the rare and hard to find books. Signed books and one-of-a-kind literature were there. Magic tomes and ancient texts were there too. And all of these treasures were guarded fiercely by the small, white dragon. A sign was posted that read: "Browse, if you like, but don't steal from here or you WILL be eaten by the dragon on duty!" No one wanted to tempt fate, especially after they saw the actual dragon.

Raven looked up at the sign above the barter countertop that read, "*All barters and trades are done here, no exceptions! Feel free to browse through our tonnage of books but no books can leave its area without having a barter ticket in hand. Thanks for being wonderful book lovers like us!*"

Raven got to the long counter and was greeted by a young man in his thirties. "Hello there! Will you be browsing or bartering today, ma'am?"

Raven shifted her box up onto the countertop and noticed the young man ogling her chest, so she leaned forward and said, "I'm bartering today. I've got some nice, juicy meats here if you want to look at them. Don't handle them too much, though, I might get turned on."

The young man, whose nametag proclaimed "Matt" stuttered for a moment as he replied, "Umm…I'll…be gentle…ma'am. Wow, I haven't seen these kinds of cuts of meats in, like forever! How did you come by these?"

"I have a good friend who's a great hunter and an even better butcher. So how many books will these fetch for me?"

"None, I'm afraid," Matt solemnly said as he longingly looked at the contents of the box.

"Beg pardon? What do you mean by that?" Her heart sank. "These are premium grade cuts of meat here! There's venison, pork, lamb, and chicken too. How can you turn these away?"

Matt gave her a sympathetic look. "I don't want to, ma'am, but lately someone has been trading meats around here that's been tainted. For our safety, we have to refuse all meat trades…even ones as good as yours."

"I see, but mine *aren't* tainted and —"

"I know this, ma'am, because yours looks way better than any of the stuff I've seen come through here. I'm not saying yours are bad; we just can't take them for barter."

Raven sighed heavily. "If there wasn't a ban on meat bartering, what could I have gotten for all this here?"

"All of it? You're serious?" When Raven nodded, Matt said without hesitation, "A lot of books! Hell, even Zytong the dragon in the Gray room would gladly trade with you for this quality of meats, and that says a lot because Zytong's guarding priceless treasures!"

"Well, fuck a frog in the eye! How are these asses tainting the meats? If I catch them, I'll taint more than just their meats!"

"Plague," Matt said firmly. "They must be harvesting their meat from animals that had died of the plague. Several people who work in the various trading posts around here got infected from either eating it or disturbing an active spore chute embedded in the meat. Needless to say, we can't accept any meat."

"I see, but still I'd like this meat not to go to waste. I'm willing to slap it around for you so you can see that there are no chutes…" She sighed again when she saw his face. "Hmm, since you won't take them in trade, I'll leave them here as a donation."

Matt looked down intently at the box of meats and grabbed it, setting it on the floor by his feet. He gave Raven a grin. "They never said we couldn't take meat as a donation. I'm sure they'll frown on me for claiming them, so I'll just keep them for myself. If I'm gonna die, it will be by a venison and lamb combo, smothered in gravy sauce."

"Thankfully, I've brought some other unique items to trade." Raven slipped her small, linen bag off her shoulder and began pouring the contents out onto the counter top.

Confused, Matt narrowed his eyes at the items. "What exactly are these?"

"Items gifted to me from an elven community. They said I could use these for trade or keep for myself."

"That's way beyond my knowledge, but Gentry should know their true value. She's a witch, after all, and their kind tends to know everything, right?" Matt wandered off to rouse a lady who was dressed all in emerald green clothing and appeared to be either meditating or sleeping.

The woman named Gentry got up and staggered over to the countertop. She had a thin figure, almost on the emaciated side. Her face had a sunken, hollow look to it, and she had thinning, blonde hair. Her clothes hugged her body but only served to give the impression she was sickly. Once Gentry made it to the countertop, she braced herself against it and clung to the edge to keep from falling over. She looked down and hissed at Matt, "You idiot! You know we don't accept meat! Do you want to kill us all?"

"I didn't barter for them. She just donated all of them because she didn't want them to go bad. If you don't want them, I plan on taking them for myself. They all look so much better than the nasty, rank meat being peddled around here."

"Get it away from me before I throw you and that stuff out!"

"Excuse me, Gentry," Raven interjected. "My name is Raven, and I apologize for the inconvenience my meats have brought you, but I can assure you that my meat is good. My friend Yonuh—"

"Yonuh?" Gentry bluntly interrupted as she narrowed her eyes at Raven. "Is that the name you just spoke?"

"Yes, he's the one who hunted and butchered these meats. Why? Do you know him?"

"Only the name. I've never actually met the man, but he's popular down by the waterfront. I hear he's a good man." She looked at the meat again and shook her head. "Even knowing they came from him, we still can't take his meats for barter. Now, though, I'm not so leery of them." Glancing over at the clerk, she said, "I'm sorry, Matt. Please put these donations in the refrigerator." She looked down at the items Raven had dumped on the counter. "Now what do we have here?"

"As you can see, I've procured some elven items," Raven said hopefully, but her stomach lurched a little from worry. If this skinny, sickly woman didn't want elven items, she had nothing else to trade. "I was hoping they would be okay to barter here."

"And what rare or magical tomes are you hoping to find today, my dear?"

Her hopes rose. "Some good fiction novels would be great, and maybe some paranormal romances—" Gentry had a weird look on her face. Again, Raven's hopes sank. "What?" she asked anxiously. "Why are you staring at me like that?"

"Seriously? A few fictional books for these priceless relics? These could easily get you into the Gray room. You could have your pick of the lot up there!"

The woman grabbed up a medallion that was a combination of rock, crystal and multiple gemstones perfectly meshed together, and it was inscribed with magical elven writing. She held it out in front of her, staring stupidly at it. "You see this? It's a healing charm that will not only replenish your life force but your overall health as well. The only thing it doesn't cure is the plague!" Now she stared at Raven. "All you want for it is a few books? This is priceless! So is the rest. You can have whatever you need here on any floor but…" She stared at the medallion again. "I can't accept something so precious for mere books!" She placed the medallion back on the counter.

Raven reached out and gently grabbed Gentry's hand and placed the elven medallion into it. "This is for you," she said in a sympathetic voice, "if you'll stop giving me a hard time over my barter. I need these books because the last few months have been one hell of a rollercoaster ride, and I need the escape. I donated the meats to you and your friends to eat, and now I want you to heal and feel better. Take this, please. You seem like you could use it the most, so maybe…it was meant for you."

Gentry held a stunned look on her face. Her mouth hung open, and her lips quivered. As tears trickled down her cheeks, Gentry asked, "Are you sure you want to do this? I can't—"

"I want you to accept it. This world has gotten cruel enough that pain has become second nature for everyone living in these times. I have my own personal healer, so what use would I need for this medallion? This is my gift to you, Gentry. We witches have to look out for one another."

Gentry flashed a grateful smile. "This is a *special* barter ticket." She handed Raven a carved piece of wood shaped to look like a book. It was colored in glittering gold paint and fit perfectly in the palm of her hand.

"Why is it special?" Raven asked as she carefully examined the craftsmanship, admiring all the attention to detail.

"It represents store credit, of course. Only one other person has ever received one like this, so don't go losing it. It entitles you to shop here until it loses it magical sparkle; it's kind of like a gift card, but this one has a *huge* spending limit. Even the Gray room items wouldn't put much of a dent into it."

"Oh wow! I guess I'll have to make a few more trips out here, but now I want my fiction fix. Thank you so very much."

Raven grabbed two hand baskets and walked up the short flight of steps to her left. She entered the Gold room where all the science fiction, horror, fantasy and mystery novels were kept. She flashed her barter ticket to one of the workers who was at his desk reading. He nodded in acknowledgment and went back to reading while Raven pranced down the aisles with a grin on her face.

As she filled up one of her baskets, Raven heard Onyx fly up behind her and giggle. Before she could turn around, he smacked her on the ass. She was in too good of a mood to complain, so she simply asked, "Did you find what you were looking for?"

Onyx hovered in front of her, shrugging his shoulders. "I got a couple of large boxes and a few new ideas about tinkering with things for our place. I lucked out and found one for the van that will come in handy."

"You're going to put rocket engines or machine guns on it, aren't you?"

"Ha! Like you would notice those upgrades, anyway. Who's to say I haven't done that already! I found schematics to convert the van into a hydro-powered vehicle, and one on how to make a hydro-station too, so fuel won't be an issue when I get finished. It's okay, you can hold your applause until it's done."

"I'll try to contain myself as you get your little, big man, masculine groove on." She grabbed a few more books and looked up at the gremlin. His nose was scrunched up. "What's wrong?"

Onyx floated down and hovered beside her. "Something or someone smells vaguely familiar, but I don't know—"

From behind them, a male voice grunted, "Ahem! Raven and Onyx, may I have a moment of your time...please?"

They both turned around and saw a young man standing by an old magazine rack. He looked haggard and out of place. He was dressed in a crimson uniform that had an inverted triangle name badge which read, *Gordon*.

Raven let the hand baskets slide off her arms and onto the nearest table. She whipped out her wand which was already sparking with magic, and she aimed it at the P.A.N.E.L. squad goon.

Onyx had his claws out and was ready to pounce. Gordon threw up a white handkerchief and begged, "Please you two, this is a peaceful meeting. I'm not here to harm either of you again!"

Onyx took flight so fast that before Gordon knew it, he was hanging off the ground. The gremlin held him up by his neck, letting his razor-sharp claws dig into the man's skin. He hissed into Gordon's ear, "I'm getting sick of you pricks showing up everywhere we go! Give me one good reason why I shouldn't tear your head off and roll it down the Hawthorne Bridge like a bowling ball!"

Gordon grimaced as he gasped for air. "You…need…me. I know…things!"

Raven walked up and roughly jabbed her wand into Gordon's chest. "What was that crack about not wanting to harm us *again*? Let me guess, you're the one who got away from Nightshade in the forest, aren't you? Did you present Yonuh's bloody shirt to your master, like a little prize? You've got a lot of balls coming for us all alone, buddy!"

"Release me. I've come…to warn you…" Gordon's eyes started to roll back in his head as he gasped for breath.

Onyx let go of him, and he dropped in a heap on the hard floor.

Raven knelt down and smacked Gordon on the head. "Warn us about what? Start talking or I'll let Onyx have his fun with you!"

Gordon rubbed his neck and felt his warm blood smear in his hand. "My master has decided to up the stakes in the hunt for Yonuh. He has sent out a deadly bounty hunter to kill you all and capture him. From what I've witnessed of it, it may do the job better than we can."

Onyx flashed his sharp teeth in Gordon's face as he hissed, "Does this bounty hunter have a name? Spit it out, dick cheese!"

Gordon's face went pale as he recalled the creature and what it had done to the men. He sputtered out, "I…don't know its…name. It's a…wraith. Zordic summoned up…a wraith!"

"Ah, shit!" Raven moaned.

Onyx nodded in agreement.

Chapter Sixteen

Onyx and Raven escorted Gordon out of Powell's bookstore, making him carry all of Raven's books. "Aww," Onyx snickered as he spoke to Gordon, "you're carrying her things already. That usually means you're in a relationship, doesn't it? How does it feel to be in love with a witch? Is it all that you dreamed it would be?"

"Your teasing won't have any effect on me, gremlin. I already get enough from the others back at the compound. I'm immune to it."

"I'm calling bullshit, right there," Onyx said as he flew backwards in front of Gordon. "I can smell the chemical change coming out of your pores that says, 'Liar! Liar! Pants on fire!' Let me guess, you're not well respected or treated as an equal, are you?"

"You could say that," Gordon said solemnly. "I'm also a coward…a yellow, chicken coward."

"If you're looking for sympathy, bark up some other tree," Raven growled. "I've had it up to here with you and your friends hunting us because your master has a hard on for my man!"

"I'm not here for sympathy. I'm looking for a mutually beneficial partnership. Like I said, I'm a coward, and that means I'm looking out for me. I happen to enjoy living, and I'm here to strike a deal with you that you can't possibly refuse."

Onyx flew over to the back of the van and opened the doors. Much to Raven's surprise, she saw that Onyx had packed the back of the van with several huge boxes of books so tall that she couldn't see the front of the cab. She gave the gremlin a stern look as Gordon sat her six bags of books in the back. "Well, I'm so glad you left me plenty of room for my books! What did you do, decide to clean them out or what?"

"Like you wouldn't have done the same thing if given half a chance! You're just mad because I shop faster than you."

"I would have gotten more, but reality decided to catch up with us in the form of a spineless man in red."

"I'm not spineless!" Gordon insisted. "I'm a coward. If I was spineless, I wouldn't be standing here at all because the master tends to rip out spines if he deems a person spineless! Cowards live longer…sometimes."

"That doesn't excuse the fact that you and your buddies take pleasure in torturing and killing people. You guys have made a sport out of it. Who gives you the right to do that shit, anyway?"

"Prophet Bob claims he was given a vision by the divine savior. He was shown that it was nonhumans who put the plague upon the Earth to kill us all so your kind could take over the world. He, the divine savior, decreed that all supernatural beings must be eliminated from this world. Only then, could our world be restored to its former glory." Gordon tried to show the usual pride when he spoke the words, but it was evident from his face that he was having doubts.

Raven noticed. "But now you aren't so sure, are you? What's got you questioning your zealous faith in this divine savior?"

Gordon was about to speak but felt a squeezing pressure on his wrists. He looked down. Onyx had slapped plastic straps on his wrists as handcuffs. "Are these really necessary? I'm not going anywhere."

"Maybe not, Gordo, but that doesn't mean you won't try something when our backs are turned. You said it yourself, you're a coward. You're only looking out for your own best interests. That means you can't be trusted. You might pull out a weapon or attack us if you feel your self-preservation is being threatened. Besides, I enjoyed doing that to you!"

Raven grabbed Gordon by his arm and escorted him to the van's open side door. As she helped him inside, Onyx slipped another plastic strap on to the middle of the one Gordon had on his wrists. The gremlin then connected it to several other straps laced around the passenger seat bracket.

Onyx glanced up at Gordon and shrugged his shoulders. "Still don't trust your ass, Gordo, so get over it!"

"Stop calling me that! My name is Gordon, you little jerk!" he growled out in frustration.

Onyx chuckled as he climbed into the passenger seat. "Ha! Not so immune now, are you? You seem to be losing that battle rather quickly."

"Onyx, behave!" Raven called out from somewhere behind the boxes in the back as she closed the rear doors. Walking around to the driver's side door, she stopped before she opened it. She looked around. "We're being watched," she whispered to herself, but still she saw nothing.

For all she knew, it could have been the wraith lying in wait for them to come out of the bookstore. She felt a sickening feeling in the pit of her stomach as she realized that Gordon could have been bait, and they had just swallowed him—hook, line and sinker.

Raven opened the door and slid behind the wheel. She looked over her shoulder. "Did you come alone or were you followed?" When Gordon didn't respond fast enough for her, she shouted, "Answer me now or we'll leave you here to fend for yourself against whatever is out there!"

Onyx gave her a confused yet inquisitive look, but she ignored him. "Now, dammit!"

"Uh, as far as I know," Gordon answered, "I wasn't followed. As for what's out there, I can't see anything."

"What are you feeling, Raven?" Onyx asked. "Do share with the rest of the class, please. I'm getting tired of having to guess at what you're thinking in that ginger-headed void you call a brain."

"I feel like I'm being watched. I felt it earlier when we first got here. When Gordon showed up, I figured he had been spying on us, and that was what I had been feeling. Now, though, I haven't got a clue. Whatever it is, it doesn't want to be seen, and it can hide pretty well from my psychic senses. Maybe you should give it a look, Onyx."

Onyx closed his eyes and scanned around with his third eye senses. Being meticulous about it, the gremlin searched the area. "Where are you feeling it the strongest?"

Raven looked around and noticed it seemed to be coming from directly ahead of them. "There!" she exclaimed excitedly. "The sewer drain is where it's coming from!"

Onyx opened his door and shot out to investigate.

Raven jerked out her wand and grabbed the door handle, readying for a fight in case Onyx needed help.

The little gremlin ripped the drain guard out of his way and shouted, "Little fucker! Come here!" He dove down into the hole.

"Do you think he's okay out there alone?" Gordon asked anxiously.

"He's capable of taking care of himself." She felt as if she was trying to convince herself of this, rather than trying to ease Gordon's anxiety. "Plus, I'm here if he needs any help."

After what seemed like a lifetime, Onyx flew out of the sewer drainage hole. He appeared to be okay, except for a few minor cuts to his face. He flew into the van and shut the door behind him. "So now can we go for doughnuts?"

"Sure, but what was down there? Are you all right?"

"Oh I'm good, but you should see the other guy — well, a shadow ghost, actually."

Raven frowned. "What the hell is it doing creeping around in the sewers? I'm mean…" She noticed the color had drained from Gordon's pale face, making it almost white. He sat nervously fidgeting, pulling at his plastic handcuffs. "Spill it, Gordon. What's got you so freaked out?"

Onyx peeked around his seat. "You're so white you look like a ghost-turd!"

"The wraith, it killed my…men, and then it seemed to have a hold on their spirits. They all changed into shadow people right before my very eyes!" Gordon's eyes darted back and forth in some sort of paranoid dance, frantically looking for the wraith or any of the shadow people.

"That shadow thing was spying on us for the wraith," Onyx proclaimed. "The wraith may have the ghosties around the area for spying, but they also need an energy source to keep them tethered here on Earth." He took a deep breath and grinned. "To Voodoo Doughnuts, woman, I'm hungry!"

As Raven popped the van into gear, Gordon frantically hollered out, "How can you think of food at a time like this? There might be more of those things, and the wraith might be lurking nearby!"

Onyx looked over the top of his seat and said nonchalantly, "It's easier to save the world when you have a full stomach. Whether you know it or not, my kind needs to eat food to live. I guess we're all flesh-eating, blood drinking monsters in your eyes."

"Yes, actually, I did think that, but now that I've been around you two, I can see my beliefs were mistaken. I don't trust Prophet Bob's visions anymore. You seem more human to me now, which I never noticed before. I even felt that way when I saw all of you in the woods that night."

"And why do you feel the prophet's visions aren't true anymore?" She scoffed and glared at him through the rearview mirror. "Especially now, after all this time, while you and your friends have raped, butchered and murdered innocent creatures?"

Wanting to change the subject, Gordon declared, "One thing I do believe is that the plague was started by one of your kind—a nonhuman."

Onyx snarled as he got into Gordon's face. "It's always someone else's fault, isn't it? Humans were fucking with nature just so they could have prettier lawns, free of pests like ants! The gene manipulation on that fungus falls squarely on you dumb humans. And when things went to hell in a hand basket, you looked for the first scapegoat you could find!"

Gordon frowned. "I've been snooping around lately, which isn't the smartest thing to do, and I've come to the conclusion that what started the plague was no accident. Something or someone made sure that a lab worker got infected with the plague."

Raven stared in the review mirror again. Gordon seemed to genuinely believe what he had said, and she wondered what exactly he had uncovered. Were there documents or a video of the incident showing the lab accident? Maybe someone bragged about ending the world single-handedly? Whatever it was, the knowledge of this was betrayal enough in Gordon's mind to want to seek out help from the most unlikely group he could find — us. With that thought, she asked Gordon, "So why us, of all people? Why work with your enemy when you know you're facing certain death now on both sides?"

"My idea is simple enough. I want you to save my life. The only way that will happen is if you and your friends can kill Master Zordic."

"Ah, I see. We kill him while you hide in the bushes watching the show and eating your popcorn," Onyx said sarcastically. "Why are you so worried about him anyway? It was you who gave him Yonuh's name, not to mention his blood, so you shouldn't be anywhere near his hit list, right?"

Gordon hesitated for a moment as he closed his eyes, remembering all the deaths he had seen by the hand of Master Zordic. "It doesn't work that way with him; he doesn't weigh in decisions based on past performances. It's more like what have you done for me lately, and did you do it right this time."

Onyx snickered. "Boohoo."

Gordon sighed, trying to ignore the gremlin, as he continued his tale of woe. "If Zordic isn't pleased, you're dead. He usually murders someone in a grand way, to make his point to everyone. For example, if you lack the courage to do something, he rips your guts out. If you try and run from him, he rips your spine out." Gordon looked at Raven, only seeing the back of her head and her eyes reflected in the rearview mirror. "He fears your kind, Raven. Zordic does his best to conceal this from everyone, but I have seen it on his face when he speaks of witches. He's not aware that I've seen his fear. I believe you can take him out and free me from the contract he had me sign so long ago."

"Yeah," Onyx replied sarcastically, "I'm sure the benefits are awesome. So why would you be his little bitch, anyway? Sounds like you should have read the fine print on the contract."

"The contract was simple enough. We got a place to live, where food and drink were in abundance, and we also got a purpose in life: rid the world of the scum who destroyed it."

"Pretty sweet deal, Gordon," Raven interjected, "but what did the demon get? No demon does anything for free, not ever."

"He wanted two things, actually. He demanded our unquestioning loyalty to him. Also, when we died, he got our..." Gordon swallowed hard, and he grimaced, thinking about his own stupidity. Finally, he said, "The demon gets our life essence when we die."

"In other words," Raven snarled, "you sold your soul."

"You have to understand," the man pleaded. "We were in dark times. The plague was everywhere. When someone makes you an offer like that, you have to jump on it because it may never come again. He trained us. He let us listen to the words of the prophet, which inspired us greatly." He sighed heavily. "Once we realized what kind of deal we had struck, we weren't allowed to leave."

"You made your bed, now go lay in it," Onyx snapped. "It's just like humans to expect us to clean up their messes!" He suddenly got excited as he saw they were quickly approaching the Voodoo Doughnuts shop.

Raven turned right off Burnside Street and onto S.W. 3rd Avenue. She parked near the entrance of the shop and shut off the van. The shop had a reputation for making delicious regular and one-of-a-kind doughnuts. When the apocalypse started, the owners had used actual voodoo magic to protect their shop from looters. Another unique trait of the shop was that you could get married there. Getting married in a doughnut shop was just one of the staples of keeping Portland weird. Even in this post apocalyptic world, people still flocked here for a wedding ceremony and two dozen doughnuts for their friends.

Onyx opened his door and looked cautiously at the street before turning around and asking, "Anything in particular you two want? I'm getting whatever I can. Yonuh and Nightshade can pick what they want later. I have a sure fire way of getting our sweets for free, if they will go for it, that is."

Raven noted the tell-tale twinkle in his eyes that told her he was feeling mischievous, which never seemed to end well for people. But since his antics wouldn't be directed at her, Raven gave him her order. "I want a couple of their Voodoo Dolls, a Diablos Rex, and I guess a regular Maple Bar."

Thinking about the doughnuts, Gordon got excited. "I love their Cock-N-Balls. When that Bavarian cream oozes into my mouth—"

Both Raven and Onyx burst into snorts and laughter.

Gordon blushed and rolled his eyes. "You guys stop laughing at me! I just happen to love their Cock-N-Balls doughnuts." He sat and pouted.

"Don't worry about it, Gordo," Onyx said, howling with laughter. "I'll have them throw in a Gay Bar doughnut too."

"Great!" he growled. "I've teamed up with immature children. If I wanted to be harassed, I would've stayed at the compound!"

Carrying a small bag, Onyx flew out the door and went straight towards the Doughnut shop entrance which already had a line forming in front of it. The intoxicating aroma of freshly fried dough assailed the little gremlin's nose. Having very little patience, he decided to thin out the line. He reached his hand into the bag and sprinkled some of the contents on the people in line.

Suddenly, the people in line screamed and fled in terror, as if some unseen monster had just shown up for coffee and doughnuts and was in a bad mood.

Laughing, Onyx landed by the doorway and walked inside the shop.

"What in the name of the divine savior did he just do?" Gordon asked as he stared at the fleeing people.

Raven opened her third eye senses and took a peek. At once, she recognized the powder. "Nightmare Dust," she pronounced. "It's a hallucinogen. It works on a person's worst fears. Too much of the stuff can cause people to commit suicide or attack their family and friends."

Gordon gulped loudly. "Why couldn't he just wait in line like everyone else?"

Raven laughed. "Onyx has the patience of a two-year-old. He has no problem causing chaos because it's in his DNA. To expect him to behave any differently would be like asking you to walk into the Willamette River and breathe underwater without an oxygen tank."

Through the rearview mirror, Raven looked back at Gordon and studied him for a few moments. "So who do you believe caused the plague?"

The man hesitated and then noticed she was being serious — something he wasn't use to getting from other people. "It was a supernatural being who started it." When he saw her tense, he quickly added, "Before you get huffy and defensive, let me explain. Then you can berate me." He took in a deep breath. "First off, the lab guy was actually sick the day of the accident, but he had been forced to go in to work which made him a prime candidate for manipulation. I know this from research I did on the plague. I checked out the computer logs and reviewed the video surveillance tapes."

"Why exactly did you research the plague? Did Zordic have you do it for him?"

"No, I did it before the plague became widespread. I'm...or was...a private investigator for the company that ran the laboratory. I kept the records and phone logs at my place and began reviewing them when word got out that an accident at the company had caused the plague. I have a copy of the accident on a disk in my pocket right now. You can review it and give me your take on what you see."

"What's the point? It won't change the past, and it won't help anyone legally sue the company since there isn't a legal system anymore."

"No, but I believe we can right a wrong that never should've happened in the first place. I've seen the video multiple times, but I never got a chance to view it with my *augmented eyes* that Zordic gave me." He sighed heavily. "I was bullied by the other men. They would have taken great pleasure in destroying the disk just as a way to push me around."

"Why would they do that to you? You seem nice enough—"

"In Zordic's world, nice is bad," Gordon hissed out his pent up frustrations. "I'm not a hardcore sociopath like the rest of them. I was a target of ridicule and humiliation because I'm a coward. Plus, I got things done more efficiently. I may have hung back, out of the action, but that was due to being a private investigator. I observe and make judgment calls on how the teams should be divided up and used based on what we were hunting at the time. It didn't help matters that Zordic put me—a coward—as the leader for the hunts!"

"I understand that your feelings were hurt badly, and now you want out. I really can't blame you either but—"

"The night I returned with all of your names, pictures and Yonuh's bloody shirt," he growled angrily, "they didn't waste any time in harassing me! Because I was the smart one—the sole survivor, they beat me, breaking several of my bones. They poured yellow paint on me and scattered white feathers all over me, calling me a chicken. They strung me up in front of the entrance to the church where Prophet Bob's flock could see me and make fun of me.

Suddenly, Raven reached out and smacked Gordon's face.

"Ouch! What was that for?"

"I've had enough, already! Bellyaching isn't going to help you. I'm sorry for all you went through, but I can't change any of it, so stop bitching or I will leave you here for the shadow people."

Gordon gave her a fierce look, but then his face softened as he realized Raven was not the enemy. She didn't deserve to hear his crap, but he wanted to be validated by her.

Out of the corner of her eye, Raven saw a blur of pink fly by. A moment later, Onyx flew into the van with six pink boxes. He gave them a huge grin and then released a long, loud burp. Setting the doughnut boxes down on the floorboard, he started rubbing his belly. "So what did I miss? You two love birds getting nice and cozy out here?"

"Arrgg! That smell! What crawled inside of you and died?" Raven pinched her nose and tried to wave away the burp's bad odor.

"That, my dear, was how I scored all these doughnuts. I made a deal with the owners. I said I wanted to take the Tex-Ass challenge. But instead of eating just one, I told them I would eat four of them in under two minutes. If I could do it, they'd have to give me my doughnut order for free!"

"What exactly is the Tex-Ass challenge?" Gordon asked.

"The Tex-Ass challenge is simply a huge doughnut that is the equivalent of six doughnuts. Anyone who can eat it in eighty seconds or less gets it for free. I upped the stakes with my challenge and all the people inside began cheering for me, wanting to see it happen. Needless to say, so did the owners and cooks, so I gave them my list of doughnut demands. They felt if I could do it, I deserved all these delicious doughnuts!"

The thought of having a sugar-wired gremlin in the van for the long road home made Raven shudder. "You ate the equivalent of two dozen doughnuts in under two minutes? How the fuck did you accomplish that?"

Onyx's eyes twinkled. "I'm a gremlin, so I worked the doughnuts over with magic first. I put a *glamour* on them so they all looked normal. But in reality, I was bending and folding them into dough balls. I quickly stuffed them into my mouth. All they saw was me eating like a zombie at an all-you-can-eat brains buffet." He laughed. "Unfortunately, the Tex-Ass doughnuts are now expanding back to normal size. I've got a little gas as well as a gooood buzz!"

"Great, just what I needed--a gassy-ass gremlin on speed!" Raven tried to roll down the window but couldn't. She looked at Onyx and saw he was wearing his Cheshire Cat grin. "You little shit, fix the windows! I don't want to smell your nasty gas all the way home!"

Onyx hovered in the air and gave her his innocent puppy dog eyes. "Moi? You think I had something to do with the windows not working? It's because I'm a gremlin, isn't it? Gremlins are always getting blamed for mechanical problems. Your view of me and my people is that of racial stereotyping! I'm so hurt by this accusation that you leave me no choice in the matter."

"You gonna fly home?" she asked hopefully.

He grinned. "Something better — much better!"

Raven narrowed her eyes. "Don't you even think about it, or I—"

"What the fuck are you doing?" Gordon hollered.

Onyx flew around inside the van like he was a racecar driver, farting and burping at the same time. All the while, he was laughing his ass off.

Gordon yanked and pulled on his restraints, wishing he could reach for the door handle. He covered his nose and rubbed his eyes which were watering from Onyx's flatulence-bombing runs.

Raven did her best to open her door, but it wouldn't budge. "Onyx, unlock the damn doors, you prick!"

Onyx let out a loud belly laugh, but when he noticed Raven pulling out her wand, he admonished her, "Now, now, Raven! No using your wand. The van is filled with gas, and one spark from your wand will create a huge fireball in here!"

"It would be worth it just to get rid of your swamp-ass perfume," she said in a nasal voice as she pinched her nose. "Open the windows and doors, or I *will* spark this van and make it light up like the Fourth of July!"

"Just give me a few more toots and…ahhh!" Onyx let out one last fart, and it was long and smelly, far worse than the previous ones combined. He sat down in his seat, with a euphoric look on his face. Glancing over at Raven, he grinned. "Damn, that last one was practically orgasmic. I feel so much better. How about you guys?"

"Onyx, roll down the windows. Now!" Raven demanded. When he ignored her, she slapped him on the back of his head.

"OUCH! What was that for—oh right, the gas! You should roll down the windows or something; it stinks in here!"

"No shit, asshole!" Gordon snarled. He thrashed around trying to free his hands, wanting to throttle the little gremlin. "Undo your fucking magic, so we can have some fresh air in here!"

"Magic? I didn't use any magic on the windows. Raven, would you be a dear and start up the van. The windows need power so they can roll down." Onyx giggled as he pointed at Raven. "You forgot to turn on the van first!"

Raven looked down and saw that the motor was off and that he was correct about the windows. She started up the van, pushed the automatic window buttons, and the windows moved down. The smell of fresh air and fried dough wafted into the van.

Raven stuck her head out of the window and inhaled deeply. "There's nothing like mother nature's sweet, pure air."

"Would someone please open my damn door," Gordon growled. "It still reeks back here!"

Raven pulled herself back into the van and looked at Onyx. "Go open his door, jackass!"

Onyx hovered in the air and floated by Gordon, who scowled at him as he went by. He opened the door and hovered outside while Gordon leaned out as far as he could, for fresh air.

The gremlin flew back in and closed the side door, avoiding a few kicks and head butts from Gordon. Onyx snickered as he climbed into his seat.

As Raven threw the van into reverse and peeled out of the parking space, Onyx sat quietly in his seat, kicking his feet and humming to himself. "Oh, Gordon," he said mischievously, "I had the guys at the doughnut shop make your Cock-N-Balls extra-large, and they were more than happy to add more of that creamy Bavarian filling. I told them how much you loved the feeling of their cream oozing down your throat. That made them laugh."

Gordon rolled his eyes. "Very funny, Onyx, but don't quit your day job!"

As she drove, Raven kept thinking about what Gordon had told her earlier. "Gordon's a detective."

Onyx snickered. "But he couldn't detect that Zordic was evil?"

Raven ignored him. "He says he has a computer disk that shows how the plague got loose."

Onyx suddenly stopped laughing. He looked from Raven to Gordon. "I guess I did miss something while I was getting our desserts. So you think you know who's to blame for all this chaos in the world? Let me guess, it was a supernatural creature, of course!"

"I'm not sure who it is on the security video because I haven't had a chance to verify it, but I have my suspicions."

"Well, aren't you just the cryptic little human. Spill the Doritos, already. Say what's on your mind!"

Gordon thought for a long moment, and then he said, "I believe it to be none other than Prophet Bob. Why else would he be in league with a demon? Like I told Raven, I haven't had a chance to review the video with my *augmented* eyes. I'd bet my life, though, that he's not only behind it, but he's also a sociopathic, supernatural monster!"

Chapter Seventeen

Depressed, Yonuh roamed around on Costco's rooftop, checking on his garden in the greenhouse or looking out at the skyline of Portland. He had betrayed Raven, and he didn't understand why. Yonuh mentally slapped himself for not resisting the necromancer and her wiles.

"No!" he said aloud. "I'm not going to blame this on Nightshade. I could have told her to go." But he had not told her to go. He had wanted her. She had needed his healing caresses, especially after what that monster Drexel had done to her, and Yonuh had used that excuse to be with her. After all, he had vowed to the Great Spirit to heal and help people.

Even the horrors that Drexel had inflicted on Nightshade wasn't excusable to Yonuh—neither was his vow to the Great Spirit. He could have healed the necromancer's psychological wounds without having sex with her. To blame it on Drexel or the Great Spirit was to lie to himself. He knew that!

He was totally to blame, and he knew that too!

Raven was his mate. His bear-spirit had marked her as his own personal territory. And, just weeks later, he had betrayed the woman he loved! His guilt was overwhelming, and he grabbed a handful of his long, black hair and screamed, "Arrgg! I'm so stupid!"

He had hurt Raven. True, she didn't know about what had happened in her absence, but she would know…and soon. He knew what he had to do. He would have to tell her. To hide this from Raven would be as much of an insult to her as his sexual tryst with Nightshade. He wasn't worthy of Raven's trust or her love. She deserved someone stronger and more faithful.

Yonuh picked a few potatoes and carrots for the stew he wanted to make for dinner tonight. With a heavy heart, he grabbed a watermelon and walked back to the dumbwaiter he had installed to make bringing his garden produce inside easier.

Nightshade was still passed out on his bed, and he decided that prepping dinner would be a good distraction for him until Raven and Onyx came back from the bookstore. He sat his produce down in a wooden crate that he had placed on the dumbwaiter. Working the heavy duty chain on a pulley, he lowered the dumbwaiter down into the warehouse. With each yank on the chain, Yonuh berated and belittled his judgment and his own character.

Once the dumbwaiter had reached the bottom, Yonuh trudged over to the ladder that was attached to the access hatch and slowly climbed down, closing and locking the hatch behind him. He carried the crate to the kitchen. The odor of venison slow cooking in a crock pot since dawn assailed his nostrils, and he realized just how hungry he was.

Once all of the produce was rinsed off, Yonuh place them all in a bowl and moved them to the prep table where he had a cutting board waiting for him, along with a peeling knife. He sat down and began peeling the potatoes when he heard soft footfalls behind him.

Gentle hands touching his tense shoulders, slowly squeezing and massaging him, forced Yonuh to close his eyes as he enjoyed the relaxing manipulation of his tired muscles. When he opened his eyes, he saw Nightshade peeking around at him, smiling brightly, and he stifled a groan.

"My big, strong bear is so tense," she chirped happily. "What's got you so tightly wound up? Is it this dinner and working alone on it doing this to you? I can help you with the prep."

She was still skyclad, and he sighed heavily. "No, just feeling guilty." He shook his head and looked away in shame. "I'm not a good person, Nightshade."

Nightshade grabbed a chair and sat down beside Yonuh. She stared at him for a long moment. "You feel this way because we had sex, is that right? You wish you had never slept with me, is that it?"

Yonuh forced himself to look away from her beautiful, naked body. Focusing on peeling the potatoes, he replied, "Yes and no. I feel bad because I went and did this behind Raven's back, like the piece of shit that I am. I enjoyed the sex with you, Belladonna. Now that it's done, though, and I'm alone with my thoughts…I see myself as a bad person who just ripped Raven's heart out and took a big shit on it!"

Tears welled up in her eyes. She hadn't meant to hurt Yonuh. She got up and grabbed another peeling knife. As she sat back down, Nightshade blurted out, "I'll tell Raven and take the brunt of her anger for you. I'll make her see that it was my fault. I came into your room while you slept peacefully and threw myself on you."

"No, Belladonna, I'll man up and tell her to her face. I refuse to let you fight my battles for me. She deserves to hear it from me, and I'll take whatever she dishes out because I'm the one who betrayed her."

With blazing silver eyes, Nightshade furiously jammed her peeling knife into the cutting board. "The hell you will! I caused this because I couldn't control my lust for you. So I will deal with the fallout if there's going to be any from her!"

Yonuh flinched at her fury.

The necromancer snatched her peeling knife up again and started to work on the carrots. With each cut, her silver eyes glowed bright.

He cringed as he watched her, suspecting that she was imagining the carrots as Raven, thinking of what Onyx always liked calling her—carrot top.

Yonuh grabbed all the potato chunks and put them into the bowl. He walked over to the stove and dumped them into the rolling, boiling water.

Nightshade snatched up a bowl and put the sliced carrots into it. Yonuh was startled at first by how fast Nightshade had chopped the carrots but, then again, she was pissed off and feeling very protective of him.

She placed the diced carrots by the crock pot. "Raven would be a damn fool to let this destroy what you two have. I admit, I wish I could have gotten to you first, but I really don't mind being the runner up. If she tries to walk out on you because of me, I *will* smack some sense into her for you."

Yonuh let out a heavy sigh as his shoulders slumped. "I'm not worth protecting, Belladonna. I—"

"Not worth protecting? I say otherwise, especially after all the crap I've put you through! You have healed and cared for me like no other person in the world has ever done. You've never asked for anything back in return. I feel like you deserved that fun surprise you woke up to today because I have no other way to show how much I appreciate you."

Yonuh hid a blush as he sprinkled a couple of pinches of brown sugar into the gravy and mixed it in. Nightshade glided over to him and put her arms around his big waist while he shredded the venison meat with a fork. She closed her eyes and enjoyed his wonderful, comforting energy he was exuding and, at that moment, she wished she could do that for him.

He tenderly massaged her arms which made her smile that he wasn't pushing her away. How could anyone truly get mad at this man? He was sweet, tender, and very nurturing. He was as fiercely protective of his friends as he was passionate in the bedroom. She felt anger rising up in her again as she thought of Raven's fury, and it would be solely aimed at Yonuh. Suddenly, she heard Raven mentally contact her.

"Nightshade, we're heading back home now with some yummy goodies. Could you please wake Yonuh up? We're bringing a…guest with us."

"Yonuh is awake. He's preparing dinner right now. I'll go tell him you guys are on the way."

"He's up? Huh, I tried to contact him but got no answer. I guess he's too preoccupied at the moment."

"Yes he is, girl," Nightshade said as she glanced up at Yonuh and noticed he was doing his best to hide his feelings and apparently blocking out Raven's psychic calls.

"Raven just told me they're on their way back now with some goodies. I should go get dressed because—"

"It would be awkward being found skyclad in my arms when she comes through the door," Yonuh said with enough melancholy to overfill the Willamette River.

"No, I was going to say that they're bringing a guest with them."

"Did she say who this person was?"

"No, but the apprehension in her voice tells me something's wrong, and we may not like who's coming to dinner with them." She leaned in and softly kissed his lips which made him put his arms around her and return the kiss. Begrudgingly backing out of Yonuh's grasp, she walked towards his room to get dressed.

Noting that it would be some time before the food was ready, Yonuh walked around aimlessly throughout the warehouse until he decided to take a quick shower. *No sense in being all dirty and sweaty before my execution.*

"Dinner will be ready shortly," he called to Nightshade as he walked by her room. "I'm going to take a quick shower."

Nightshade's silver eyes glowed with arousal as she replied, "Sounds like fun! May I join you?"

He ducked into the bathroom without replying. Methodically stripping off his clothes, he placed them on a nearby free standing shelf.

He took a deep breath as he gazed at his reflection in the mirror and muttered, "You don't deserve Raven, you piece of filth!" He sighed and stepped into the shower. He turned on the hot water and let it cascade down his back as he leaned against the wall under the shower head, letting his tears mix in with the water. "She's gonna leave me," he whined. "And I don't blame her one bit."

Nightshade stood by the bathroom and gently put her hand on the door but didn't open it. Hearing a noise behind her, she turned and saw Onyx. He was flying towards the kitchen with two clear sacks that had pink boxes in them.

Onyx flew back towards the door again. A moment later, Raven and a guy walked in, both carrying several bags in each hand. Nightshade looked closely and saw this unknown man was wearing all crimson. They had brought home a P.A.N.E.L. stooge for dinner! *What the hell is this world coming to?*

Nightshade strolled up to Raven and the man beside her and hissed, "What's this ass doing here? Did he hurt you guys? I'll tear his soul out and send it to a place worse than Purgatory if he has!"

The man blanched at the threat and dropped the sacks he was carrying, spilling the books out onto the floor. Trying to hide behind Raven for protection, he tripped over his own feet and landed on his ass beside the books.

Raven chuckled as she looked down at the crimson heap on the floor. "Gordon, I'd introduce you to Nightshade, here, but you already know her from the forest, don't you?"

Surprised, Nightshade exclaimed, "You? You're the one who shot me? I should've known that already from the way you ran and hid like a little bitch! I guess I'm even more terrifying in the light, aren't I?"

"Please don't hurt me!" Gordon pleaded pitifully. "I...I came in peace and with a warning too!"

Nightshade raised an eyebrow as she squatted down by Gordon, making him even more physically uncomfortable by her closeness. Her silver eyes flared as she gazed into his fearful eyes without blinking, making Gordon squirm even more.

Raven bent down and collected her books off the floor. She did her best not to laugh at his reaction and Nightshade's obvious torture of him.

Her eyes still locked on Gordon, the necromancer smiled and said to Raven, "You mentioned you were bringing home some goodies, but I wasn't expecting this delightful treat!" She growled and snarled for Gordon's benefit. "Mm, oh the fun I can have with him. It ought to last for hours—if not days!"

"Pew! What's that smell?" Onyx cried out as he flew into the room. Pinching his little, round nose, he exclaimed, "Damn it, Nightshade! You know better than to scare the new puppy; he isn't house broken yet!"

About that time, Raven got a whiff. "Eww, Gordon! Really? You couldn't have done that outside or in the bathroom?"

Not only had Gordon pissed his pants, but he had soiled them as well. Pleased with herself, Nightshade stood up, still malevolently grinning at him.

Raven sighed. "Leave him alone, alright? He has information we need about Zordic. He says he has a computer disk showing who caused the plague to happen. Where's Yonuh?"

The necromancer's voice was barely above a whisper, and it had taken on a sympathetic tone. "Yonuh needs you, Raven...now more than ever. He just stepped into the shower." Suddenly, she frowned and glared at Gordon, her voice rising and harsh. "What difference does it make if he has evidence of who started the apocalypse? It's not like it'll change anything!"

"True," Raven replied as she walked toward the direction of the bathroom, "but it may shed light on what actually happened. If the culprit is still around, we can bring them to justice and let the world know by showing them the video."

"What good will the video do if no one can see it? Most of the world has no electricity anymore—"

"We can use the video broadcasting system that Prophet Bob uses to preach on. It's been set up in various hotspots where most humans live now. He had Master Zordic create a network of screens and visual aids so everyone in the world could hear his gospel and make them want to fight for his cause."

"Well, aren't you a fountain of knowledge," Nightshade said to Gordon as she held out her hand to help him up to his feet. "Let me show you to one of the other bathrooms, so you can clean up. Onyx, would you mind finding something for our guest to wear?"

"Sure thing, toots! What size of Depends do you wear, Gordon?" Onyx snickered as he flew off.

Gordon warily grabbed Nightshade's hand, and she helped him up. Only, after the man was up, she didn't let go of him. Instead, she leaned in and coldly whispered into his ear, "The wound you inflicted on me is the only free shot you get. You attack me again, and I'll be sliding my black dagger into your heart and stealing your soul for my amusement." She looked at him with cold, silver eyes. "Now let's get you cleaned up. I'm not letting you out of my sight, so you'll have to strip in front of me, big boy!"

Gordon's eyes widened in shock, and he gulped loudly.

Raven pushed the bathroom door open and immediately was smacked in the face from the sauna-like heat that was trapped in the room.

She could hear not only the shower running, but also a sad growling. Raven's heart sank.

She couldn't stand that Yonuh was in so much emotional turmoil. She began to undress. Raven wasn't going to just talk to him out here, she wanted to see his face and help him get through the pain.

Placing all of her clothes next to Yonuh's, on the free standing rack, she walked softly towards the showers. As she got to his stall, Raven peeked in and saw Yonuh under the shower, his body turned away from her. She also noticed his body was twitching a lot—a sign of his emotional upheaval.

Raven stepped in quietly and grabbed a bottle of body wash. Lathering up a bath sponge, she touched his back with it.

He gasped in surprise and whirled around. Seeing that it was her, he pulled her to him. "I'm not worthy of your love, Raven," he moaned.

"You let me be the judge of that, you big, sexy bear of mine!" She began washing his belly with the sponge and caressing it with her free hand.

Yonuh groaned with pleasure but felt torn by what he had done earlier with the necromancer. "I did you wrong, Raven. I had sex with Nightshade while you were gone. I'm so weak and pathetic that I…I can't even control myself for the few hours that you were away. I deserve your full fury, Raven. I—"

"Shhh, just let me do this, Yonuh. You need this now," Raven said in a soothing voice as she pressed her body against his, causing Yonuh's member to spring to life.

"But you don't understand. I betrayed your love and trust! How can you be so calm, so caring of me when you should be trying to kill me or worse?"

"And why do you assume I feel betrayed or hurt, Yonuh?" Raven asked as she turned him around. She dropped to her knees and started scrubbing Yonuh's ass which she couldn't help but nibble on.

Yonuh flinched and squirmed as he enjoyed her being so playful, but he still felt confused at her complete acceptance of what he had done to her. "Because I'm a piece of garbage that can't control himself when he wakes up with a naked woman in his bed and she's not you! OUCH!"

Raven spanked his ass hard several times. "Bad bear! How dare you degrade yourself in front of me! If you do that again, I'll turn you around and smack you in the balls until you stop it!"

"Maybe you should do that; I deserve it!" Yonuh said coldly. He felt Raven slide her hand up between his legs and grip his member firmly which made him groan with pleasure as she stroked it.

"I would never hurt you, Yonuh...let alone this yummy piece, right here! I'd rather fuck you than cause you anymore grief than you're in right now!"

"I'm confused. I confessed, but...you act like...it's no big deal. Why?"

"Because Nightshade told me all about it and how she found you later, practically shredding yourself apart with the notion that you hurt and betrayed me."

"What? I wanted to tell you to your face! I didn't want you to hear about it like that--OOF!"

Raven spun him around and pinned him to the shower wall. Water ran down her head and body, making her skin glisten. The sight of her beautiful, naked body made Yonuh want her even more.

"I was shocked at first, and I thought Nightshade was trying to gloat about it. She told me how you felt and that I had to come home and take proper care of you. I must confess that I'm attracted to her as well, and I totally understand how you had difficulty resisting her wiles. She's used them on me, and I can't stop myself either. Besides, I'm also glad for her."

Confused, Yonuh asked, "What do you mean by that, Raven?"

"Other than what that leech Drexel did to her, you are the first man she has ever been with. She's had to stick with women her whole life because no guy was man enough to want to be with her. Don't get me wrong, she's definitely a lesbian—it's her nature." She paused for a moment. "Well, now that I think about it, I guess she's bisexual. Anyway, I'm glad she got to have you as her first man because now she can know what it's like to have a real man inside her, one who will treat her 'like a queen in bed.' Her words, not mine." She smiled lovingly up at him.

"It won't happen again; I swear it, Raven! I'd rather die first than—"

"Shhh..." Raven placed a finger on Yonuh's babbling lips to silence him. "How can I be mad that you went and fucked Nightshade when I've done the deed with her too? That would be hypocritical of me, now wouldn't it? I feel more comfort in knowing you had her and not some random skank out on 82nd Avenue because that would really upset and hurt me. Does that make any sense?"

Yonuh nodded which made Raven grin at him, but she got taken by surprise as he grabbed her and pinned her against the shower wall with her arms above her head. Yonuh nibbled on her ear and neck, making her moan with want as he spread her legs apart. He slipped a finger inside her slick core and began thrusting it slowly, making her squirm as she moaned, "Oh Yonuh, we have...a guest here. We can't keep him...waiting—OH GODS!"

"We won't be long. First, though, you're going to get a preview of coming attractions later tonight. I hope you don't mind the appetizer right now?" Yonuh slid a second finger inside Raven's core and thrust harder and faster.

"Oh fuck! Oh damn, Yonuh! Your magical fingers— AHHH! GODS!" Raven arched her back as she started coming which only urged him on to go faster and harder.

"That's it, my sexy witch. Come for me, my love. Enjoy the energy coming from my fingers and explode for me!"

She exploded with a full blown orgasm as her core clinched around Yonuh's big, meaty fingers. He continued to thrust them inside her, making her orgasm last longer. When he stopped, Raven slid down the wall and onto the floor. She felt like the whole room was spinning and had trouble focusing.

Yonuh shut off the water and stepped out of the stall for a moment. He returned with several towels for Raven and one draped on his shoulder. He grabbed Raven by her waist and effortlessly lifted her to her feet, which didn't help her vertigo go away.

"Damn, the room is still spinning!" Raven groaned as he helped to dry her body off. "Don't lift me up like that after you've made my head explode, okay?"

Yonuh chuckled as he continued to dry her off. She could feel how much he loved her with the simplest of gestures, like this, and she knew there was no way he could ever care this much for anyone else. Even if he did this for Nightshade, she wouldn't feel jealous — well, maybe a little bit. She smiled.

When her body was dry, Yonuh took her hand and led her to their clothes. As she got dressed, she took in the sight of him drying off that golden brown, Native American skin of his. She wanted to lick, kiss and caress him with each swipe of his towel. Once she was dressed, Raven grabbed his clothes and held them out for him. She debated on tackling him and going for another round with him but, unfortunately, they had company, and she wasn't sure how bad Gordon was being tortured by Nightshade.

"Who's here?" Yonuh asked with a chipper smile.

"A P.A.N.E.L. squad guy named Gordon. He's asking us for our help and has other information that you need to hear. If what he says is true, then we're very lucky he's the cowardly sort and sought out our help."

"I see." Yonuh zipped up his pants and shrugged into his shirt. "Let's go see whether his claims are legit or not."

Raven and Yonuh walked out of the bathroom holding hands. Onyx was on the floor, rolling around laughing and holding his belly. As they approached him, they found Nightshade coming out of one of the other bathrooms with Gordon. He was wearing bed sheets like a toga and had on Depends as well. His face was beet red from embarrassment.

"HA HA! Very funny, asshole!" Gordon growled as he adjusted the Depends briefs.

Onyx kept shouting, "TOGA! TOGA! TOGA, MOTHER FUCKER!"

"So this is all you could find for the poor man to wear?" Raven asked. "Gordon, I hope you didn't piss on your recording."

"Nightshade has it," Gordon said gruffly. "Now that we've had our fun, can we please go watch it?"

"No," Yonuh told them, "we'll eat first. We can watch the video later. I'm starving after all the...fun I've had today, and I'm sure the rest of you are as well."

"I'm practically ravenous for something to eat," Nightshade chimed in.

"Homemade stew and Voodoo doughnuts, you can count me in, Yonuh!" Onyx hollered as he took flight towards the kitchen.

"Gordon, are you hungry? You're welcome to have a bowl or two with us," Raven said and got surprised by his reaction.

Gordon started to cry which made Nightshade put a comforting arm around him. She escorted him towards the kitchen. Glancing back at Yonuh and Raven, she shrugged. "What can I say? The pathetic worm is growing on me."

Raven pulled Yonuh along with her to the kitchen. "We have much to discuss about our little trip to Powell's, and most of it won't be pretty, either."

Chapter Eighteen

Everyone at the dinner table howled with laughter as Onyx regaled them with tales of their adventure to Powell's and Voodoo Doughnuts. He embellished a lot but neither Raven nor Gordon had the heart to say otherwise. Things got worse as he explained the Tex-ass Challenge Doughnut and how he scored the free doughnuts.

Gordon dipped his spoon into his bowl for another bite of Yonuh's venison stew. As he chewed, he acted as if he hadn't had a meal this great in forever. Yonuh noticed how the man's eyes rolled back in his head as he ate. "Nothing beats the real thing, does it, Gordon?"

"Beg pardon?" Gordon said, startled. He wasn't used to being spoken to without harassment. He looked sheepishly around the table, feeling everyone's eyes were upon him, making him uncomfortable.

"I didn't mean to upset you, Gordon. I only meant that during your time with Zordic, he provided food and drinks magically. It's not the same as the real deal, like what you're having now. It only sustained you and gave you more energy to do his bidding, but in the end, I'm sure you could tell the difference."

"Yes, this is a more filling and nourishing meal than I've had in a long time."

"Actually, that's the point of the demon's food," Nightshade interjected her knowledge. "It keeps you wanting more of what he has to offer. Kind of like a drug, in a sense. I'm sure when you were starving that his banquet was too much for you to turn down."

"But it tasted so real at first, but then I found I needed more and more. He had us hunting tirelessly way before you came into the equation. His magical food gave us extra strength and endurance to do things that would have made most people collapse from exhaustion."

"It was real food, actually," Nightshade said, "but I'd rather not go into it here at the dinner table. Suffice it to say, he took old foods and drinks and cast his spell on them, making them seem fresh. You're an intelligent man, Gordon. I'm sure you'll figure it out." She gave Gordon a flirty smile that unnerved him.

"I'd rather not think about it right now; I'm enjoying this great meal, and I don't want any of it to go to waste. Thank you, Yonuh, for allowing me to sit at your table and eat your wonderful food."

Yonuh nodded his head at Gordon. "You're a guest in our home, and it would be wrong not to offer you food and drink. Besides, it's not often we get a member of the P.A.N.E.L. squad in here who wants to talk, rather than trying to kill us. I'm sure when you met up with Raven and Onyx today you weren't met with open arms."

Gordon unconsciously rubbed his sore neck. His hand came away covered in dry flakes of blood. He looked at his hand and brushed it off as he spoke. "No, I wasn't, but I can't blame them for their reactions towards me. I may have come under a white flag of truce, but when you people have been burned enough times by my former squad associates, it's understandable that you would shoot first and not ask any questions later. Thankfully, there wasn't any shooting at all, just sharp claws on my neck."

Yonuh rose and walked around the table. Standing behind Gordon, he asked, "May I see your neck?"

Gordon complied by turning down his collar as Yonuh bent down to inspect.

He saw Gordon's neck had small puncture marks that were caked with dry blood. There was also swelling around some of the wounds too, meaning there was a chance infection was setting in.

Yonuh looked at Onyx who was already defending his actions. "Hey, how was I to know he was actually going to play nice? I admit, I did want to rip his head away from his neck earlier, but that's in the past. Don't you be judging my actions, buddy!"

"I wasn't," Yonuh assured him. "Are there any toxins or poisons in those claws of yours?"

"Poisons? Are you saying I'm going to die?" Gordon exclaimed in a panic. He wanted to jump up and run away, but Yonuh put his hands firmly on his shoulders and held him down in his chair. As soon as Gordon felt the healer's warm, comforting energy flow through him, he immediately began to calm.

He looked up at Yonuh and asked, "How are you doing this to me? One moment I'm scared out of my mind, the next I'm calm as a baby sleeping safely in a crib. Please, tell me."

Onyx was looking at his little hands. He shrugged. "As far as I know, there aren't any poisons or toxins, but that doesn't mean they're sterile claws either."

Yonuh nodded as he cupped his hands on Gordon's swollen neck and started chanting. Gordon felt lightheaded as healing energy coursed through his head and neck. He even felt the chaffing marks on his wrists mend and saw them disappear. Yonuh stopped his chanting. "Do you feel better now, Gordon?"

Amazed and awed, Gordon examined his wrists. He rubbed his neck and felt no pain. There were no longer any wounds; only the dried flakes of blood remained.

Gordon looked up at Yonuh as he smiled and nodded at him. "What are you, exactly?"

The healer shrugged. "I'm just a simple man trying to make my way in the world the best I can, just like you."

The others around the table snickered which made Gordon uncomfortable, mainly because it was usually directed at him.

Nightshade finally spoke up. "If you believe that, then I'm nothing more than a harmless, little kitten. Yonuh doesn't like to brag about his talents because that's how he is. He's a shape-shifter as you already know, and he's also a Native American energy healer too. He's a rare breed indeed. He's changed and affected all of our lives here in many ways."

"That just barely scratches the surface of what he truly is," Raven insisted. "Yonuh may be a shape-shifter and a healer, but he's also our friend who's extremely protective and would die just to ensure we were all safe from harm."

Onyx flew up with his chest bowed out and pointed at Yonuh. "The day we met, we were all in a nasty jail. I tried to kill Yonuh because I didn't know him. I didn't even know where I was, just that I had been tranquilized. I was ready to fight." Tears came to the gremlin's eyes. "That same day we busted out of that jail, he gave me a room here. He also gave me all the tools in this place as a gift because that's what he does! When one of your fucktard friends shot me, he saved my life. As far as I'm concerned, Yonuh is a fucking God because he gave me Doritos! That sums him up in my book better than what you ladies just said!"

Yonuh tried to hide the blush that was creeping up his neck, heading straight for his face.

"I must say your friends hold you in high esteem," Gordon said. "Do you require anything from them to stay here with you?"

Yonuh was about to speak, but Raven beat him to the punch. "We're here because we choose to be here. We're not here against our will or obligated to Yonuh in any way. And if you think Nightshade and I are only here by trading sexual favors for a roof over our heads, then you're absolutely clueless! I had a home of my own until your *friends* decided it would be fun to burn it to the ground and drag me off to that jail. Nightshade had her own place too, but she decided it would be safer if we all banded together against your friends. Onyx…he's here because — hell, I'm not sure exactly why he's here. I have no clue, but he chooses to hang out here and stay safe, helping us watch our backs!"

"So what's your story then Onyx, why are you here?" Gordon asked with genuine interest as he ignored Raven's little tirade.

"I'm here because they can't get rid of me. I'm a fly in the ointment, a monkey in the wrench, and a pain in the ass. I was given my own room all to myself with access to a garage and all the tools in this place were given to me whether I stayed here or not. How stupid would I be if I turned that down? Plus, Yonuh gave me Doritos that sealed the deal in my mind!"

"I see…I think," Gordon said. "But why would he want you here in the first place?" He eyed Raven. "I'm only curious and not trying to start a fight."

But it was Yonuh who wanted to explain. "I wanted companions in my life. I had been living here in seclusion for far too long. When I got abducted and met them, I felt I should offer my home to them. I wanted to offer it as a way of saying thanks for helping me escape the jail. I couldn't have done that on my own, and I know that!

"This place has more than enough stuff in it to barter with. I told them that they could use anything here for themselves or use it to barter for things they needed. I hid from the world because I've been taken advantage of in the past, so inviting them to live here was a big step for me." He sighed heavily. "Now it seems your master wants to take advantage of me as well."

Gordon nodded slowly as he sat back in his chair, crossing his arms over his chest. Nightshade stood up and started clearing the table of the dirty dishes. "I'm going to get these soaking in the sink. When you're done, put your dishes in there too. I'll do them later."

Onyx grabbed his plate and put it in the sink. He started filling it with hot water and soap as Nightshade made her way to the sink. She smiled and patted Onyx gently on his little head.

Raven leaned over next to Yonuh and whispered, "I still want to know what's going on between them. He hasn't been the same since the night in the elven community."

"We had an enlightening conversation, Raven," Onyx said as he flew slowly by her, grabbing her and Yonuh's dirty dishes. "Gordon, are you done?" The gremlin hovered next to the man. "If not, help yourself to more stew. You can bring your bowl with you and eat as we watch what's on your disk."

Gordon's lips parted, and he seemed to be on the verge of tears. "Oh, come on," Onyx protested. "I didn't say anything that was that bad, Gordon! What gives man? Why are you such a bawl-bag right now, huh?"

Gordon wiped his eyes. "You don't understand, Onyx. For the first time in a long time, I feel like I'm being treated as an equal. As much as you've taunted and threatened me today, I feel like...like I'm with family." More tears flooded his eyes, and he tried to wipe them away with his napkin. "I may be the black sheep here, but you people still welcomed me into your home like nothing had happened between us."

"Technically, you're more like the crimson sheep of the family," Onyx said and chuckled. "But that's just how we operate around here. We're a family, albeit a strange one. We tease and fight with each other." Onyx hovered by Gordon and put his little hand on his shoulder.
"I don't trust you yet, Gordon, so I'll be keeping a sharp eye on you, as well as an even sharper ear on you at all times. Any signs of betrayal, and I *will* take your head off. Got it, baa, baa, crimson sheep?"

Gordon nodded as he got up to get more stew from the crock pot. As Yonuh sprayed down the table with a bleach water mixture, Raven wiped it down. Gordon felt like he was at home with these people, which was more than he could say for living in the barracks. Suddenly, Gordon froze. Did I say *people*? The longer he was around them, the less he could see them as the vile monsters Prophet Bob and Master Zordic preached about. Hell, those two were more monsters than Yonuh and his...family. Even that word *family* felt right to say.

After Gordon finished ladling the stew into his bowl, he was escorted to an area of the warehouse that had been partitioned off to look like a living room. It had a sixty inch flat screen TV, a few game consoles, and a DVD player connected to the TV. There was a beige couch and loveseat set in an L-pattern with a glass coffee table sitting on top of a throw rug.

Onyx placed the pink Voodoo Doughnut boxes on the coffee table and grinned. "Hey Gordon, I got your Cock-N-Balls right here!"

"Onyx," Nightshade said with an amused look on her face, "I could have sworn you didn't swing that way. It's okay, Gordon, if you do. I'm not judging you, so feel free to be with whoever you want to be with."

Gordon blushed. "He's referring to the doughnuts I ordered today. They're my favorites, and they taste divine. Just for your information, though, I prefer the company of a lady, even though it's…been a while."

Nightshade smiled at Gordon and patted the cushion on the couch next to where she would be sitting. He obeyed her direction and sat down where she wanted him. Yonuh and Raven curled up together on the love seat. Nightshade turned on the TV and took off her cloak, draping it over her arm. She bent over and put Gordon's disk into the DVD player, making sure to take a peek at the man over her shoulder. She was rewarded with a stare that only a man could give when he saw something he wanted. Even though Gordon was human, he was definitely a man, so why not have fun teasing him with her goods.

He gulped when he saw her svelte figure, and when she swayed back and forth in front of the TV, his heart thundered in his chest, and he felt his member getting hard.

She turned and sauntered over to the couch, sitting down next to Gordon. Onyx landed in Nightshade's lap and asked, "Can't you be any more slutty, Nightshade? I'm not sure he's getting your message."

"Actually," the necromancer replied, as she pulled Gordon up close and put her arm around him to cuddle, "I haven't even begun to show off my slutty side. If he plays his cards right, then I just might do that tonight!"

Onyx sniffed the air with his sensitive nose. "Trust me, girl, he's game whether he wants to admit to it or not." He chuckled. "OUCH! What was that for?" He rubbed the side of his head where she had boxed him.

"For being nosey as usual," she said in a haughty voice. "Now press play for me, my dear?"

Onyx slipped off her lap and grabbed the remote and a couple of doughnuts. He handed Gordon one his Cock-N-Balls doughnuts and snickered as he plopped down beside him.

Gordon held it up to his mouth to eat, but he suddenly stopped when Nightshade leaned over and licked the doughnut at the opposite end.
He gasped and nearly dropped it. She swirled her tongue along the chocolate shaft and said in a sultry voice, "Mm, tastes divine, indeed, Gordon."

A moan of desire escaped the man's lips, and he thought his male member was going to burst through the Depends she had forced him to wear.

The gremlin heard the soft moan and grinned.

"Onyx, you can press play any time this century," Raven growled.

"Yeah, yeah! Keep your skirt on, carrot top. Have a doughnut and hush because the show's about to begin. There won't be any breaks, so all who need to go potty, go now." He chuckled. "Gordon, I guess you went earlier."

"Onyx!" Yonuh growled irritably.

The gremlin let out a deep belly laugh and pressed play on the remote. The screen flickered and was snowy. "Give it a moment," Gordon advised. "It'll get better. I had to rip this in a hurry because the company was trying to erase all the security recordings."

"You sure it was the company trying to do that?" Onyx asked with skepticism.

Gordon thought about it and finally said, "No, but that's what I thought initially as they were really good at covering up accidents. Now that you mention it, though, I'm thinking it could have been Prophet Bob."

As they watched, the picture cleared up, but there was no sound. They could see the inside of a lab where several people were working either with microscopes or transferring vials to a reach-in fridge that had three glass doors. The workers didn't look special or out of the ordinary. They were dressed exactly how one would imagine a lab worker to be dressed: white lab coats with multiple pens in the breast pocket, dark slacks and dress shoes. Each one had their own tasks to complete, and they seemed like single-minded drones, working away without worrying about the others.

There were several long, black countertops in the room, and each one had a sink and a couple of microscopes on it. There were several pieces of equipment in the lab that weren't familiar to Gordon or the others. A file cabinet sat at one end of the room, with stacks of paperwork and boxes that contained empty vials and slides atop it.

"Boo!" Onyx cried out. "This show stinks. Can we watch more re-runs of paint drying because that has more excitement than this?"

"Hit fast forward and I'll tell you where to....stop!" Gordon gasped as he felt Nightshade move her hand up under his sheet and tease his member with her finger.

Raven rolled her eyes. "Behave, Nightshade!"

"What's wrong with molesting a man wearing a toga and a diaper?" the necromancer asked, giggling.

"Depends..." Onyx commented and then went into a cackling fit.

Gordon blushed. "Press play, Onyx! This is close to where the incident occurs."

Onyx pushed the play button as he wiped tears from his eyes and tried to stop giggling. The video showed the same lab room, except now there was only one lab worker gazing into a microscope while writing on a pad of paper to his right. Suddenly, he jerked his head up from the microscope and looked all around the room as if he had heard a noise. After a moment, he went back to his observations.

Gordon picked up the remote and paused the video. "This is where I noticed the anomaly the first time around. At first, I thought it was just a glitch or a corrupted part of the recording. Look just behind the man. See that dark spot? It's in multiple frames, so pay attention to it because it's responsible for the accident."

"Just from looking at that dark spot, I can tell it's no glitch," Yonuh said as he leaned forward. "Can you feel it, Raven?"

"Yeah I do, and it's something nasty, that's for sure." Raven narrowed her eyes as she studied the dark spot.

Gordon had a baffled look on his face, so Nightshade decided to clarify things for him. "If your senses are open like ours are, or if a human is sensitive to the supernatural, you can use your third eye and gaze at that spot and actually receive a tingling sensation from it. That tingling can help you determine what's causing the spot."

"How is this creature invisible in the first place?" Gordon asked.

Onyx chimed in with his usual sarcasm, "The big, bad hunter doesn't know his prey? No wonder you and your buddies suck at your jobs! It's in a different plane of existence. That's where we all used to be before the plague hit and it made it easier to go undetected. Most of the human race didn't believe we existed, except in fairytales. The world would have been a different place if everyone's third eye was open, and they could see the other realities."

"Now that we're out in the open people see and fear us," Raven added. "Their ignorance and hatred is easier to accept than the idea that *we* have always been here among them since time began."

Gordon nodded as he pressed the play button. For no apparent reason, a beaker suddenly slid off the countertop and shattered on the floor. The worker stared at the broken glass for a few moments and then glanced around the room with a confused look on his face. Finally, he left the frame for a few minutes and returned with a dustpan and a broom. As he swept up the glass, the dark spot appeared beside the man once again. Busy at the trash can, the man didn't see that the door to one of the refrigerator units opened up.

Gordon leaned in, using his augmented eyes to observe the dark spot.

The lab worker leaned the broom against the wall and placed the dustpan on the floor beside it. He turned around to go back to his work area and froze. Noticing, for the first time, that one of the refrigerator doors was open, he looked around the room. As he grinned, his lips moved. He seemed to be speaking to someone, but no one was in the room.

Probably thinking someone was playing a trick on him, he ran around the room several times, looking in different places, searching for the trickster. Finally, after not finding anyone, he walked over to close the refrigerator door. As he reached for the door to shut it, a plastic box flew out of the refrigerator, striking him hard enough in the chest to physically knock him backwards and onto the floor.

Yonuh and Raven both leaned forward, eyeing the scene as it played out.

The man frantically tried to wipe the spilled contents of the box off his chest while scooting backwards on his rear end and out of frame. The dark spot seemed to take on more of a corporeal form, but only just.

Gordon paused the recording and looked closely at the creature. His mouth opened in shock as he recognized it. Sitting back hard on the couch, he covered his face with his hands in despair.

Nightshade looked at the screen. "That's Zordic, isn't it?" she asked in a cold, vicious voice. "I'm getting a demonic vibe from that image. Gordon, do you see Zordic?"

He let out a huge sigh as his hands dropped away from his weary face. The words Gordon uttered sounded like that of someone who had been betrayed in the worst way. "I'm such a fool for hating you guys. All this time, I've been serving the one who killed off most of humanity! How can I go on? I guess the Prophet Bob was right when he said it was the supernatural creatures that caused the apocalypse because it was Zordic — a demon — that unleashed the plague."

"Many roads seem to be leading back to him and Prophet Bob," Yonuh said as he rubbed his chin.

"My question is did Zordic act on his own or was he under orders from Prophet Bob, by way of some demonic pact?"

Onyx flew up into the air with his arms crossed on his chest. "Why don't we go down to that church and ask Prophet Bob about this security video in front of the mindless drones he calls parishioners? We'll ask him to explain why his good buddy, the demon, killed off most of the world's population."

"Yeah, I'm sure he'll openly admit to everything," Raven scoffed. "We can't even make out Zordic's image on the video. All we see is a demon, and we don't see that very well. If we can't see Zordic's *public image,* Prophet Bob's followers sure aren't gonna see it either. They'll probably want to lynch us all on the spot for such an accusation!"

Onyx flew down and ejected the disk. He looked over his shoulder as he walked away, strutting with his trademark mischievous grin and twinkle in his little, yellow eyes. He twirled the disk on the tip of his finger.

Confused, everyone looked at each other and, one by one, they got up and followed the gremlin. "What's he up to?" Raven asked.

"I don't want to think about it," Yonuh answered.

Onyx made his way to the long countertop that used to be for customer service. He pulled out one of the laptops they had taken when they escaped Zordic's jail. Onyx flew up and squatted on the countertop. He laid the disk down and fired up the laptop, whistling as he waited for it to load.

"What's he doing?" Gordon asked.

Nightshade smiled and replied, "What he does best — electronic mischief!"

The moment he had access, Onyx's little, yellow eyes glowed brightly as his fingers moved at lightning speed. His eyes darted back and forth as a Cheshire grin plastered itself to his little face.
Multiple pages of code shot from his fingers to the keyboard and before long, Onyx had created a program and named it, "Gremlin's Rock Art!"

"May I have the disk please?" Onyx asked. He stood like an operating surgeon with his hand out, waiting for an instrument.

Raven grabbed the disk and slapped it into the gremlin's hand.

Sliding it into the disk drive, Onyx hummed to himself as it loaded. He then ripped the video recording to the laptop and ejected the original copy, replacing it with a blank disk.

"Watch and learn children because I'm only doing this once," the gremlin announced. He sped up the recording towards the end and found the place he wanted which was where the black spot assaulted the lab worker. Onyx highlighted the black spot and clicked a tab called "I see you" which made the black spot's distorted view materialize into a more corporeal body, adding lines and definition.

"Ladies and gentlemen, I give you the one, the only, sore dick!" Onyx announced and pointed to the screen. "You can applaud later or, better yet, give me Doritos."

"Yeah, that's him all right!" Gordon agreed excitedly as he stared at the laptop's screen.

"I guess you *have* been working for the killer of humanity all this time, Gordon," Yonuh said softly.

A flash of anger shot through Gordon, but it faded away immediately when he noticed that Yonuh was giving him a look of sympathy and not mocking him as he had first thought.

Onyx burned the newly enhanced video, and when the drive ejected the disk, Onyx slapped a label on it that read, *"The Tale of Sore Dick!"*

"Shall we pay old sore dick a surprise visit tonight?" the gremlin asked as he hopped down from the counter.

"I'm sure the prophet's sheep would enjoy this home video!" He began gyrating and spinning the disk on his finger.

"People won't believe it's him," Gordon said knowingly. "He's got glamour on at all times. Prophet Bob's followers don't see his true demon self. They only see a rather large human enforcer. How will you convince them that he's actually a demon?"

Raven shifted to hold Yonuh's hand. "Magic," she explained. "We can break his glamour spell, and the people will see his true form." She turned to Gordon. "So where's this church at exactly? I don't know about the rest of you, but I'm ready to kick some demon ass!"

Gordon felt a wash of relief covering him, knowing these beings before him were prepared to save his life. "The church is a few miles from here. It's across the street from the compound that Prophet Bob prefers to use on a night like tonight. Because it's considered a holy day of the week, a live video feed will be shown to those places in the world that have his television setups. No matter what service it is, though, Zordic will be there with Prophet Bob under the guise of security, so he won't be hard to find."

Onyx floated in the air and stated with a grin, "If you guys can make a distraction for me to go undetected, I can have this video streaming so that people can see and judge for themselves."

As everyone grabbed their weapons and walked towards the garage, the red lights on the ceiling suddenly started flashing. Yonuh was about to head to the surveillance room, but Onyx put a hand up, stopping him. "I'm on it, Yonuh!" He flew off.

Raven looked at Nightshade. "Do you feel it too?" she asked anxiously.

"Yes, something is trying to penetrate the building," the necromancer said. "It can't get in because of our protections and wards. Whatever is out there, it's definitely not human!"

Without warning, a portal appeared out of nowhere, and Gordon yelped in fear. As Yonuh and the others scrambled to draw their weapons, preparing for a fight, four elves, Sabic, Sicca, Nesara, and Xenon rushed through the opening.

Xenon was the last to come through, and he promptly closed the portal behind him. All the elves looked haggard and bloody, their clothes dirty and shredded. They each held their drawn weapons as if they were in a battle.

"What's happened?" Yonuh demanded. "Are you all right?"

At that moment, Onyx flew back and joined the others. He saw the elves but didn't seem to care. His normally dark face was pale, and he looked worried.

Nightshade noticed and grimly asked him, "Do I really want to know what's out there?"

"Hundreds of shadow people are everywhere!" he exclaimed. "They're all probing and testing the building, trying to find an access point."

"I was afraid of that," Xenon said with a defeated look on his face. "Yonuh, we need to get you to safety. Our community was wiped out by a wraith, and those shadow people are under his control. They're his army! If they know you're here—"

"The wraith already knows he's here!" Nesara hissed irritably. "That's why his ghost army is out there, trying to get inside." Suddenly, a renewed fire blazed in her eyes, and she growled, "I'm not letting that thing take you, Yonuh; I'll die before I see that happen!"

"If it wants Yonuh, why did it come after your people?" Raven asked. "It doesn't make sense."

"Apparently, it's tracking Yonuh by using his blood or some form of DNA," Xenon explained. "It attacked swiftly and those elves it killed, it converted their souls into more shadow people." His hands shot up and covered his face, and he wailed in despair, "We lost so many!"

"The wraith is very powerful," Sabic told them. "Nothing we threw at it had any effect on it at all. It absorbed our magic like a black hole sucks in stars. The wraith just kept laughing and calling your name, Yonuh."

"Yonuh, you must escape from here and hide," Sicca warned.

"I'm not going anywhere," the healer proclaimed. "Zordic sent this wraith to do his dirty work. The demon thinks he has claim to me because he's addicted to my blood. No matter where I go, the wraith will find me. I have to do battle with this thing, and I've got no choice but to make my stand here." He turned to his mate. "Raven, my love, would you mind making a black salt circle?"

Raven nodded. "I'm on it, Yonuh, but—"

"Just make it big enough for two people to stand in." He glanced at Sabic. "You say it absorbed your energy attacks—your magic?" The elves all nodded in unison.

A deadly cold smile washed across Yonuh's lips. "Good, then I know what to do!"

Chapter Nineteen

They all looked at the monitors in the surveillance room and watched as the shadow people not only grew in numbers but were still probing and swarming the building. Yonuh knew very little about shadow people, but the more he gazed at them, the more confused he felt. These being weren't very threatening, he thought, but there was something about them that put an uneasy feeling in his gut.

"Can someone explain to me what these being are?" Yonuh asked but still couldn't take his eyes away from the monitors. "I've never encountered them before; what's so special about them?"

"They're ghosts that have more negative energy in them than the usual ghost should," Raven replied as she sat at the desk mixing a bowl of salt with ashes from the charcoal grill to make black salt. "This is due to the person's nature when they were alive, whether they were mean and cruel or just downright evil."

Yonuh frowned. "But I don't think that's what I'm seeing here, especially if most of these came from the elven community."

Nesara leaned against the table. "Your right, Yonuh, these are different because the wraith killed them, and their souls have been corrupted. These were good people once, but now they're at the beck and call of the wraith, feeding it energy."

"Wait a second," Onyx chirped up. "If this wraith is so badass, why does it need to be a fucking leech in the first place?"

"It needs them because it's not of this world and they are," Sicca replied as she felt anger welling up inside her.

"In its own realm, there would be no need of this. Here on Earth, it needs a sustained energy source. They're like batteries for it, and the chaos and negative feelings they create in others only adds fuel to the wraith's ability to stay here."

"So what would happen if we took out all of those shadow people?" Yonuh inquired.

"Normally, if that happened and the wraith couldn't sustain enough energy, it would end up leaving this world and head back to its own realm by default. This one is different, somehow, because when it attacked us, it didn't have this many at its disposal. In other words, it was powerful before it added the elven ghosts."

Gordon made an "O" with his mouth as his eyebrows shot up in surprise. "It's part of the deal it has with Zordic, the demon! When he summoned the wraith, he gave it two globes of…" Gordon paused, trying to put what he had seen in to words. "I believe the globes were filled with energy. Plus, Zordic added the men who surrounded the circle as payment for the wraith's services. How Zordic came up with all that energy, is still a mystery to me."

Yonuh looked at Gordon inquisitively and wondered how he couldn't know of his master's collection. But then he recalled from his visions that Zordic preferred to be alone for that part, so he decided to give the man a pass. "Zordic collects the life essence of all he kills, whether they're human or supernatural creatures. Didn't you ever wonder why he kept all his interrogations private?"

"Of course I did!" Gordon snapped defensively. "We weren't privy to all his machinations. Do *you* know for sure that's where the energy came from? Where's your proof?"

"I was there and had many visions of what Zordic did to those on his steel table," Yonuh growled. "You and your good friends hunted down shape-shifters exclusively!

I felt EVERYTHING he did to his victims — all the skin flaying, the rapes, the carving of the inverted triangle from *my* chest to the abdomen. I even felt the painful anguish of his victims when he pulled out their life essence while they each watched in horror as he placed it in those DAMNED GLOBES!" Yonuh screamed as his face reddened. His eyes glowed gold with very little brown left in them.

Raven took Yonuh by his hand and turned him to her. He had said the word "my" when he talked about the inverted triangle being carved into the victims' bodies. Yonuh had internalized every horror he had felt as the other shape-shifters screamed in unbearable pain. Now, those feelings lay heavily on his soul. She could see his beast was chopping at the bit to be unleashed, and she knew it wanted to take a chunk or two out of Gordon, one of the men who had chased down the innocent shape-shifters. Raven cradled her hands behind Yonuh's head and pulled him down to her so she could kiss him and make his beast forget Gordon…for the moment.

"So how does this human in Greek attire…and diaper fit into all of this?" Xenon asked which prompted a snicker from Onyx.

Gordon glared and took a swing at Onyx but missed as the gremlin flew safely to the ceiling where he mocked, "He's one of the demon's little goons. He came to us with his tail between his legs, wanting our help. He was the only survivor from that night in the forest, by the way."

Sabic and Sicca both drew their daggers simultaneously. They grabbed Gordon and slammed him hard against the wall, holding on to his neck.

Xenon shook his head and commanded, "Enough of this, everyone! This is exactly what those shadow people are doing to us. They're sending negative energies in here and putting us all at each other's throats. We're feeding the wraith! I know your wards and protections are strong, but with all the shadow people at your doorstep, the bad energy is still getting in!"

Raven held Yonuh to her as she watched the altercation over his shoulder. She noticed Nightshade looking up at Onyx with a calm but sad face as she held out her hand, beckoning him to come down to her, which he did without question. Maybe she could sweet talk the elves into using a truth spell or potion on Onyx so he would tell what kind of hold Nightshade had over him. It just didn't feel right to Raven, and it had started to fill her up with anger, which she wasn't sure where that was coming from.

"You're being affected by the shadow people too, my love," Yonuh whispered into Raven's ear as he kissed and nibbled on her earlobe.

"You two should get a room or a cave," Nesara teased.

Onyx flew up on the table and gazed at the monitors. He noticed all the shadow people were moving apart. Suddenly, Onyx saw a dark mass flow through the path they had just made. The little gremlin folded his arms over his chest. "Did anyone order a dingy, black, tattered bed sheet? It's slinking its way to the garage door!"

Sicca let go of Gordon to look at the monitor. "It's the wraith!" she exclaimed with a shaky voice.

"No shit!" Onyx growled. "I kind of figured that out when the shadow fuckers went all Red Sea and parted for it!"

Yonuh backed away from Raven's arms. Leaving the room, he called back to her, "Make the circle, Raven. I'm going to call Fruxendall. Hopefully, he and his friends will come. We need help in getting rid of these shadow people." He looked at the others and said in a cold, angry voice, "Everyone, prepare for battle because this ends here!"

Raven nodded as she reached for her bowl of black salt. "They'll come, Yonuh; I just hope they bring an army with them when they do."

Yonuh began to chant.

Trying as much as it could, the wraith couldn't enter the building. The wards and protections held firm, but that didn't stop it from calling out in a demanding, cold voice that would send chills up an iceberg's back. *"Yonuh...I'm heeere for you...and only you....Come out now, and I shall...spare your frieeeends! This is a...one time offer...fail to come out...and ALL shall dieeee!"*

Onyx and Nightshade walked out of the surveillance room, with the elves following closely behind. The necromancer drew her black dagger and muttered a spell over it, charging it up. Sicca and Xenon drew their swords while Nesara and Sabic took defensive positions near Yonuh. Gordon walked out of the room last. Uncomfortable and feeling out of his league, his eyes darted around the huge room, searching for the wraith, afraid it would get past the wards.

"Looking for a way out, Gordon?" Onyx asked grimly. "I hate to burst your bubble, but the safest place to be is in here right now, so suck it up and pull your diaper a little higher because the shit is about to get wild!"

Yonuh opened his eyes and saw that everyone seemed ready for a fight. He didn't like this at all and felt the weight of responsibility slamming hard onto his shoulders. The elves all had their weapons charged and ready, as did Nightshade. Raven stood by the black circle she had made. She held her unsheathed athame in her right hand and the charged up wand in her left.

He walked up to Raven and looked at the black salt circle. "I'll be in the circle, and I'll draw the wraith in here with me and trap it."

Raven was about to protest that it was too dangerous, but Yonuh put up a hand to shush her. He continued, "Fruxendall and his people are waiting for my signal to come and attack." He glanced at the gremlin. "Onyx, I'd like for you and anyone else to help them. The faster we can shred the shadow people, the weaker the wraith will become. I'd rather it be trapped in here with us than out there fighting us."

"I'm on it!" Onyx flew to the ceiling where the roof access hatch was located and waited. He yelled back down, "All of you, be careful, or I'll kick your asses!"

Yonuh focused on the wraith and called out, "If you want me that badly, come in here and take me!"

The wraith made a sound that could have been a chuckle. It made Yonuh's hackles rise as it replied, "*I would, but you…have to let meee in first.*"

The wraith's voice had an eerie quality about it that made Yonuh shudder and think of death in a way he'd never really considered before. He forced himself to concentrate on fighting the horrid thing and glanced over at Raven and Nightshade. They were both focusing on one particular ward, making a hole in it just big enough for the wraith to come inside.

The wraith felt the ward weakening and floated over to it. When the hole was big enough, it cackled viciously and slithered through it, like a nightmare coming true. Several of the shadow people made their way inside too just as Raven and Nightshade were sealing the hole shut again.

When Yonuh saw the wraith, he psychically ordered, *"Go, Onyx! Fruxendall, attack now! We have the wraith inside! "*

"Ah, more elves…to add to my collected army….how deeelightful!" the wraith hissed out. *"You won't eeescape meee…again. I – "*

"That's because, for you, there won't be a next time," Sicca cried out. "You destroyed our village and killed my friends. I will have my revenge!"

Yonuh concentrated on the black salt circle and chanted softly, building up energy around him. He felt that if he played ignorant and left the salt circle open just a little, it would fool the wraith into believing the circle was weak in that spot. The open spot had to have weak energy in it, or the wraith would become suspicious and start investigating the entire circle, and Yonuh didn't want the vile thing looking closely at the center. He hoped the wraith's arrogance would actually make it cross into the circle after him. He pooled the potent energy on the floor and did his best to cloak it from the wraith.

Yonuh was willing to take this risk to protect the others, but the elves were already going full on attack with the wraith. Raven and Nightshade took to shredding the shadow people that had made their way into the warehouse when the wraith had entered.

With each slash and jab of the elves' swords, the wraith seemed to get better at avoiding them. It shifted and dodged, merely playing with the elves. As it got bolder, it called out, *"Your eeentire village…did this as well….Seeee where they…are now? You will join them…shortlyyy….All of you will."* The wraith dodged several more blows from Sicca before it cackled again and shot out a dark energy that resembled a spear. The energy spear pierced her heart, and the elf gasped loudly, completely surprised.

"SICCA! NOOOO!" Xenon howled in anguish as he watched her collapse to the floor like a marionette doll whose strings had just been cut. He pulled out an energy bomb and cast it at the wraith. The wraith took the blast full on and absorbed it, much to the shock of Xenon.

"I seeee you miss her…" the wraith mocked as it shot out another black energy spear in the blink of an eye. Xenon tried his best to parry it, but he failed, and his sword only passed through it. The black spear pierced Xenon's chest unhindered, and he screamed in pain. *"Join…your elven…wife!"*

The wraith seemed invincible, and that made Nesara and Sabic back off in fear of it. Yonuh could barely hear Onyx, who was now outside, as he cried out to the shadow people he was fighting, "Eat my claws, you sorry ass-balls!"

The wraith shifted slowly as if it was looking over a shoulder, which it didn't have, and in an instant, it roared out in pain and flew to the wall, trying to leave the building. But just as it had been sealed out by the wards and protections of Nightshade and Raven, the wraith now realized that it was sealed in by that same magic. It turned and saw its shadow people, who had made their way inside, easily destroyed by Nightshade and Raven.

The wraith growled and said with false bravado, *"Necromancer…how sweeeet. Your soul will make…a great trophyyy!"*

Gordon stood behind the long countertop, fretting and worrying the whole time. He had watched the wraith turn its attention to Nightshade, and he worried even more. Even though she knew he had been the one who had shot her, she had forgiven him and had actually flirted with him. As she moved closer to the counter to be in a better position, Gordon wanted her with him. "Come behind the counter. It'll protect you," he called out to her.

With her black dagger held out in front of her like a shield, she focused all her attention on what the wraith was doing and ignored Gordon.

Thinking she hadn't heard him, he called out to her again, "Come behind the counter." Gordon gasped as he saw the wraith slither and maneuver closer to Nightshade. He hurried to the end of the counter, too frightened to go out around it where the battle was taking place.

Without warning, the wraith shot out a spear at Nightshade, but her black dagger absorbed the energy. She backed up closer to Gordon and the end of the counter.

"*Very impressive…*" the wraith chuckled manically, "*but let's seeee…how you handle this….*" The wraith fired another black energy spear.

Again, the necromancer's blade absorbed it.

Suddenly, another energy spear snaked out of the wraith. It was smaller and faster than the others.

Nightshade saw it but didn't have time to react. In the blink of an eye, the second smaller spear had pierced Nightshade's hand that held her dagger, disarming her. As the sound of her blade hitting tile echoed off the counter, the necromancer dropped to her knees, screaming out in pain. She held her right hand close to her breast, and reached for her dagger, but it was too far away. With blazing eyes, and in unbearable pain, she did the only thing she could. She chanted a spell of protection. Before she could finish her spell, though, the wraith fired yet another black spear at her. She saw it coming, and she knew beyond a shadow of a doubt she was about to die.

"NOOOOO!" Gordon screamed as he leaped in front of Nightshade, taking a direct hit from the black spear. He fell hard on the floor before her and sputtered violently as he slid the black dagger to her. Dying, he said in a raspy voice, "This is the one…time I could…be brave…for you. I'd do it…again…in a heartbe—" Gordon lay motionless but had a smile on his face as a single tear escaped his eye.

As Nightshade stared in horror at Gordon, the wraith mocked her. *"How touching, saved by a…human. Was he your…lover? I…hope so!"*

Suddenly, the wraith screamed out in anger, *"Aaaargh!"* It could feel energy draining from its soul as its shadow people were being destroyed outside.

Raven ran over to Nightshade and helped her to her feet. They tactically fell back towards Yonuh and the other two elves.

The wraith looked outside and cried out, *"What…is this? Sasquatches…attacking my…children? How…is this…possible?"*

"That's what happens when you fuck with us," Onyx heckled with a grin as he flew down from the ceiling. "You're nothing but a two-bit, hand-me-down, Halloween rag!" He stopped speaking as he carved up two shadow people at one time. "Oooh, I bet that stings, doesn't it?" Done with that task, his taunts at the wraith began anew. "You're an ugly, overgrown rat turd!"

The wraith twitched and shook every time a shadow person was shredded outside, making it feel weaker and weaker.

Yonuh smiled. Now it was time he took on the wraith. "I'm still waiting for you to come and take me away. Are you no longer up to the challenge? You're not, are you?" he taunted. "Can't even bring your demon master a simple shape-shifter? Wow, I just realized you're nothing but his little bitch-dog. Here, girl, fetch!"

Intense anger and frustration coming from the wraith shot out at Yonuh. The horrid thing flew away from the wall and sailed towards him. It stopped every few feet, jerking and writhing as more energy was torn from it by the battle outside.

Raven held a sobbing Nightshade in her arms, trying to comfort her over Gordon's sacrifice for her. She worried, though, that Yonuh's plan was too risky and that he might end up dead like Gordon, sacrificing his own life for those he loved. And that was something she knew her mate would do.

"I know you're scared, Raven," Yonuh spoke to her psychically in her mind. *"Just remember it has to take me alive. I'll need you and Nightshade to start shredding it when I trap it."*

She looked at her mate and nodded that she would. *"Okay, but seeing this play out is tearing me up inside, Yonuh."*

"*I don't like it either, but this has to end now. I'm not letting it slink back off to its own realm.*" He paused for a moment, giving her a reassuring smile. "*Nightshade, if you're up for it, can you help us shred this thing when I trap it?*"

The necromancer wiped the tears from her eyes. "*With pleasure, Yonuh. I have to honor the sacrifice Gordon made to protect me. He saved me and died a hero. The wraith will NOT get away from me!*"

The wraith stopped just shy of Yonuh and the black circle. The healer could feel it probing the circle's power and considering. The wraith seemed hesitant to make a move, so Yonuh taunted, "You're right. I'm completely safe from you inside this circle. Better go back to Zordic and whine that you're so weak, you can't touch me. You can bawl about it like the little baby, bitch-pup that you are!"

The wraith hissed at the insult but then chuckled, "*Your circle…may beee black, but…it's weeeak enough. I'll have no…problem collecting my bounty…on this day!*"

Before it made its move towards Yonuh, the wraith let out a growl of anger as it felt more shadow people being destroyed outside.

Yonuh smiled as he heard Onyx call to him mentally, "*Bam, baby! The shadow people are no more. Kick it where it hurts, Yonuh!*"

With that, Yonuh handed out an ultimatum. "Come and get me if you wish to die, but I'm giving you one last chance to leave and never return. If you refuse my offer, then stay and suffer our wrath, wraith!"

The wraith no longer hesitated, and it pushed its way into the black salt circle at its weakest point. It cackled as it reached for Yonuh, feeling ever more confident that it was inside the circle. "*Your circle is…weeeak, shape-shifter. You are now…mine! I tire of…theeese games.*"

"I agree with only part of your statement," Yonuh replied as he revealed the swirling vortex of energy on the floor. He pushed more of his energy into the weakest part of the black salt circle, closing it fully and making it even more powerful. "It's time you pay for your evil. I'm afraid you'll not be heading back to your own realm when we're done with you!"

"Brave you are…but foolish. What have you…done in heeeere?" the wraith asked warily as it felt a shift in its energy.

"Oh nothing that will cause me any harm." Yonuh beamed a smile at the wraith. "The energy in here will do to you what you did to that energy bomb. You're nothing more than a black hole. Energy goes into you, but it never returns. The balance in life dictates that if you exist, then so does the opposite of what you are. So enjoy this white hole as it eats and purifies your energy."

"Bounty…or not, I will…kill you for…this!" The wraith stretched different parts of its body like multiple tentacles, shooting them out at Yonuh. As they got close, Yonuh drew upon the energy vortex and created a shield over his body. The tentacles wrapped around the healer, but then they all retreated back to the wraith. It howled in pain as its body burned away into nothingness wherever it touched the shield.

In its anger, the wraith fired a barrage of black spears at Yonuh. Each one of them dissolved on contact with the shield, shocking the wraith.

At that moment, Fruxendall and his people entered the warehouse, with Onyx following close behind them. The gremlin hovered by Nightshade and Raven. He noticed Nightshade's injury and put his hand tenderly on her shoulder. "I'm sorry I wasn't here to protect you."

"I'm fine," she assured him. "We're just waiting for Yonuh to give the word for us to strike. I think he's enjoying the idea of shocking the hell out of the wraith though."

Yonuh said coldly, "I believe it's time to stop all the nonsense and end this, don't you agree, wraith?" He focused on the energy vortex and his shield, making them both grow stronger. "I'm a peaceful man, but you and your demon boss have really pissed me off! It's time to show you what I can do!"

Yonuh lunged forward and grabbed the wraith with both hands. It bellowed in pain as Yonuh yanked it up to his face and growled menacingly, "Does this hurt? I'm sure it does because it's called karma, and you're going to take it like the little bitch you are!"

"This is...impossible! How are you...ARRHHGG...able to...do this? No...shifter...has...this power!"

"Old Zordic failed to mention that I'm also an energy worker, didn't he? It sucks going on a job without all the facts. You look terrible, and since I shift into a bear, I think I'll give you a big bear hug. What do you say to that?"

The wraith screamed in terror as Yonuh engulfed it. It violently twisted one way and then the other, trying desperately to get away.

It looked to Raven as if Yonuh was cuddling with a dingy, black sheet that was quickly disappearing before her eyes.

Onyx nodded as he watched the wrestling match and seemed to be agreeing with himself. "Now that's one hug the wraith will never forget! I wonder if this will lead to spooning. Ouch!"

Nightshade thumped Onyx on his head and said with a grin, "Be nice, will you? The wraith will be lucky if Yonuh's bear doesn't hump it!"

Raven and Nightshade both moved forward, each holding their respective weapons in hand. Once Yonuh let go of the wraith, all that was left of it was a gray, thin sheet of energy that was its life essence.

The women took turns slicing pieces off of the wraith and letting them fall into Yonuh's energy vortex, dissolving them into nothingness.

Onyx walked up to the circle, pointing as he taunted what was left of the wraith. "That's what you get for coming in here and fucking with our badass family!"

Yonuh held the last bit of the wraith's essence and said coldly, "You killed my friends and hurt my family. I have no mercy for you!" He made energy claws appear from his hand that resembled a bear's claws and swiftly slashed at the essence until none remained to cut. Yonuh pushed all the built up energy back into the Earth as well as the energy that charged the black salt circle. He then broke the circle by pushing through the salt with the tip of his shoe.

Yonuh stepped out of the black salt circle and into Raven and Nightshade's waiting arms. They held him tightly, but he wasn't sure why until he noticed he was losing his strength. "Can I please get a chair to sit in?" he asked in a weak voice as weariness covered him.

Onyx took to the air and flew towards the long countertop to fetch a chair. He took a moment to survey the scene before him. The two elven lovers had died in the name of vengeance for their people. Gordon had died out of sheer bravery by acting as a human shield for Nightshade. Most of Fruxendall's kin were in the building, silently waiting and weirdly swaying from side to side—all in unison.

Onyx came back rolling an office chair on the floor while he flew behind it, pushing it. Yonuh sat down in the chair with Raven and Nightshade's assistance. He felt they were being more like mother hens, fussing over him, but he decided to let them do it if it made them feel better. Hearing the soft footfalls of a Sasquatch coming towards him, he looked up. "Are you and your people okay? Anyone hurt or in need of healing?"

"No, the ghosts of dark weren't a problem for us," Fruxendall said mentally inside Yonuh's head. *"As for healing, the necromancer appears to need it, but it would be best to do it later when you've rested."*

"Nightshade, are you hurt?" Yonuh asked in surprise. For the first time he saw blood smeared all around on her right hand.

"It's nothing," she lied, more concerned for him than her hand.

Raven glanced up at Fruxendall. "Thanks for coming out and helping us tonight. We greatly appreciate it, especially on such short notice."

"Not a problem. We're allies, and that's what allies do. Your enemy becomes our enemy, my sweet fancy. It was a pleasure destroying that big ghost of dark."

"We were going to track down the demon, Zordic, tonight and confront him and Prophet Bob about a video that shows the demon causing the plague to occur. But then all this crap happened."

"That's how it goes when one fights the darkness. There's always something lurking about and waiting to pick a fight. I must say that Yonuh handled that nasty wraith quite well; he's a gifted friend, isn't he, my sweet fancy?"

Raven blushed. *"That he is, Frux. That he is."*

When Nightshade saw Yonuh gazing at her hand and frowning, she immediately tried to hide it by moving it behind her back. It didn't work; he held out his hand to her, and she knew exactly what he wanted. Shaking her head, she said, "I'm fine, Yonuh. You need to rest after what you just did. This can wait awhile."

"I'm worried that it could get infected," Yonuh gently pleaded. "We don't know what kind of nasty things the wraith left behind in that gash."

"Seriously, you should rest—OUCH!" Nightshade yelped as Onyx smacked her hard on her ass. The gremlin pushed her towards Yonuh, causing her to topple into his lap.

"Quit your bitching and let the man heal you! I'm tired of this banter already, so just do it and get it over with. SHEESH!"

Nightshade glared at the gremlin. He stood there with arms folded across his chest, ignoring the daggers her eyes shot at him. Yonuh pulled her close to him, pinning her next to his body, and brought her hand up so he could see it better.

He closed his eyes and started chanting. Nightshade felt his warm, healing energy course through her body, and her eyes rolled back in her head. She grunted in pain as the tendons and muscles shifted and mended together. Yonuh's chanting slowed as he felt the wound sealing up with new, pink skin. When her injury had thoroughly healed, he stopped his chant and leaned back in his chair, feeling drained. He still held on to Nightshade, though.

"Thanks, Yonuh, but you really weren't in any kind of shape to do a healing now, were you?"

"Maybe so, but it was worth it. I couldn't leave you in pain."

A slight grin creased her lips. "I seem to be in pain a lot which I apologize for, by the way. But I guess it's a great excuse to find my way back into your arms."

Yonuh chuckled as he released Nightshade, allowing her to slip off his lap. She turned her gaze to Onyx who quickly hid behind Raven. "Hey at least now you're not going to be so cranky," he protested. "I did you a favor so layoff already!"

Raven eyed Yonuh and felt a pang of worry hit her gut. She walked over to him, which caused Onyx to take to the air and out of Nightshade's reach. Raven knelt in front of the healer and took his hands in hers. Yonuh looked down at her and gave her a tired smile. "I'm fine, my love," he told her. "I just need some rest…and maybe some chocolate."

Onyx didn't hesitate to volunteer as he zipped away yelling, "I'm on it, buddy!"

Fruxendall shambled over to Yonuh and Raven. *"I see you are exhausted, my friend. Will we be going after the demon tonight or should we wait?"*

Yonuh looked up at the huge Sasquatch and thought for a moment. "I'm going tonight," he decided. "If we wait any longer, there's no telling what other creatures Zordic will send after us."

"You are in no shape to do anything at this time," Fruxendall pointed out. *"Why do you feel you must go? My people and your tribe can go in your stead. We will take care of this matter."*

"I'm the one he wants, and I'm the one responsible for all of them if they end up becoming collateral damage!"

"Yonuh, my love," Raven chimed in, "Frux is right. You're spent, and it shows. If you go with us in your weakened state, there's a greater chance you'll be captured. I can't allow you to go!"

As Onyx flew up, landing beside Yonuh, he handed him several chocolate bars. The healer nodded in appreciation as he tore off the wrapping and quickly ate them.

With his arms folded across his chest, Onyx looked Yonuh over. "You look like shit! You've spent all your energy trapping the wraith. You need to recharge your batteries, dude. About all you would be good for is bait to trap the demon; although, he doesn't have the balls to come out himself and grab you. You need to stay put and rest, my friend."

Nightshade stood behind Yonuh and put her hands on his shoulders. They were tensed up tighter than a piano string, she thought. She pursed her lips, feeling bad for the man, knowing all the tension was caused from everyone telling him to stay behind. "They're right, Yonuh," she added gently but hated saying it. "We can unmask the demon in front of the humans for the world to see. I...I don't want you to get hurt, especially in your exhausted condition right now."

Yonuh growled in frustration as he tried to stand up. He got only part way up before he collapsed back down onto the chair. He glared at everyone around him as he snarled, "I'm not helpless! I can help out. I'm quite capable of taking care of myself. I just need a short nap and then we can deal with Prophet Bob and Zordic."

"Dude, you need more than a nap!" Onyx exclaimed. "You need a week off. Hell, you can't even stand up at this point which tells me the battle with the wraith did more of a number on you than you're willing to admit to."

Nightshade looked down at Raven, who still knelt in front of the healer. The witch's hand was on her wand, and she guessed what Raven was about to do. The necromancer took her hands off Yonuh's shoulders and leaned around to his left, so she could see him better. "If we were in the shape you are in right now, you'd do the same to us, wouldn't you?"

Yonuh turned his head towards her. The look on his face was enough to break her heart. Through his exhaustion, she could see the mental pain and turmoil this was causing him. He couldn't stand the thought of his loved ones leaving without him, fighting his battles, yet he couldn't even rise from the chair. Though Yonuh would disagree, Nightshade knew what Raven was about to do was the right thing.

Tears streamed down the healer's face as he choked out, "But...but this is all my fault! I...I can't let you all—" Yonuh's head slumped to his chest as he fell unconscious in mid-sentence.

After she had sleep-spelled him, Raven slipped her wand back into her pocket and helped Nightshade adjust Yonuh in the chair.

"Damn, carrot top!" Onyx shouted in surprise. He shook Yonuh a few times then let out a low whistle. "Man, he's going to be pissed when he wakes up. I still can't believe you did that to him!"

Raven let out a heavy sigh. "I had no choice; it was for his own protection. I didn't want to, but—"

"You made the right call, Raven," Nightshade said as she put a hand on her shoulder. "He needs to be guarded while he's spelled." She turned to the others. "Who'll watch over him?"

"I'll do it," Nesara said without hesitation. "He risked his life to save mine, so it's only right that I protect him in return."

Raven eyed the elf, not trusting her. She finally sighed and turned to Fruxendall. "Would you be willing to carry Yonuh to his bed so he can rest more comfortably?"

The big Sasquatch nodded and shuffled over to Yonuh. He easily picked up the healer. He turned towards Yonuh's room but then stopped. *"My sweet, little fancy,"* he psychically said to Raven inside her head, *"I would gladly carry him to the ends of the Earth without hesitation. Yonuh will have one of my kin here to watch over him too."* Fruxendall walked off quietly.

"Sabic, you stay here with the Sasquatches," Raven ordered. "When we make it to Prophet Bob's church, we'll use the summoning charm. Open a portal and then you guys can join up with us there."

Sabic nodded curtly. Fruxendall's kin acknowledged her plan by nodding and grunting. Raven looked at Nightshade and Onyx. Her eyes blazed green, and she had a malicious smirk on her mouth. "Let's go show them what a real battle looks like. After tonight, Prophet Bob, Zordic and his P.A.N.E.L. goons will be wishing they had never heard of us!"

Chapter Twenty

"Tonight's the night!" Prophet Bob proclaimed with his arms raised high in the air. He was a muscular man in his early fifties. About five foot five, he weighed in around one hundred and seventy pounds. His salt and pepper hair was slicked back, and he had a regal face that seemed like it had been chiseled to perfection. Bob had a commanding presence in any setting, but the fact that he could see into the future and predict events before they unfolded with scary accuracy made people respect him even more.

People who followed him clamored to hear about the visions and messages he received from the divine savior, especially during the height of the plague. Prophet Bob gave hope to millions around the world as he preached on how the world could be restored if all the blights on humanity were cleansed from the Earth, meaning people should kill supernatural beings.

It was a packed house tonight. Cameras were in place to capture the different angles of Prophet Bob, and the video feed of the service was being broadcast all over the world. There was a huge screen that hung on the wall behind him, so people in the back of the large church could see him better. It also showed what was being recorded.

"What's going to happen?" a lady called from her pew.

"What news does the divine savior have for us tonight, Bob?" an elderly man asked with a rapt expression on his face.

"I've had a vision—a vision like no other!" Bob made a gesture with his hand towards Zordic. "My associate has a recording of my vision, and if things play out as I know they will, this night shall mark the beginning of the end.

The road to peace and prosperity shall be paved with the blood of the supernatural beasts that now roam freely throughout our world!"

A roar of cheers and applause erupted as soon as Prophet Bob finished speaking. Several people fell to their knees, crying tears of joy as they held their arms up towards the ceiling, mouthing, "Thank you. Thank you!" Many of the parishioners gave out excited hugs and happily shook the hands of their neighbors.

During the midst of all the jubilation, a small boy walked up to the prophet as he put on his microphone headset and asked, "How will we know when it starts?"

The prophet gave the child a grandfatherly smile and patted the boy on the top of his head. "Let's just say you will know it when it begins, my child. It will not be pleasant to see, but I assure you, you will know." The prophet turned and walked over to Zordic. "Is everything ready and in order?"

"As ready as it's going to be, Bob. Now we wait and let things unfold as you've foreseen."

"Tonight the world will change. No longer will we fear the supernatural creatures that prowl and stalk us from the dark, my friend. Soon, we shall walk as free beings in *our* new world!"

"Oh, you have no idea how right you are!" Zordic said as he cast a greedy, maniacal gaze over the parishioners.

Raven parked the white van between a bar and an old gas station that overlooked the church. They were able to see the gated compound that Gordon had described. The compound's church was huge; it took up a full city block. But the main church, which was just out of sight, was massive in comparison. From this vantage point, only the large, golden steeple that rose out from the center of the main church could be seen.

Nightshade surveyed the grounds with her excellence night vision and noted that all the walls were black. The extra strong chain link fences were held together by huge brick and mortar posts.

Along the fencing were cedar trees trimmed and groomed for the sole purpose of privacy. Clearly, it wasn't easy for onlookers to see inside the compound. Each of the driveway gates was controlled by an electric key pad, and there appeared to be only two. Besides those gates, there were several smaller entrance gates, each with its own key pad.

"Allow me to do a little reprogramming on those gates," Onyx said and grinned. "After that, I'll go to work on the streaming feed inside the main church, if that's where it's coming from. If not, I'll find a way around it!" He opened his door and gently closed it behind him before lifting off and soaring across the street. He dove into a thick cedar tree beside one of the smaller gates. He waited to see if he had been seen before making any move towards the key pad.

"Guard coming your way!" Nightshade called out mentally.

"Yeah, I can smell his cheap after-shave a mile away. Plus, the idiot is whistling! Some guard he is, letting everyone know he's coming."

"No one ever said that these humans had to be intelligent to work for a demon," Nightshade interjected.

"Can you use those beautiful, silver eyes of yours and look into those tall trees in the yard?" Onyx asked. *I'm not sure from my vantage point, but I believe there could be guards up there too."*

Nightshade cast her gaze up and methodically probed each of the evergreen trees. They were so tall that if one fell, it would stretch as far as the compound's length. She noticed several tree stands set in strategic places so the guards could see anyone coming from the four corners of the compound. Those stands that she could see were occupied. She shook her head in disbelief. The guards up in the trees were smoking! Trails of cigarette smoke wafted out from the branches, easily pinpointing where the guards in the trees were stationed.

"Our van may have already been spotted by the guards up in the trees,"
Nightshade said aloud to Raven, "but I don't know why they haven't sounded an alarm yet."

"It's possible they recognize this van as one of their own and don't feel anything is off," Raven answered in a hopeful voice. She peered up into the evergreens but only noticed the orange glow of a cigarette.

"Maybe," Nightshade said and shrugged. "They'll notice us as soon as we make our move on them. Unless…"

Raven grinned. "What are you planning? I see those wheels turning already."

"Like our jailbreak — so I need a few dead bugs."

"Onyx!" Raven psychically called out to him. *"There're several guards in the trees as you suspected. Do you think you can snatch a few…dead bugs for Nightshade?"*

"Why? Is she getting hungry?" Onyx snickered. *"Are dead bugs a good snack? Has she turned into Renfield?"*

"No, jackass, I need them for my spell!" Nightshade boomed her voice mentally. *"I'm trying to save us a lot of trouble by making those guards my slaves, like I did in jail when we all first met!"*

"Whoa! Tone it down, sugar tits! You're giving me a damn migraine from hell! Just hang on to that pretty little thong of yours, and you'll get the bugs, you freak!" Onyx said with a pained voice.

Raven looked back at Nightshade who had a smirk on her face. "It would serve him right if he did have a migraine. He's dropped back to the undead cracks again, and if he doesn't watch it, I may make him eat those bugs!"

Raven snorted. "You're losing control over the little guy."

Nightshade stared blankly at Raven. "What do you mean by that? Nobody controls Onyx except Onyx. I may have to have another enlightening chat with him after this is all over but—"

"And what exactly is this enlightening chat anyway?" Raven felt frustrated with all the secrecy. "I wish you would enlighten me on how you've had him behaving for you."

They felt the van rock as Onyx opened the door and slipped onto the passenger seat. He grinned as he held out an assortment of bugs. "Dig in while they're still warm, my little—"

"Say it and I *will* force feed them to you on a Dorito!" Nightshade shot back with a cold hiss.

Onyx was about to speak but then thought better of it. He meekly handed them over to Nightshade.

She looked down at the dead bugs in the palm of her hand. She held a couple of crickets, three moths and a ladybug. Nightshade looked over at the gremlin.

"Bite me," Onyx growled. "It's all I could find on such short notice, okay?"

Nightshade pulled her black dagger out and gave her finger a small prick, drawing blood. "At least most of them can fly." She gathered a dab of her blood on the black dagger and held the tip of the blade directly over the bugs, letting her blood drip on each one. "It would be a bitch if they were all crickets." She slowly made a circular, counter clockwise motion with the black dagger as she began her incantation.

"I could go and loosen up their tree stands," Onyx offered. "It would be funny as hell seeing them fall out." He snickered as he mimicked a tumbling gesture with his hands.

"No," Raven said, "this'll be better because she can command them to shoot their friends. It'll be like having our own set of snipers on top of them, and they won't realize it until it's too late."

They both watched silently as Nightshade built up a swirl of energy around the blade. Her eyes glowed brighter, and Onyx chimed in, "Uh, you might want to close your eyes. We don't want them noticing an obvious sign of a non-human."

Nightshade closed her eyes and tapped each of the dead bugs gently with the tip of her dagger. One by one, each of the bugs came back to life and turned to look at her with the patience of the dead, awaiting her orders. Nightshade finished her incantation and looked down at her little minions with an evil grin.

"That was quick!" Raven said with an impressed look on her face. "It seemed like it took longer at the jail."

"That's because I didn't have my dagger. It helps me focus my magic. Plus, it's great for defense against magical attacks by absorbing them, like it did against the wraith." Nightshade opened the side door and let the bugs loose. Closing the door again, she sat back and concentrated. As she held her black dagger in both her hands, she heeded Onyx's warning and closed her eyes.

Raven sat back in her seat and watched as Onyx fidgeted around with his tools, waiting for his chance to cause mischief and mayhem.

Nightshade smiled as she shifted her black dagger to her left and then moved it up towards the roof of the van. "I could have one of the guards open the gates for us, but I know you have your little heart set on it, Onyx."

"If I had known it was going to be this easy, I would've grabbed more bugs," Onyx said and giggled. "I'd love to see old sore dick's face as we march in with his militia under our command!"

"That would be great, but I'm already taxing myself with the few I have under my spell. I'll have a hell of a time using them and keeping out of the other guards' gun sights."

The necromancer let out a gasp and opened her eyes when she felt a small hand on her thigh. "We won't let anything happen to you, Nightshade," Onyx promised. "We'll try and get those pricks in your zombie crosshairs. They won't know what hit them!"

Raven gave him a speculative look as he sat back down. Onyx shrugged. "I'm not letting either of you die on my watch. Yonuh is out of commission at the moment, and protecting you ladies is exactly what he would want me to do. Someone's got to protect the *skirts* around here!" He giggled.

"I'll give you a really nice charm bracelet if you'll slap him silly," Raven offered.

"Hey!" Onyx exclaimed in a pout.

Nightshade smiled. "He's already silly." She closed her eyes again and concentrated. "I've got them under my control now. Onyx, go have fun and don't get hurt. Raven, I believe it's time to call in the troops."

"Way ahead of you." Raven grinned as she opened her door and walked behind the van.

Nightshade opened her eyes and then her door, stepping outside. Onyx zipped past her, grinning as he smacked her ass. She turned to swat him, but he had already taken flight. She quietly closed her door and silently crept behind the van where she found Raven squeezing the elven artifact. She relayed to the witch the info she had on the guards under her control.

Moments later, a portal appeared five feet away from them, and Sabic walked through. The Sasquatch army slipped through quickly and quietly. Their stealth was legendary, and Raven hoped the guards would have a hard time detecting them. Each of the Sasquatches had a large tree branch in his hand. She stared at the massive clubs, glad the hairy creatures were on her side.

"Onyx is disabling the gates and will go to work on the streaming video feed next," Raven told the newcomers. "Nightshade has several of the guards under her control, so if you see any standing around like a zombie, their eyes vacant, then you'll know they're with us. Four of Nightshade's zombie guards are up in the trees, so we have snipers at our disposal. Plus, there are two on the ground."

Raven and Nightshade turned and watched Onyx soar through the air, giving them a thumbs-up as he went off in search of the source of the streaming video feed. Raven turned to speak but noticed that the only one there was Sabic. The elf held her bow ready with an arrow notched.

"Damn, they ghost out quick!" Raven exclaimed as she heard the guards' screams and the sounds of total carnage and destruction by the Sasquatches across the street.

"That's our cue," Sabic calmly spoke as she glided past Raven and Nightshade. "I'll do my best to keep you both from harm."

"Payback time," Raven growled. "I'm going to enjoy burning these houses to the ground!" With her wand drawn, ready for a fight, she urged, "Let's go." The two women ran side by side toward the compound.

Nightshade gave her a sideways glance and replied, "Just don't get yourself killed over revenge, or I will summon you back to life and kick your ass!"

They both skidded to a halt as several bloody bodies landed in front of them, the guards' heads lolling at unnatural angles. The Sasquatches shifted in and out of this dimension, looking more like they were teleporting all over the compound.

As they entered the grounds, two men walked up to them with glazed-over, zombie eyes and patiently waited. Nightshade quickly gave them their orders. "Walk into each of the barracks alone and kill anyone wearing the crimson uniform." Each man walked in separate directions, heading for the closest barracks to him.

From behind them, Raven and Nightshade heard a woman screaming. They turned and saw a shapely, athletic blonde running down the street completely naked, trying her best to cover her top-heavy breasts with her hands but failing. They looked up the road but didn't see anyone chasing her, so both Nightshade and Raven turned their attention back to the chaos in the compound.

Raven took a steady aim at one of the larger two-story barracks and hissed out, "*Incaendium!*" Her wand sent out sparks, and the barracks caught fire near the stairs. She swished her wand, controlling the flames, making them jump to the side of the barracks.

"Nice. I'll have to remember that one next time I need a campfire started," Nightshade teased. Suddenly, gunshots rang out, and screams assailed their ears. With their weapons drawn, a small group of crimson thugs spotted them and advanced toward them. Nightshade squinted at the men and, one by one, they dropped dead from her silent commands to her men in the trees.

Raven cast more fire spells at each building she came upon. "Not so funny when it's your home burning, is it?"

"This is so much fun!" Fruxendall mentally called out with delight. *"One would think they had never seen a Sasquatch before. The looks on their faces before we smash them are priceless!"*

Nightshade looked to her left and saw one of the Sasquatches grab two squad goons by their throats. He lifted them up like they weighed nothing and slammed them both down on the pavement face first with an audible crack. Howling and roaring with a guttural laughter, other Sasquatches swatted squad members like they were flies, having way too much fun as they did.

Arrows whizzed by in bunches as Sabic leaped from the different rooftops, killing anything in crimson that moved into her peripheral view. She made it to the smaller church that was shaped like a military barracks and wedged her body into a defensive crouch between the main church and its annex, firing more arrows.

"I've got everything ready for the big reveal," Onyx called out mentally. *"Get your asses across the street!"*

"Are you okay, Onyx?" Raven asked. *"I haven't heard your sarcastic remarks for so long, I thought you were dead."*

"Ha ha, very funny, carrot top! I had a few disagreements over here at their headquarters, but they were nothing I couldn't handle. One lady thought she could take me on and was so full of herself that I had to teach her a lesson!"

"Was she a top heavy blonde, by any chance?" Nightshade asked and grinned.

Onyx snickered. *"Ah, that she was. I take it you saw her too. A real beauty — but loud. She'll remember me for the rest of her life…I have that effect on women!"*

Raven and Nightshade exchanged bemused looks as they ran past the smaller church. Unleashing more arrows than her quiver appeared to hold, Sabic gave them a nod as they ran by. When they reached the main gate, they saw the larger church just across the street. The structure was an octagonal shape in the center and had rooms and offices added on to its opposite ends. Out front was a water fountain with multi-colored lights submerged in the water. The fact that a demon used the church meant it had been desecrated. How else could Zordic be on the grounds, let alone inside the church itself?

At that moment, the church's main entrance pushed open. With their weapons drawn, more of the P.A.N.E.L. members came rushing outside.

Nightshade smiled as her silver eyes glowed. "I've got this one!" She expertly swished her black dagger around, making a circle of energy in the air. Stabbing the exact center of the circle, she cried out, *"Culpa et terrorem!"* A blast of energy shot out at the oncoming thugs and covered them.

The P.A.N.E.L. members froze. With their eyes wide and frantically darting, they looked as if they were surrounded by something that only they could see. Some of the men dropped to their knees crying remorsefully while others turned and ran away, wildly discharging their weapons at whatever they thought was chasing them.

"That's different," Raven said nonchalantly as they strolled past a pile of shaking and shrieking men, all dressed in crimson.

"The terror spell would have done the job just fine, but I thought about Gordon. The guilt of what he had been forced to do to survive ate away at him, so I added a guilt spell to the incantation. As you can see," Nightshade motioned around her as someone shot themselves in the head, "guilt can be just as bad or even worse than any of the terrors these goons inflicted on the innocents."

"How long will the spell last?" Raven asked as they made it to the glass double doors of the church.

"It depends on the person...on how much they can handle before they come to grips with their evil deeds, but I'm not sure about the guilt phase. This is the first time I've used it. Could last forever, I don't know."

Raven grabbed the door handle and waved Nightshade in first. "You ready to freak out the holy rollers and expose a demon?"

"If everything goes right, we may not have to do anything. The people may lynch both Zordic and Prophet Bob."

Raven nodded in agreement as she followed her into the church. They walked into the vestibule that was decorated with fake flowers and plants. The sconces that hung on the walls even held fake candles. Images of the divine savior—according to what Prophet Bob said was his true likeness—adorned several places in the room. When Raven saw the paintings and sculptures, she frowned. The divine savior looked a lot like Prophet Bob!

This place isn't inviting at all, the necromancer thought as she glanced around the room. It bespoke of trickery and a fake façade to keep the prophet's sheep feeling happy and secure while he preached about murdering innocent supernatural creatures. And, all the while, he had a demon at his side. Hypocrisy and religion tended to be in bed together, and this was no different.

Both Raven and Nightshade kicked open the wooden double doors, making a grand entrance and startling everyone. The parishioners turned around, gasping and gaping.

"Oh, I'm sooo sorry," Raven announced loudly so everyone could hear. "We didn't mean to be late for tonight's service." She tried to say the words with a confident air but felt them faltering under so many eyes, all flickering with a mixture of anger and fear.

The octagonal-shaped room had many rows of pews situated along each wall, giving the room an amphitheater effect. Prophet Bob stepped out from behind his pulpit as Zordic trotted up just a few arm lengths away.

Several people stood up, ready for a fight. One shouted, "How dare you invade the sanctity of our blessed church! We should kill them as the divine savior has ordered!"

More people found courage in numbers and shot up out of their seats, with righteous malice in their eyes. Prophet Bob held his arms up in the air and commanded, "Please calm down, my children. All this has been expected. No need for alarm. Even though we're in the presence of filth, we should hear what they have to say."

"No need for you to get in a tizzy," Raven announced. "We're here to shine light on how the plague started!"

"We already know it was your kind that did this to us!" A young woman screeched out, pointing an accusing finger at Raven.

Nightshade stood silently, staring at Zordic. Something was wrong; she could feel it. He should have been angry for the interruption. He should have been excited and ready to kill. But he wasn't. He just stood there on the platform, calmly looking at the intruders. A cold chill shot up the necromancer's spine.

"Watch and learn the truth on the big screen there!" Raven retorted. "We have a video of what happened, and it shows who's responsible."

"*It's go time, Onyx,*" Nightshade ordered. *"Roll the video now before we get lynched!"* Even knowing there was a video that exposed him, Zordic still remained calm.

The video stream of the service was interrupted, and everyone turned to look back at the big screen behind the pulpit. They stared at the screen, but the tension in the room only seemed to thicken even more. Finally, someone irritably cried out, "Where's the sound?"

"It's a view from a security camera, not a YouTube homemade movie," Raven explained. "They had no microphones, probably out of paranoia that what they were creating would be stolen by a competitor." People gasped as the image of a shadowy figure popped in again and again.

Zordic looked up in time to see the scene where the worker had his "accident." He seemed to enjoy his handy work. As the worker backed out of view, the shadowy figure began to coalesce into a solid form — Zordic's solid form.

"See? This shows your kind did this to us!" someone hollered. "Thanks for proving —"

"We aren't done with our little show and tell, are we Nightshade?" Raven cut the zealot off.

Nightshade smiled wickedly as she extended her arm, pointing her black dagger at Zordic. "*Detego,*" she muttered. As she lowered her arm, people began to scream. Zordic's glamour charm broke, and they recognized him as the one up on the screen. Prophet Bob turned and stared at Zordic. "My dear friend, what have they done to you?"

"What? What's everyone looking at?" Zordic asked. "It's obviously computer trickery up on the screen as you—" His voice fell silent as he gazed at the screen and noticed it was a live feed on him, and he was no longer in disguise. He fell to his knees crying, looking at his clawed, red hands.

"There's the one you should be pissed off at!" Raven called out angrily and pointed an accusing finger at Zordic. "He's been here with you the whole time. He's been working hard at killing any of us who could actually get rid of him. That, boys and girls, is a demon in the flesh and out in the open for the whole world to see."

Zordic stood up with a threatening glint in his black eyes. He looked around the deadly silent room, seeing the shocked faces of the parishioners. In a booming voice, he cried out, "So you cast a spell on me, and now I look like a demon— a demon that resembles the one in your photoshopped video. Seems like a great coincidence that I would take this form, like the one you obviously created in that recording. You creatures are here to ruin and discredit the prophet, aren't you? You're trying to make it seem as if he's in league with demons!"

"You *are* indeed a demon," Raven shot back.

"So how did this evidence come about anyway? You must be bored if this is what you want to do in your spare time." Zordic held his chin up in defiance, trying to save face.

Nightshade hissed out coldly, "We got it from a man wearing a crimson uniform. He went by the name of Gordon."

Zordic hesitated when he heard the name but quickly recovered. "Ah, him! He couldn't handle the job of protecting Prophet Bob. He's a coward, so he ran off. Please tell him he won't be getting his old job back, ever!"

"Gordon died warning us about the wraith you summoned to kill us!" Nightshade narrowed her eyes and goaded, "He had more balls than you'll ever have; you can't even do your own dirty work, can you? You've been revealed as the…cowardly, yellow chicken that you are, Zordic, and it's time for you to fry!"

Zordic's jaw tightened and twitched as he saw Nightshade raise her dagger and slowly walk toward him. He knew this was bad and that the live feed had shown his true form, but he wasn't stupid. He knew exactly what he had to do.

At that moment, several parishioners in the congregation gasped. Prophet Bob held his chest as blood pooled and stained his white shirt. He looked down at his chest, the blood stain getting bigger by the moment. He glanced out at his followers with a panicked look on his face. As he started to collapse, he called out in a shaky voice, "As I've foreseen…from the…divine savior…this night…" He crumpled in a heap on the platform.

Raven and Nightshade stood together in the aisle, both stunned at what they had just witnessed.

Zordic knelt down by Prophet Bob's prone body and let out a long, devastated moan. The demon plucked Prophet Bob's microphone headset from his head, so everyone could hear him as he said in a cold voice, "The prophet is dead at the hands of these two evil sorcerers! This was his vision that he spoke of earlier tonight.

With his death, these two have just started what will be known as *'The Great Cleansing,'* and if you follow me, the world will indeed return to its former glory!

As of this moment, all supernatural creatures are to be killed on sight." He glanced over at Raven and Nightshade and saw confidence fade from their faces, only to be replaced with wariness and then fear. "Bring these two creatures before me so all of you can mete out justice in the name of our fallen Prophet Bob and the divine savior!"

Raven gasped and turned, starting for the door. Nightshade took her cue from the witch and turned around also. But it was too late. The congregation swarmed around them like sharks around blood in the water. They were angry about their murdered prophet, but they were also very wary of the creatures. The two were obviously very powerful.

Zordic grinned maliciously as he spoke, "Ladies and gentlemen, if you look under the pews, you'll find adequate weapons that will kill these creatures — all courtesy of the late Prophet Bob."

In a loud roar of voices, the parishioners excitedly flung the pews over. To the horror of Raven and Nightshade, there was an assortment of weaponry from guns to swords and everything in between. The men scrambled to get the guns while the women seemed to prefer the swords. Even some of the older children took up daggers. The congregation, which was now armed with weapons and had evil glints in their eyes, closed in on the witch and the necromancer.

"I say we burn them alive!" an older man cried out.

"They need to suffer in the fires of Hell," another called loudly. "They put the rest of Mankind through hell!" A cheer of agreement rang out.

Just as the angry parishioners reached them, everyone froze. The men preventing the two ladies from leaving were picked up and thrown at the crowd, hitting several people and knocking them down.

A circle formed around Raven and Nightshade — a very hairy circle. The Sasquatches howled and swung cleaving swats with their massive tree branches, keeping the humans at bay.

Fruxendall appeared behind Raven and Nightshade, and he gently lifted them into his arms. *"You two didn't think we were going to leave you with these close-minded fools, did you?"* He took several steps forward and vanished. The crowd gasped in surprise. The other Sasquatches gave the congregation one last, long howl, scaring them and vanished also. The parishioners sighed in relief.

"Marcus, my child, play the video recording I gave you earlier while I tend to the prophet," Zordic said calmly, using the microphone. The crowd turned and looked at the front of the church where Zordic was kneeling. They watched him toss the headset aside as he tenderly picked up the prone body of the prophet and went toward a side entrance. "My children of the divine savior," he called out over his shoulder, "please stay here and watch the recording of Prophet Bob's last vision. It was his most fervent wish that you see it."

The image of the prophet came on the screen, and Bob spoke in a voice with much conviction. *"My children around the world, if you're seeing this then the vision of my assassination at the hands of the supernatural creatures has come to pass, and I am no more. The vision showed that in my absence 'The Great Cleansing' of the world begins now. My blood that was spilled marks these creatures' intent in silencing me and the word of the divine savior. They fear you and want this world to lie in ruin, so they can prey on all of you and your children! I urge all of you to take up arms and snatch this world back from their sickly claws. You must restore the world to its former glory and get back the peace that was stolen from humanity!"* He paused, and the crowd cheered.

"My friend Zordic will lead you to victory and glory in the name of the divine savior, but you must act now! There are special logbooks that everyone around the world must sign so that they may receive the gift of sight from the divine savior.

The church in which you are seeing this video will have logbooks on the altar. Your signature will allow you to see your enemies no matter where they hide. All the divine savior asks of you is to be under the command of Zordic and that you willingly give all your energy for the cause. Once you sign up, you'll see these creatures by using the eyes of the divine savior. He demands justice for the entire human race! Go forth, unite as one, and smite them all!" The video stopped.

The congregation cheered, and they all ran to the front of the church. They swarmed the logbook that had been placed on the altar in front of the pulpit, eagerly shouldering their neighbors out of the way, so they could sign the book first. Beside the logbook was a pure white dagger and a sign that read, *"Sign up for the divine savior's holy army. Simply prick a finger with this consecrated dagger and place your blood on the logbook. He will grant you His sight and protection."* One by one, the humans obeyed.

In his personal office, Zordic placed the prophet's body on the floor and walked over to his own logbook. He saw the number of names growing exponentially as each person put their blood in the logbooks all around the world. *ALL MINE!* Zordic thought greedily before turning back to the prophet. He waved a hand over the body, and it instantly crumpled into a pile of red clay under all the clothes.

Zordic stared at the lumps of clay and said coldly, "Your services are no longer needed, my friend!" He let out a maniacal laugh. "Now I rule this world, and all other supernatural creatures will no longer pose a threat to me or my new slave children. Soon, I shall find where my Yonuh is hiding, and he will be MINE!"

This series is continued in
"A Beacon of Light Arises:"
The Yonuh Trilogy
Book 3

Contact Joshua Griffith on Facebook
Follow him on Twitter

Made in the USA
Columbia, SC
22 December 2022

73578448R00159